Justin Winsor

The Reader's Handbook of the American Revolution

1761-1783

Justin Winsor

The Reader's Handbook of the American Revolution
1761-1783

ISBN/EAN: 9783337226961

Printed in Europe, USA, Canada, Australia, Japan

Cover: Foto ©Andreas Hilbeck / pixelio.de

More available books at **www.hansebooks.com**

THE

READER'S HANDBOOK

OF THE

AMERICAN REVOLUTION:

1761-1783.

BY

JUSTIN WINSOR,

LIBRARIAN OF HARVARD UNIVERSITY; PRESIDENT OF THE AMERICAN LIBRARY
ASSOCIATION; FORMERLY SUPERINTENDENT OF THE
BOSTON PUBLIC LIBRARY.

BOSTON:

HOUGHTON, OSGOOD AND COMPANY.

The Riverside Press, Cambridge.

1880.

RIVERSIDE, CAMBRIDGE:
STEREOTYPED AND PRINTED BY
H. O. HOUGHTON AND COMPANY.

PREFACE.

I WISH the user of this Handbook to understand its purpose and limitations. It is like a continuous foot-note to all histories of the American Revolution. It points out sources, but it includes also the second-hand authorities, though not all of them. Its references are made because the books referred to are the best; or because for some reason they are significant above others, though perhaps in minor details; and sometimes simply because of their greater accessibility. Any one disposed to follow its guidance will find that, with the more common books at his command, the course of events can be understood; while with the larger resources of our greater public libraries within reach, he can compass the subject much more thoroughly. Complete guidance to all details would have been possible by much more extensive subdivision and much greater analyzing of the books. The work seems large enough for the purpose, as it is. I could hardly have named more of the smaller general histories and other books, but slightly connected with the subject, except by swelling the volume without proportionate gain.

The special student will, however, find here his starting-point. The ordinary reader can survey the field and follow as many paths as he likes.

I began the making of these notes when the first fervor of the centennial period impelled a good many readers at the Public Library of Boston — which at that time was in my charge — to follow the history of our Revolutionary struggle. To aid that impulse some portions of this Handbook, in a less perfect state, were printed in the Bulletins of that Library. I believe it a part of the duty of a public librarian to induce reading and gently to guide it, as far as he can, because I know that as a rule there is much need of such inducement and of such guidance. I am no great advocate of courses of reading. It often matters little what the line of one's reading is, provided it is pursued, as sciences are most satisfactorily pursued, in a comparative way. The reciprocal influences, the broadening effect, the quickened interest arising from a comparison of sources and authorities, I hold to be marked benefits from such a habit of reading. It is at once wholesome and instructive, gratifying in the pursuit, and satisfactory in the results.

It is intended, if the system of this Handbook proves practically useful, to follow this initial volume, with others covering themes of History, Biography, Travel, Philosophy, Science, Literature, and Art.

JUSTIN WINSOR.

HARVARD UNIVERSITY, GORE HALL, *Sept.* 1879.

AMERICAN REVOLUTION.

1761–1775.

In Massachusetts, 1761–1765. — Writs of Assistance.

SHORTLY after the close of the French war, when the British government was no longer dependent on the friendly assistance of the colonies, and revenue was to be got from enforcing the acts of trade, the application of the agents of government for " writs of assistance " was met by James Otis in his plea against the grant. Tudor's Life of Otis makes that patriot the centre of interest at this period, and the legal aspects of the case can be studied in Horace Gray's Appendix to the Reports of Cases in the Massachusetts Superior Court, 1761–1772, by Josiah Quincy. The third volume of Hutchinson's History of Massachusetts, 1750–1774, gives the governmental view, while in Minot's History of Massachusetts, 1748–1765, the patriot side is sustained, and this view is represented in the Lives of Josiah Quincy, John Adams, and Samuel Adams. In its broad relations, as indicating the temper of the people, it is discussed by Bancroft in his History of the United States; by Hildreth in his History; by Frothingham in his Rise of the Republic; by Barry in his History of Massachusetts, etc. There are delineations of the causes of the Revolution in many popular and lesser histories, like Ridpath's, p. 285, etc. The same ground is gone over in McCartney's Origin and Progress of the United States, and better in G. W. Greene's Historical View of the American Revolution. A statement of the grounds and motives is in J. P. Thompson's United States as a Nation. There are several contemporary publications on the existing political condition of the colonies, like Almon's publication, London, 1775, on the Charters of the British Colonies in America, and Anthony Stokes's Constitutions of the British Colonies, London, 1783; also see William Griffith's Historical Notes of the American Colonies and the Revolution, 1754–1775. Political tracts of this period are numerous.

Of the many tracts preceding the commotion of 1765, that of James Otis on the Rights of the British Colonies asserted and proved, published at Boston, 1764, is typical of the best of them.

On the general subject of taxing the colonies, see the Parliamentary History, the Speeches of Chatham and Burke, May's Constitutional History of England, ii. 576, and the whig and tory views as shown respectively in Massey's and Adolphus's Histories of England.

In the South, 1761–1765.

For the progress of events and illustrations of the spirit of the people, see David Ramsay's Revolution in South Carolina; Moultrie's American Revolution; R. W. Gibbs's Documentary History of the American Revolution, 1764–1776; Drayton's Memoirs of the American Revolution in South Carolina (ending in 1776), and later histories of that State like Simms's; Jones's Defence of the Revolutionary History of North Carolina; W. D. Cooke's Revolutionary History of North Carolina; Foote's Sketches of North Carolina; Martin's History of North Carolina; Caruthers's Life of Dr. Caldwell; R. Purviance's Baltimore town during the Revolutionary War.

Illustrative details will be found in the Bland Papers, edited by C. Campbell; and in later records like Wirt's Patrick Henry, etc.

Stamp Act, 1765–1766.

To the general authorities named in preceding sections may be added, for local coloring, the chapters in the histories of Boston by Drake and by Snow, and in Lossing's Field-Book of the Revolution. See also Tudor's Life of Otis, ch. 14; extracts from Josiah Quincy's Diary in the Proceedings of the Massachusetts Historical Society, April, 1858. In the same Proceedings, June, 1872, there is a fac-simile of Andrew Oliver's oath declining

the stamp office. There are letters of the Stamp
Act times in the Historical Magazine, May, 1862.
Cf. also files of the Boston newspapers of the day,
like the Boston Gazette and Evening Post.

The Examination of Franklin relative to the
repeal of the act was published in full, and in this
connection consult the Lives of him by Sparks,
Parton, Bigelow, etc., the latter reprinting the
Examination of 1767.

The Annual Register and the monthly magazines in London, like the Gentleman's, reflect the
phases of English public opinion about the opposition in the colonies. The histories of England
for that period (typical among the later ones may
be taken the Pictorial History, Massey's, and Earl
Stanhope's), together with the lives and correspondence of the prominent political actors of the
day, throw light from that side. Cf. Rockingham
and his Contemporaries, i. 250; Fitzmaurice's
Life of Lord Shelburne, i. 319, and·ch. 7 for the
repeal of the act, and Protests of the Lords, ed.
by J. E. T. Rogers, ii. 77.

For the effect of the Stamp Act in Connecticut,
see Stuart's Life of Jonathan Trumbull. .

For the effect of the Stamp Act in New York
and Virginia, see the Magazine of American History, June, 1877, and the Pennsylvania Magazine
of History, ii. 296. Consult also the Memoirs of
General Samuel Lamb; and the histories of New
York City and State. Almon's Collection of

Tracts, London, 1773, gives in vol. i. the proceedings of a Congress held in New York, in answer to a call from Massachusetts, which was also printed separately in New York in 1845. Considerable light on the way in which New York was forced into opposition to Great Britain is thrown in the Collections of the New York Historical Society for 1876.

A large number of political and controversial tracts were printed at this time, both in the colonies and in England. Those in America will be found set down in Haven's pre-revolutionary Bibliography of the American press, which is appended to the American Antiquarian Society's edition of Thomas's History of Printing. The English ones are mostly enumerated from month to month in the monthly magazines of the time, published in London. Some part of all these are to be found in the catalogue of the Sparks Collection, now in Cornell University library; in that of the library of Parliament, Toronto, p. 1421; the catalogue of George Brinley's library, 1879, No. 181, etc., 2116, etc.; those of the library of Congress, New York Historical Society, Massachusetts Historical Society, etc.

Regulators in North Carolina, 1768–1771.

Beside the general histories, see Rev. Dr. Hawks's Battle of Alamance and the War of the Regulation, in W. D. Cooke's Revolutionary

History of North Carolina. See also Caruthers's Life of Dr. Caldwell; Foote's Sketches of North Carolina; Martin's History of North Carolina; The New England Historical and Genealogical Register, Jan. 1871; Lossing's Field-Book of the Revolution, ii. There is a tale, " The Alamance," by C. H. Wiley.

In General, 1767–1775.

This period and its patriotic movements, so far as relates to Massachusetts, are made the special theme of Frothingham's Warren and his Times; and in the same author's Rise of the Republic, the action of the patriots is viewed as tending to form the national spirit. A chapter in Tudor's Otis is given to characterizing the people of Boston at this time, and in the collection of contemporary documents called Niles's Principles and Acts of the Revolution, the spirit of the people can be read in their own words. A file of Papers relating to public events in Massachusetts, 1765–1774, was printed a few years ago by the Seventy-six Society, the originals of which are now in the Massachusetts Historical Society's Cabinet. See their Proceedings, Jan. 1878. Alden Bradford's Massachusetts State Papers, 1765–1775, gives the addresses of the Executive during this period. What is known as Almon's Collection of Papers also gives public documents, 1764–1775. Mercy Warren was a sister of James Otis, and in her

History of the American Revolution we have the characters of the most distinguished of the patriots drawn by one who knew them closely. Her estimate of John Adams in this work was not satisfactory to Adams, and the letters that passed between them thereupon are given in the Massachusetts Historical Society's Collections, 5th series, vol. iv. Eddis's Letters from America, 1769–1777, London, 1792, reflect the feelings of the colonists.

The influence of the press is traced in the third era of Hudson's History of American Journalism, in J. T. Buckingham's Specimens of Newspaper Literature, and the aspects can be studied in the files of the five newspapers published in Boston at that time: —

Fleet's Evening Post, patronized both by the whigs and the government.

The Boston Newsletter, the only paper which continued to be published during the siege.

The Massachusetts Gazette, the chief organ of the government.

The Boston Gazette, devoted to the patriots.

The Massachusetts Spy, devoted to the patriots.

The most important journal in Massachusetts, out of Boston, was the Essex Gazette.

For the influence of the clergy, see Thornton's Pulpit of the Revolution, and the Patriot Preachers of the Revolution, 1860.

As before, the lives of leading patriots must be

consulted: Wells's Life of Samuel Adams; the Life and Diaries of John Adams; Quincy's Life of Josiah Quincy; Austin's Life of Elbridge Gerry; Stuart's Life of Jonathan Trumbull; Bigelow's Life of Franklin, from his own writings, and other Lives of Franklin by Sparks and Parton; and the general histories, like those of the United States by Bancroft and Hildreth, and those of Massachusetts by Minot and Barry, etc.

The third volume of Hutchinson's Massachusetts Bay still gives the tory view, and the later British estimates of the period are found in Mahon's (Stanhope's) and Massey's Histories of England. See also the paper on Col. Barré and his Times in Macmillan's Magazine, Dec. 1876; or Living Age, No. 1699; and the Lives of Chatham and other parliamentary defenders of the colonists.

For the local associations of the Province House, Green Dragon Tavern, etc., see Shurtleff's Description of Boston, and Drake's Old Landmarks and Historic Personages of Boston.

Some letters on the condition of things in Boston, sent to the ministry by Bernard, Gen. Gage, and Com. Hood, between Jan. 1768, and July, 1769, were printed in London, and drew out from Samuel Adams a Vindication of the Town of Boston, 1770. Cf. Wells's Life of Samuel Adams; but this tract has sometimes been ascribed to James Otis. See Proceedings of the Massachusetts Historical Society, i. 485.

Kearsley's American Gazette, London, 1768, il-lustrates the condition of affairs in Boston, and gives a journal of transactions there.

Letters describing the state of feeling in Boston were written by Gov. Hutchinson and Lt. Gov. Oliver to friends in England, and these finding their way into Franklin's hands were transmitted, in Dec. 1772, to the patriots in Boston, and were made to support an address to the King for the removal of the Governor and Lt. Governor, as persons who were using their position to increase the discontent. These letters, with the proceedings thereon, were printed in Boston, 1773, and in London, 1774. See papers on their history in the Massachusetts Historical Society's Proceedings, 1878, p. 42. There is a synopsis of these letters in Parton's Franklin, i. 560. See also Campbell's Lives of the Chancellors, vi. 105; Massey's England, ii. ; Adolphus's England, ii. 84, for English views. Franklin's own account of his connection with these letters was first printed in W. T. Franklin's edition of Franklin's works, 1817, and is reprinted in Bigelow's Franklin, ii. 206; but see also pp. 130, 161, 193, 200.

John Dickinson of Philadelphia represented at this time the responsive sympathy of the Middle Colonies, and his tracts need to be considered: Address to the Committee of Correspondence in Barbadoes, defending the Northern Colonies, 1766; Farmer's Letters to the Inhabitants of the

British Colonies, 1767, arguing against the right
of taxation; and his Essay on the constitutional
power of Great Britain over her colonies, 1774.
Cf. Bancroft's United States, viii. The condition
of affairs in New York is seen in Gov. Tryon's
and Lt. Gov. Colden's letters to Lord Dartmouth,
printed in Documents relative to the Colonial
History of New York, viii., and in Jones's New
York in the Revolutionary War, i. with notes, pp.
468, 502; and p. 506 begins a reprint of a very
rare volume, Proceedings of the last Provincial
Assembly of New York, Jan. 10 to April 3, 1775.
Cf. Sparks's Life of Morris, and documents in
Force's Archives. Parton, Life of Jefferson, depicts the condition of affairs in Virginia at this
time. Cf. also Wirt's Patrick Henry.

The feeling of antipathy in the whigs against
the tories is well shown in Trumbull's Hudibras-
tic epic, McFingal, of which there is an annotated
edition by B. J. Lossing. On the origin of the
poem, see the Historical Magazine, Jan. 1868.
For the loyalist feeling of New York, see Jones's
New York in the Revolutionary War, published
by the New York Historical Society, 1879, and
the Life of Peter Van Schaack. The aspects of
southern toryism can be traced in Jonathan Boucher's Views of the American Revolution, a series
of discourses preached during this interval in Virginia, and which, when subsequently published, he
dedicated to Washington.

Boston Massacre, March 5, 1770.

Frothingham, in his articles in the Atlantic
Monthly, June and Aug. 1862, and Nov. 1863,
on the " Sam Adams Regiments," traces carefully
the progress of events from Oct. 1768, which cul-
minated in the massacre in March, 1770, and this
matter is epitomized in his Life of Warren, ch. 6.
Bancroft treats it in all its relations, in ch. 43
of his sixth volume; and it is the subject of
a special monograph, The Boston Massacre, by
Frederic Kidder, and is described in the introduction to Loring's Hundred Boston Orators. A contemporary Short Narrative, with an appendix of
depositions and a folding plate of State Street at
the time, was printed by order of the town in Boston and also in London in 1770. It was reprinted
in New York in 1849. A Fair Account published
in London, 1770, supplements the Short Narrative.
Isaiah Thomas's Massachusetts Kalendar for 1772
had a woodcut representation of the massacre.
Capt. Preston, the royal officer who commanded
the soldiers, was defended at his trial by John
Adams and Josiah Quincy, and the Lives of these
patriots treat of their defense. John Adams's
brief, used at the trial, is in the Boston Public
Library. A report of the trial, taken in short-
hand, by John Hodgson, was printed in Boston
the same year. Accounts of the trial are found
in the histories and in P. W. Chandler's Amer-

ican Criminal Trials, vol. i. The plan of the ground used at the trial is in the possession of Judge M. Chamberlain, of Chelsea.

The collection of orations delivered on succeeding anniversaries is necessary to a full understanding of the event. The earliest collection of these orations is that made by Peter Edes in 1785, which passed to a second edition in 1807. Some of these orations and other contemporary accounts can be found in Niles's Principles and Acts of the Revolution. Other documents are in the Historical Magazine, June, 1861. Cf. titles in the Brinley Catalogue, Nos. 1655–1665.

See also Snow's History of Boston, the Lives of Otis, Samuel Adams, etc., and the general histories. There is a descriptive letter by Wm. Palfrey, addressed to John Wilkes, in the Proceedings of the Massachusetts Historical Society, March, 1863, where will also be found a letter of Gov. Hutchinson.

Crispus Attucks, one of the slain, usually called a mulatto, is held to have been a half-breed Indian, in the American Historical Record, Dec. 1872.

There was published in Boston the same year the Proceedings of his Majesty's Council of the Province concerning what passed in consequence of the unhappy affair of March 5th.

Rhode Island.

There is a History of the destruction of the schooner Gaspee in Narragansett Bay, June 10, 1772, by John R. Bartlett, Providence, 1861 ; and a documentary history of the event was compiled in 1845 for the Providence Journal, by W. R. Staples. See also the histories of Rhode Island, and Parton's Life of Jefferson, ch. 14 and 15. This was one of the earliest acts of violent resistance.

The Tea Party, December, 1773.

Frothingham, in his Life of Warren, ch. 9, has given the details, and in his Rise of the Republic, ch. 8, has shown its political significance, and has again taken a general survey in his Centennial paper, in the Proceedings of the Massachusetts Historical Society, Dec. 1873. See also under Oct. 1877, for a diary of this time and also the Collections of this Society, 4th series, vol. iii.

In ch. 2 of Reed's Life of Joseph Reed, and in Sparks's Washington, the relations of the patriots of Boston to those of the other colonies at this time can be studied.

Bancroft gives to it ch. 50 of his sixth volume ; and Barry, ch. 15 of his second volume. Geo. R. T. Hewes, an actor in the scenes, has given an account of it in his Traits of the Tea Party ; and there is a paper, " Information of Hugh Williamson," among the Sparks MSS. in Harvard

College Library.   There are illustrative documents in Force's American Archives, vol. i. ; in Niles's Principles and Acts of the Revolution; and the contemporary account and records have been reprinted from the Boston Gazette of Dec. 6, 1773, by Poole, in one of the Massachusetts State Registers.

See, further, Tudor's Life of Otis, ch. 21 ; Snow's Boston; Niles's Register, 1827, vol. xxxiii. p. 75, from Flint's Western Monthly Review for July, 1827 ; Lossing in Harper's Monthly, vol. iv., and also in his Field-Book of the Revolution, i.

A letter about the punch bowl, used by the patriots before going to the wharf, is given in the Proceedings of the Massachusetts Historical Society, Dec. 1871.

Mrs. Caroline Howard Gilman printed, in 1874, an account of a private centennial celebration of the Tea Party in Cambridge.

There is a chapter on the Boston Tea Ships in Fitzmaurice's Life of Lord Shelburne, vol. ii.

For debates in Parliament, see The Parliamentary History ; and later views in May's Constitutional History of England, ii. 521 ; Massey's England, ii. ch. 18.   The first accounts received in England are given in the Gentleman's Magazine, 1774, p. 26, and are quoted in Carlyle's Frederick the Great, vi. 524.

Tory views of the events of this period are given in Peters's History of Connecticut, and in

the appendix by McCormick to the reprint of it,
— to be taken throughout with caution.   Cf. the
article " Lying as a Fine Art " in Scribner's Magazine, June, 1878.   See a foreign estimate in Hilliard d'Auberteuil's Essais historiques, 1782.

Boston Port Bill, 1774.

General Gage arrived in Boston in May, to
put the provisions of this bill in force, June 12th.
Its political bearings can be traced in Bancroft,
and in Frothingham's Warren, ch. 10, and in his
Rise of the Republic; and the military sequel in
Frothingham's Siege of Boston.   See also Tudor's
Otis;   Wells's Samuel Adams;   Life of John
Adams; Life of Josiah Quincy; Pitkin's United
States, i. App. 15; Grahame's United States, iv.
358.

Illustrative documents will be found in Force's
American Archives, vol. ii.   See the diary of
Thomas Newell, in Boston, Nov. 1773 to Dec.
1774, in Proceedings of Massachusetts Historical
Society, Feb. 1859, and in their Collections, 4th
series, vol. i.   The correspondence of the Boston
Donation Committee, relative to the supplies sent
to the embargoed town from other places, is given
in the Massachusetts Historical Society's Collections, 4th series, vol. iv.   Col. A. H. Hoyt has
given, in the New England Historical and Genealogical Register, July, 1876, an account of these
donations during the period 1774–1777.   This
tract was also printed separately.

For correspondence of the Boston patriots with those of the other colonies, see Frothingham's Rise of the Republic; Reed's Life of Joseph Reed.

The Suffolk Resolves, passed at Milton, Sept. 9, 1774, can be found in the Appendix to Frothingham's Warren.

The Provincial Assembly of Massachusetts met at Salem, Oct. 5, 1774, and A. C. Goodell delivered an address at the centennial celebration of the event.

Josiah Quincy, Jr., and others discussed the political bearings in published tracts. Quincy's is reprinted in his Life by his son.

For its effects in New York, see Lives of Jay by Jay, i. 24, and by Flanders; Force's Archives, 4th series, i.; for results in Connecticut, Hollister's History, ii. ch. 6.

For the feeling in the South at this time, compare the general histories; McRee's Life of Iredell; Thaddeus Allen's Origination of the American Union; McSherry's Maryland, ch. 7; Read's Life of George Read, pp. 86, 101; Rives's Madison, ch. 3; Life of R. H. Lee, i. 97; Randall's Jefferson, i. 85; Parton's Jefferson, 130.

Continental Congress, 1774.

This was held at Philadelphia, Sept. 5th–Oct. 26th, to devise plans for a redress of grievances, and for the restoration of harmony. The idea of a Continental Congress is said to have originated with Franklin. Sparks's Franklin, i. 350. Cf. Bancroft, vi. 508; vii. 40, 63.

Brief notes of the debates were kept by John Adams. Cf. Works, ii. 366, 370, 382, 387, 393. Also Adams's Life by C. F. Adams, Works, i. 150; ii. 340, his Diary; ix. 339, 343, Letters; and his Correspondence with Mercy Warren, Massachusetts Historical Society's Collections, 5th series, iv. 348.

Histories of the United States by Bancroft, vii. 127; Grahame, iv. 373; Hildreth, iii.; Pitkin, i. ch. 8. Frothingham's Rise of the Republic, 335. Histories of Massachusetts by Barry; of New York by Dunlap, i. ch. 29 and 31; of Pennsylvania by Gordon, ch. 20; of New Jersey by Mulford, p. 389.

Biographies of Samuel Adams, by Wells, ii. 218; of Patrick Henry by Wirt, p. 105; of R. H. Lee by Lee, i. 106; of Washington by Marshall, and by Irving, i. ch. 35; of Jefferson, by Tucker, i. ch. 3, and by Parton, ch. 17; of Elbridge Gerry by Austin, ch. 5; of William Livingston by Sedgwick, ch. 5; of George Read by Read, 93; of John Jay by Jay, and by Flanders in his Chief Justices, and also in the latter the Life of Rutledge, ch. 5 and 6; of Josiah Quincy by Quincy.

Documents will also be found in Force's American Archives. The instructions to the Virginia delegates are in Jefferson's Writings, i. 122. The relations of the Congress to the Provincial Congress of Massachusetts are set forth in Frothingham's Joseph Warren, ch. 12. John Adams's Diary gives glimpses of the state of society in Philadelphia at the time.

The Declaration of Rights which the Congress put forth is given in John Adams's Works, ii. 535, with the original draft also.

On the 28th of Sept. Joseph Galloway introduced his plan of adjustment, embracing a union between Great Britain and her colonies. It was printed in a pamphlet, and later, in 1779, in his Rise and Progress of the American Rebellion. Cf. the Lives of Washington by Marshall and Sparks; of John Adams by C. F. Adams, ii. 387; of Samuel Adams by Wells, ii. 218; of Jay by Flanders, 100; of Patrick Henry by Wirt. Also cf. Franklin's Works, viii. 144, and Frothingham's Rise of the Republic.

Jones's New York in the Revolutionary War, edited by De Lancey, i. ch. 2, depicts the relations of the loyalists to the Congress; also pp. 438, 449, 477, 490 for notes.

R. H. Lee drafted the Address to the People of Great Britain, adopted by the Congress. Cf. Lee's Life of R. H. Lee, i. 119; Pitkin's United States, i. App. 17; and Jay's Life of John Jay, i. App.

John Dickinson wrote the petition to the King, agreed upon in the Congress. Cf. American Quarterly Review, i. 413 ; John Adams's Works, i. 159. This paper was signed in duplicate, — one copy is in the State Paper Office, London ; the other is mentioned in Henry Stevens's Bibliotheca Historica, p. 87. Franklin printed it in the App. to his Account of the Proceedings of the Congress, London, Jan. 1775.

The Proceedings of the Congress were printed in Philadelphia, by order of Congress, and at once reprinted in Boston.

The Congress was attacked in two tracts, Free Thoughts on the Proceedings, and Congress Canvassed by a West Chester Farmer, — both by Seabury, a loyalist, subsequently Bishop of Connecticut. Alexander Hamilton, who was practicing his pen in criticism on the Ministry in Holt's Journal, replied in A Full Vindication, 1774. This was replied to in a View of the Controversy, and again answered by Hamilton, in The Farmer Refuted, 1775. Cf. J. C. Hamilton's Republic of the United States, i. 65.

Political Agitation.

On the tory side, a writer in the Massachusetts Gazette, signing Massachusettensis, now known to have been Daniel Leonard, but generally supposed at the time to be Jonathan Sewall, presented the strongest front. These papers were reprinted in a pamphlet in Boston, again by Rivington in New York, and in 1776, again in Boston during the siege.

John Adams answered in the Boston Gazette, signing Novanglus. Almon abridged these papers and printed them in his Remembrancer as a History of the Dispute with America. They were twice reprinted before they were given at length in Adams's Works.

In 1819 both of these controversial series appeared in Boston, in one volume, with a preface by John Adams, in which he supposed his opponent to be Sewall. See Quincy's Life of Quincy, p. 381. Frothingham in his Rise of the Republic says they present accurate views of the arguments as the Revolution reached the stage of physical force.

There has been some controversy about the origin of the *Committees of Correspondence*, a device for the interchange of information and encouragement, and for mutual assistance between the various colonies. Cf. Frothingham's Rise of the Republic, pp. 284, 312, 327; Wirt's Patrick Henry, controverted in the North American Review, March, 1818; Randall's Jefferson, i. 80; Tucker's Jefferson, i. 52; Kennedy's Memoir of Wirt; Life of R. H. Lee, i. 89; Wells's Life of Samuel Adams, i. 509, ii. 62; Grahame's United States, iv. 338.

The general political movement all through the colonies at this time is depicted, drawing largely upon the newspapers of the day, in Frothingham's Rise of the Republic, p. 396. For the feeling in

Massachusetts, see the histories of that State by Bradford and Barry; Lincoln's History of Worcester, ch. 6 to 9; Gordon's Thanksgiving Sermon in Thornton's Pulpit of the Revolution; Hancock's Oration on the Anniversary of the Boston Massacre, which Wells, in the Life of Samuel Adams, ii. 138, says was largely composed by that patriot. Cf. Loring's Hundred Boston Orators.

For the feeling in New York, see the reports Governor Tryon made to the home government, and other documents from the British Archives, given in the Documents relative to the Colonial History of New York, viii.

For sentiments prevailing in Virginia and the South, see Rives's Madison, i.; Randall's Jefferson, i. ch. 3; Wirt's Patrick Henry; and various papers in Force's American Archives.

Effects and Movements in Great Britain, 1767–1775.

The debates in Parliament are the best exponents of feeling at this time. Read's Life of George Read, p. 76, gives a synopsis of arguments for and against taxation of the colonies. The Cavendish debates of the House of Commons, May, 1768, to June, 1774, give reports taken at the time by a member, and edited by John Wright in 1841. Cf. reports in that collection under Nov. 1768; Jan. and Feb. 1769; March and May, 1770. Debates are also given in the

Parliamentary History; and scantily in the Gentleman's Magazine and other periodicals. Summaries are in the Annual Register. Contemporary impression and hearsay accounts, tinged with positive whiggism, can be found in Walpole's George the Third, edited by Le Marchant, and in his Last Journals, edited by Doran.

Pictures of the contestants in these debates, with a tory coloring, are drawn in Adolphus's History of England, ii. ch. 24, and the strong ministerial sympathy which pervades Adolphus can be offset by Massey's History of England, a later work, with opposition views. Cf. also Campbell's Life of Loughborough, in his Chancellors. Burke as a speaker is depicted in Wraxall's Historical Memoirs, ii. 35; and in the Lives of Burke, by Bisset, Prior, and Macknight. For other accounts of the opposition leaders and policy, see Rockingham and his Contemporaries; Russell's Memoir and Correspondence of Charles James Fox, book iii., and his Life and Times of Fox, ch. 4.

The culmination of the Tory argument can be traced in Dr. Johnson's tract, Taxation no Tyranny. Moore's Life of Sheridan, ch. 3, gives the outline of an intended answer to Johnson. In Dean Tucker's writings, we have the advanced liberal views. Macknight's Life of Burke, ii. 115. The writers on the American controversy are characterized at some length in Grahame's United

States, iv. 320. The book-lists in the current numbers of the Gentleman's and other magazines, chronicle the numerous political tracts as they appeared.

Dr. Franklin was at this time maintaining in London the side of the colonists. See his letters on the Boston Resolutions of 1768 in Sparks's Franklin, vii. 375. In vol. iv. Sparks gives Franklin's different writings as they came consecutively out. In 1772 the Boston Resolutions against the bill for paying the salaries of the judges by the Crown were reprinted in London by Franklin, with a preface on the condition of the colonies, which is given in Sparks's Franklin, i. 350.

The news of the Tea Party in Boston had reached London, Jan. 19, 1774, and the accounts were printed in the London papers, Jan. 21st. Lord North, on March 14th, brought in a bill to remove the government from Boston to Salem, and to close the port of Boston ; on the 31st it received the royal assent. Cf. Parliamentary History, xvii. 1163 ; Donne's Correspondence of George III. and Lord North, i. 174 ; Annual Register, xvii. 1159 ; Protests of the Lords, edited by J. E. T. Rogers, ii. 141 ; Adolphus's History of England, ii. 59 ; Massey's History of England, ii. ; Pictorial History of England, Reign of George III. i. 159 ; Russell's Life and Times of Fox, ch. 5 ; Life of Lord Shelburne, ii. 302 ; Chatham

Correspondence, iv. 342; Rockingham Memoirs, ii. 238; Macknight's Burke, ii. 50.

In 1774 General Gage was impressing on the King his disbelief in the colonists' earnestness. Cf. Donne's Letters of George III. and Lord North, i. 164, and the Parliamentary History, xviii. for the speeches.

In July Governor Hutchinson held an interview with the King, and an account of what passed is in the Massachusetts Historical Society's Proceedings, Oct. 1877. Cf. Donne's Correspondence of George III. and Lord North, i. 194.

The King dissolved Parliament Sept. 30th, and after elections a new Parliament assembled Nov. 30th.

Meanwhile Franklin was maintaining intercourse with Chatham and trying to arrange a plan of pacification. Cf. Lives of Franklin by Sparks, Bigelow, and Parton. He had deferred returning to America until the results of the Congress of 1774 were known, and it devolved on him to present its petition to the King. Cf. Sparks's Franklin, 372; Quincy's Life of Quincy; Bancroft's United States, vii. 186. Walpole in his Last Journals, i. 439, describes the effect of this Congress upon the parties in England.

Josiah Quincy made notes of speeches he heard in Parliament, Jan. 20, 1775, by Chatham, Camden, and others. Cf. Quincy's Life of Quincy, 318, 335. Also see Gordon's American Revolution, i.

298; Force's Archives, 4th series, i. 1494; Walpole's Last Journals, i.

Before leaving London Franklin wrote some articles for the Public Advertiser on the Rise and Progress of the Difference between Great Britain and her American Colonies, which are reprinted in Sparks, iv. 526.

In March, 1775, Franklin left England, and on his voyage home he wrote out for his son an Account of the recent negotiations with the British Government for a reconciliation, which is printed in Sparks, v. 1, and in Bigelow's Franklin, i. 256.

January — March, 1775.

For the interval before the actual hostilities at Concord, still follow Frothingham's Siege of Boston, ch. 2, and consult for illustrative documents Force's American Archives, vol. i., where will be found De Berniere's narrative of his explorations towards Worcester to get information for General Gage.

For particulars of Leslie's expedition to Salem, in March, see C. M. Endicott's article in the Proceedings of the Essex Institute, vol. i., with a contemporary letter, also published separately; the Life of Timothy Pickering, vol. i.; George B. Loring's Speech and other addresses at the centennial celebration, 1875.

The contemporary evidence relative to the expedition to Marshfield can be found in Force's American Archives.

E. E. Hale's popular summary, One Hundred Years Ago, begins with these preliminaries of war.

Lexington and Concord, April, 1775.

The best eclectic account is that in Frothingham's Siege of Boston, and in his Appendix will be found a chronological list of the principal authorities.

Paul Revere's expedition on the night of the 18th, to give notice of the morrow's march, which is the subject of Longfellow's poem, was narrated by himself, and appears in the Collections of the Massachusetts Historical Society, 1st series, vol. v., and more accurately in the Proceedings, Nov. 1878. There has been some controversy as to the tower from which the lantern, which was the signal to Revere, was shown, and on this point see the pamphlet, Paul Revere's Signal, by John Lee Watson, with remarks by C. Deane (see Proceedings Massachusetts Historical Society, Nov. 1876) ; and one entitled Alarm of April 18, 1775, by Richard Frothingham. The question is also discussed by W. W. Wheildon, in his History of Paul Revere's Signal Lanterns, 1878, and in H. W. Holland's William Dawes and his Ride with Paul Revere, vindicating Dawes's claim to be considered one of the two who roused the country. See, in this connection, on the escape of Hancock and Adams, Loring's Hundred Boston Orators, and General Sumner in the New England Historical and Genealogical Register, vol. viii. p. 188.

The narrative and depositions ordered by the Provincial Congress were printed in the Journal of the third Provincial Congress, 1775, in the London Chronicle, and in various Boston newspapers; and the whole reappeared in a pamphlet, issued at Worcester, in 1775, by Isaiah Thomas, and entitled A Narrative of the Incursions and Ravages of the King's Troops on the Nineteenth of April; and they are given in Force's American Archives, 4th series, vol. ii.; Shattuck's History of Concord, p. 342; and portions are given in Frothingham's Siege of Boston; Remembrancer, 1775, vol. i., etc. The original depositions were signed in several copies, and some of them are in the Lee Papers in Harvard College library. See the Calendar of the Lee Papers, published in the Bulletin of Harvard College library. Other originals are among the Lee Papers in the library of the University of Virginia. Cf. Sparks's Washington, iii. 35.

This matter constituted the account sent by the Congress to England, with the Essex Gazette, which was the chief newspaper narrative, and which reached London eleven days ahead of General Gage's messenger; and in this connection, see the Proceedings of the Massachusetts Historical Society, April, 1858. Other accounts and depositions can also be found in Dawson's Battles of the United States; in Frank Moore's Diary of the Revolution. See an account of the expresses sent

South in Christopher Marshall's Diary, p. 18. In the New England Historical and Genealogical Register, Oct. 1873, p. 434, is the dispatch sent April 19th, from Watertown, conveying tidings of the conflict, to which are appended the indorsements of the authorities of the towns through which the express passed. An original of one of these dispatches is in the Pennsylvania Historical Society's library. Some of the contemporary accounts are given in Niles's Principles and Acts of the Revolution. A fragment of a diary by Dr. McClure is given in the Massachusetts Historical Society's Proceedings, April, 1878. Cf. Military Journals of two private soldiers, 1758–1775, Poughkeepsie, 1855.

The Rev. William Gordon, May 17, 1775, prepared An Account of the Commencement of Hostilities, which is in Force, and this, with additions and abridgments, forms part of his History of the Revolution. A contemporary letter, probably by Dr. Foster of Charlestown, is given in the Proceedings of the Massachusetts Historical Society, April, 1870.

The Rev. Jonas Clark delivered a discourse in Lexington on the first anniversary in 1776, and appended to it a narrative of events, which was reprinted in 1875. A brief account was also prepared by the Rev. William Emerson of Concord, a witness of the events at Concord, and this was printed in R. W. Emerson's Commemorative Discourse in 1835, which has been printed separately, and in the American Historical Magazine, New Haven, 1836. Other anniversary sermons were delivered in Lexington, in 1777 by Samuel Cooke, and in 1782 by Phillips Payson, both of which are in the Boston Public Library.

Of the British accounts, Col. Smith's report will be found in the Appendix to Mahon's (Stanhope's) England, vol. vi. Various English accounts are given in Force, and in The Detail and Conduct of the American War. General Gage sent to Governor Trumbull, a "Circumstantial Account," which is printed in the Massachusetts Historical Society's Collections, 2d series, vol. ii., while in vol. iv. will be found a reprint of a pamphlet entitled General Gage's Instructions, etc., originally printed, in 1779, from a manuscript left in Boston by a British officer, which gives Gage's instructions to Brown and De Berniere, Feb. 22, 1775, with an account of their journey to Worcester and Concord, and a narrative of the "Transactions" on the 19th of April. A contemporary account is given in The Rise, Progress, and Present State of the Dispute, published at London, in 1775. In a work published at Dublin, 1779–1785, in three volumes, entitled History of the War in America, there is a large folded sheet of the numbers of the killed, etc., of the British forces at Concord, Lexington, and Bunker Hill. An engraved likeness of Earl Percy, is given in Andrews's History of the War. The third report of the Commissioners on Historical MSS., in England, 1872, cites various papers of the Percy family touching the events, etc., of the American War, 1775–1777.

Stedman, in his American War, and the other British writers claim that the provincials fired first at Lexington; and Pitcairn's side of the story is given from Stiles's Diary in Frothingham, and in Irving's Washington.

Late in the day General Heath exercised a general command over the provincials, and his memoirs can be consulted. Colonel Timothy Pickering's Essex Regiment was charged with dilatoriness in coming up, and this question is discussed in the Life of Pickering, ch. 5, by his son.

The semi-centennial period renewed the interest in the matter, and the question, whether the provincials returned the fire of the British troops at Lexington, was discussed with some spirit. This having been denied, a committee of the town of Lexington authorized Elias Phinney to publish, in 1825, an account of The Battle of Lexington, to which was appended depositions (taken in 1822) of survivors to establish the point. This led the Rev. Ezra Ripley and others, of Concord, in 1827, to publish The Fight at Concord, claiming the credit of first returning the fire for Concord, and this was reissued in 1832. In 1835 the story was again told in the interest of Concord, in Lemuel Shattuck's History of Concord, which was examined in the North American Review, vol. xlii. In this account, as well as in that by Ripley and others, it was claimed that the part borne by Captain Davis of Acton was not fairly represented, and Josiah Adams, in his centennial address at Acton, in 1835, and again in a letter to Shattuck in 1850, presented the merits of Davis, and gave depositions of survivors. In 1851 James Trask Woodbury made a speech in the Massachusetts legislature on the question of appropriating money to erect a monument to Davis and his fellows, which was printed by the town of Acton. The parts borne by other towns have also been commemorated: for Danvers, by D. P. King, in 1835; for Cambridge, by Rev. A. McKenzie, in 1870; and also see S. A. Smith's West Cambridge on the 19th of April, 1775, Boston, 1864.

At Lexington, Edward Everett delivered an address in 1835; but see also his Mount Vernon Papers, No. 47. There is an account of the celebration in Niles's Register, vol. xlviii. A plan of the Lexington field can be found in Josiah Adams's letter, and in Moore's Ballad History of the Revolution, part 1. Compare Hudson's History of Lexington, ch. 6, of which he published an abstract in 1876; a popular narrative in Harper's Monthly, vol. xx.; accounts in association with landmarks in Lossing's Field-Book, and in Drake's Historic Fields and Mansions of Middlesex. See also R. H. Dana's address in 1875; the centennial Souvenir of 1775, and A. B. Muzzey's paper, The Battle of Lexington, with personal recollections of men engaged in it, in the New England Historical and Genealogical Register, Oct. 1877, and subsequently printed separately.

At Concord, Edward Everett delivered an address in 1825, and much of interest in connection with this anniversary was printed in the newspapers of that day; and Lossing in his Field-Book, and Drake in his Middlesex, should be consulted for much illustrative of the events of 1775. Popular narratives can be found in Frederic Hudson's illustrated paper in Harper's Monthly, May, 1875, and the article by G. Reynolds in the Unitarian Review for April, 1875. Read George W. Curtis's oration in 1875, and James R. Lowell's ode, in Atlantic Monthly, June, 1875. Also the Rev. Henry Westcott's Centennial Sermons, 1875.

The town of Concord, in 1875, printed an account of the Centennial Celebration, giving a facsimile of pages from Rev. William Emerson's contemporary diary of these events, and having for an Appendix an account of the literature of the subject, by James L. Whitney, which was printed separately.

The events of the 19th of April also form important chapters in Bancroft's United States, vol. vii.; in Elliott's New England, vol ii.; in Barry's Massachusetts, vol. iii.; and in other general works on the Revolutionary period. Consult Dawson's Battles of the United States; E. E. Hale's One Hundred Years Ago; and Potter's American Monthly, April, 1875. The events of the day make part of the story of Hawthorne's Septimius Felton.

Amos Doolittle's contemporary engravings are reproduced in a new edition of Clark's narrative. See also Moore's Ballad History, part 1; and Potter's American Monthly, April, 1875. There is a view of Concord taken in 1776, in the Massachusetts Magazine, July, 1794, which is fac-similed in the separate issue of J. L. Whitney's Literature of the Nineteenth of April.

An account of Jonathan Harrington, the last survivor of the fight, is given in Potter's American Monthly, July, 1875. Compare Lossing's Field-Book and De Lancey's note to Jones's New York in the Revolutionary War, i. 552. There is in the Historical Magazine, July, 1860, an account of a musket captured from a British soldier at Lexington, which belonged to Theodore Parker, and now hangs in the Senate chamber of the State House at Boston.

Claims have been raised for other places as having been those where blood was first shed in the war, for which see Potter's American Monthly, April, 1875. Dawson gave a paper on the affair at Golden Hill, in New York City, Jan. 19–20, 1770, in the Historical Magazine, iv. 233, and

more at length in the number for Jan. 1869. See
page 5 for the battle of the Alamance, and the war
of the Regulators in North Carolina. There is an
account of the Westminster Massacre in Vermont,
March, 1775, in the Historical Magazine, May,
1859.

Mecklenburg Declaration, May 20, 1775.

Whether the declaration of independence passed
by an assembly in Mecklenburg, North Carolina,
is supported by credible evidence has been a matter of controversy. It was denied by Jefferson,
and J. S. Jones published a Defence of the Revolutionary History of North Carolina against the
aspersions of Jefferson. The alleged resolutions
of May 20th would seem to be the uncertain rec-
ollection, twenty years later, of some that were
passed May 31st, a wrong date given them, and
alterations made under the influence of the continental declaration of July 4th. Cf. Frothingham's
Rise of The Republic, p. 422; Randall's Jefferson, iii. App. 2; North Carolina University Magazine, May, 1853; J. C. Welling in North Amer-
cian Review, April, 1874; Hawks's Lecture in
W. D. Cooke's Revolutionary History of North
Carolina; and passages in the general histories.

May and June, 1775.

The events of the interval between Concord and
Bunker Hill can best be studied in Frothingham's
Siege of Boston, and in his Life of Joseph Warren,

ch. 15. Particularly on the affair at Noddle's Island, May 27, 1775, see Force's American Archives, Humphreys's and Tarbox's Lives of Putnam, Sumner's History of East Boston; and a chapter in Dawson's Battles of the United States. Letters written from Boston in May are in the Proceedings of the Massachusetts Historical Society, June, 1873.

Com. F. H. Parker, in the Magazine of American History, i. 209, gives an account of the capture of the Margaretta at Machias in June.

The effects of Lexington and Concord on the other colonies are depicted in Stuart's Life of Jonathan Trumbull, and generally in the standard histories. The news was received in New York April 23d. Cf. Jones's New York in the Revolutionary War, i. 39, 487; Documents relative to the Colonial History of New York, viii. 571.

A letter of Joseph Warren to his wife on the day before the battle of Bunker Hill is given in the Proceedings of the Massachusetts Historical Society, April, 1871.

Bunker Hill, June 17, 1775.

Frothingham, in an Appendix to his Siege of Boston, enumerates in a chronological order the chief authoritative statements regarding the battle. Dawson devoted the whole of the June, 1868, double number of the Historical Magazine, to a collation of nearly all the printed accounts, authoritative and compiled, and from his foot-notes can be gleaned a full list of articles and books which at that time had been published.

Earliest Accounts. — The affairs of the 19th of April had among other results precipitated the removal of the newspapers published in Boston to other places, and the number for April 24th was the last of the Evening Post published in Boston. Edes's Boston Gazette, which was thus removed to Watertown, the seat of the Provincial Congress, gave in its issue for June 19th the earliest account of the battle which appeared in print. The Massachusetts Spy, which had been removed to Worcester in May, had its first account in its number for June 21st. That same day the Connecticut Journal had its first intelligence, and though it was several days later before the New York papers published accounts, on this same 21st a handbill with the news was circulated in New York. In F. Moore's Diary of the American Revolution, there will be found a list of the contemporary newspapers publishing these accounts, and from which he derives in part the matter of his book which begins Jan. 1, 1775. Many of these accounts will be found reprinted in Dawson's Historical Magazine article; and some of them have been reproduced in fac-simile in the centennial memorials of 1776. Frothingham reprints that of the Massachusetts Spy in his condensed narrative of the battle, and it is in fac-simile in the Centennial Graphic.

Prof. Winthrop, June 21st, sent a brief account to John Adams, then in Philadelphia, which is given in the Massachusetts Historical Society's Collections 5th series, iv. 292.

The Rev. Mr. Thacher was a spectator of the action from the north side of the Mystic River, and within a fortnight afterwards, depending in some measure upon Prescott's assistance, prepared an account, the manuscript of which is now preserved in the American Antiquarian Society's collection at Worcester. This had been used by Frothingham and others, but was never printed in full with all its corrections indicated, till Dawson included it in his Appendix in 1868. This narrative of Thacher's was made the basis of that which the Committee of Safety prepared for transmission to England, and this latter narrative is given with much other matter in The Journal of the Third Provincial Congress, 1775, and has been reprinted by Ellis (in 1843), Frothingham, Swett, Dawson, etc. Force's American Archives, vol. iv., is another repository of these and various other contemporary accounts, several of which are copied by Dawson in his Battles of the United States, as well as in his Historical Magazine article; and by F. Moore in his Ballad History of the American Revolution, part 2.

Colonel Prescott's own account is contained in a letter dated August 25, 1775, and addressed to John Adams, and this can be seen in Frothingham, where it was first published, and in Dawson. What is called the Prescott manuscript, which is said to have been prepared in the family of the colonel, and in part with his approval, was first printed in full in Butler's History of Groton, p. 337, etc., and it has been reprinted by Dawson, p. 437. Frothingham and Sparks had the use of the manuscript known as Judge Prescott's (son of the colonel) memoir of the battle ; but it was never printed in full till it appeared in Frothingham's centennial narrative, 1876.

Contemporary feelings will be found expressed in the letters which passed during the war between John Adams and his wife Abigail Adams, which, having been some years ago published separately, were reprinted in one series by their grandson, Charles Francis Adams, in 1876.

President Stiles, then of Newport, kept a diary of events at this time, which is preserved at Yale College. He first heard the news on the 18th, and began his account on that day, to which he added from day to day, as further corrected tidings reached him. This was printed at length for the first time in Dawson, but has been used by Sparks, Frothingham, Bancroft, etc. This diary also copies the letter of Peter Brown, dated June 25th, to his mother, which is considered by Frothingham, who gives it, as the most noteworthy description written by a private soldier engaged in the battle, and is printed from the original in

Potter's American Monthly, July, 1875. Another
letter, of date June 21st, is given in the Proceedings of the Masachusetts Historical Society, Feb.
1870; under Oct. 1876, p. 108, will be found a
brief account from Fenno's orderly-book; and under March, 1877, another from Thomas Boynton's
Journal.

Colonel Scammans's account of his court-martial is given in the New England Chronicle, Feb.
29, 1776, and is reprinted in Dawson, p. 400.

Governor Trumbull in a letter, Aug. 31, 1779,
gave a sketch of the action, and it is printed in
the Massachusetts Historical Society's Collections,
vol. vi. See also Stuart's Life of Jonathan Trumbull, ch. 16. Colonel John Trumbull, who afterwards painted the well-known picture of the battle,
was not in it, but saw the smoke of it from the
Roxbury lines, and in his autobiography, published in 1841, has an outline narrative. General
Heath's memoirs, published in 1798, have a brief
account. The narrative in Thacher's Military
Journal is entered as having been written in July,
1775. The Memoirs of General James Wilkinson,
printed in 1816, give in ch. 19 a "rapid sketch,"
embodying his own knowledge and other evidence
which had reached him at first hand, as he went
over the field in March, 1776, with Stark and
Reed, and conferred with Major Caleb Stark.

Other testimony of eye-witnesses was gathered
too long after the battle to be wholly trustworthy,

in 1818, at the time of the Dearborn controversy, later to be mentioned ; and numerous depositions were taken from survivors attending the semi-centennial celebration, which are preserved in three large volumes, but are considered by those who have examined them as of little or no value. The recital of the Adventures of Israel R. Potter, who was a participator in the battle, and who published the first edition of his narrative at Providence, in 1824, was put into literary shape by Herman Melville. There is a long account in the Columbian Centinel of December, 1824, and January, 1825. An account by Oliver Morsman, a revolutionary soldier, was published at Sackett's Harbor in 1830; and Mr. Charles Coffin published at Portland, in 1835, an account compiled from the narratives of Generals Heath, Lee, Wilkinson, and Dearborn. Mr. Needham Maynard contributed the recollections of a survivor, which were printed in a Boston newspaper as late as 1843.

British Accounts. — Of the British accounts, the entries in Howe's orderly-book are given in Ellis's sketch (edition of 1843). The Gentleman's Magazine (London) of the same year gave an account with a somewhat erroneous plan of the redoubt, which has been reproduced in Frothingham's monographs. General Gage's official report was printed in Almon's Remembrancer, accompanied with strictures upon it, and it has been reprinted by Ellis (edition of 1843 with the strictures), Force, Swett,

Frothingham ; by Dawson, in his Historical Magazine and in his Battles; in Frank Moore's Ballad History, etc. Burgoyne saw the action from
Copp's Hill, and his letter to Lord Stanley, dated
June 25, 1775, has also been given in Fonblanque's
Life of Burgoyne; in Dawson; in Ellis, edition
of 1843; in the New England Historical and
Genealogical Register, April, 1857; in an appendix to Pulsifer's Sketch of the battle, and is also
given in Samuel A. Drake's Bunker Hill, the
Story told in Letters from the Battle-field, in
which also will be found, together with various
other minor British accounts, the Impartial and
Authentic Narration, originally London, 1775,
by John Clarke, "a first lieutenant of marines,"
who gives what purports to be a speech of Howe
to his troops previous to the advance, which with
much else in this somewhat extended narrative
is considered rather apocryphal. This narrative
by Clarke was reprinted privately in 1868. The
compiled account in the Annual Register has been
thought to have been written by Burke. Cf. William Carter's Genuine Detail of the Royal and
American Armies, with a plan of the works on
Bunker's Hill, London, 1784. Carter was a lieutenant of the Fortieth Foot, and there is a note on
the curious details connected with the book, in the
Brinley Catalogue, No. 1789. Force, Ellis (edition of 1843), and Dawson, gather various contemporary royalist accounts, and some particulars can

be found in the separate historic records detailing the careers of some of the royal regiments in the action, like the Fourth, Fifth, Tenth Foot, etc. Moorsom's Fifty-second Regiment gives a brief account of its share in the battle, with plates of their uniform at the time. See also Lushington's Life of General Lord Harris, pp. 54–56; Sergeant Lamb's (Welsh Fusileers) Journal of Occurrences during the late American War; and the Detail and Conduct of the American War, for a letter from Boston, July 5, 1775, with other English reports. The British accounts first took regular shape in Stedman's History of the American War, published in 1794. Howe's conduct of the battle is criticised in Lee's Memoirs of the War in the Southern Department. Mahon's (Stanhope's) History of England, vol. vi., represents in an account, otherwise fair, that the Americans then and since have considered the battle a victory; but, when called upon to substantiate such an assertion, relied chiefly (see his Appendix) on the reports of British tourists of a subsequent day. A loyalist's statement of Howe's obstinacy in attacking in front, is in Jones's New York in the Revolutionary War, i. 52.

See a French narrative in Hilliard d'Auberteuil's Essais historiques, 1782.

Later Special Accounts. — In 1858 Mr. Henry B. Dawson published a popular account of the Battles of the United States, giving a chapter, based on the ordinary authorities, to Bunker Hill. In 1868, in the Historical Magazine, an American periodical then edited by him, he gave a special study of the battle, in which the "colonists" of the earlier work became "insurgents," and the royal troops were represented as fighting "in support of the constitution, the laws, the king and the government, and in defence of the life of the nation." Differing from other authorities, he represents that the attack along the beach of the Mystic was a preliminary attack. He has elaborately collated the various contemporary and later compiled accounts, and has appended numerous illustrative documents by English and American writers, derived from Almon, Force, Ellis, Frothingham, and others, to which he adds several printed for the first time. The fac-similes of Page's, De Berniere's, and Dearborn's maps, which are mentioned in his text as given with his account, were never appended to it.

Of the more extended descriptions, that in Frothingham's Siege of Boston is distinctively marked for its dependence chiefly upon contemporary accounts, and its avoidance of the mingled recollections and self-deceptions of the survivors of all grades, who in 1818 furnished so many depositions, over forty years after the conflict, to perplex the truth-lover. These confused recollections, added to the local jealousies of the partisans of the troops of Massachusetts, New Hampshire,

and Connecticut, and to the facts narrated by different persons as having taken place in positions
so disconnected as the redoubt and the rail fence,
have done much to render the sifting of evidence
very necessary; and it all gave some ground for
Charles Hudson, in 1857, in his Doubts concerning the Battle of Bunker Hill (see also Christian Examiner, vol. xl.) to attempt a logical vent-
ure somewhat after the fashion of Whateley's famous argument on the non-existence of Napoleon.
When, later, Frothingham wrote the Life of Joseph
Warren, he took occasion to summarize his longer
narrative in a chapter of that book, and his whole
description has again been recast in a popular
form in his centennial Bunker Hill, where he has
added much new matter, in letters, incidents, etc.

Anniversary addresses have often rehearsed the
story, occasionally adding a few details to our
stock of information, and the most significant
among them have been Webster's, in 1825 (see
also Analectic Magazine, vol xi.), at the laying of
the corner-stone of the monument; Alexander H.
Everett's, in 1836, which subsequently was in-
woven in his Life of Warren, in Sparks's series;
the Rev. Dr. George E. Ellis's, in 1841, which
was subsequently issued in 1843, anonymously, as
a sketch of the battle, with an Appendix of illustrative documents, some of which were printed for
the first time, and has again, in 1875, been recast
in a centennial History without the illustrative

documents (see also his account in the New York Herald, June 8, 1875); that by Edward Everett; and that by Judge Devens in 1875. A succinct narrative of the battle was also once or twice printed by Alden Bradford, in connection with his studies in the history of Massachusetts. A New History of the Battle, by W. W. Wheildon, traces two separate engagements constituting the battle. Recent years have produced condensed summaries, like that of Pulsifer and S. A. Drake; that by James M. Bugbee, in Osgood's Centennial Memorial; an article by H. E. Scudder, in the Atlantic Monthly, July, 1875; one by Launce Poyntz, in the Galaxy, July, 1875. The story also makes ch. 4 of E. E. Hale's One Hundred Years Ago, and is retold in the Centennial numbers of Frank Leslie's Pictorial, in the Centennial Graphic, and in various other popular memorials of 1875. It is gone over discursively in the illustrated paper, by Rev. Dr. Samuel Osgood, in the July (1875) number of Harper's Monthly.

Particular reference is given to *landmarks* in Lossing's Field-Book of the Revolution, vol. i., which account also appeared in the first volume of Harper's Monthly; in S. A. Drake's Historic Fields and Mansions of Middlesex. Finch, in an article in Silliman's Journal, 1822, gave an account of the traces then existing of the works of the British and Americans in the siege of Boston, and this has been reprinted by Frothingham. The

Report of the Bunker Hill Monument Association, 1876, gives a plan showing the position of
the monument and the present landmarks of the
neighborhood, relative to the lines of the old fortifications. See also the section below on Maps and
Plans.

Accounts in General Histories. — The battle
has necessarily given a subject to chapters in the
general histories of the war and of the State. The
earliest American historian of the war was Gordon
(see Loring on Gordon's History in Historical
Magazine, February and March, 1862), and he
followed closely the account of the Committee
of Safety. Ramsay's American Revolution was
published in 1789. Mrs. Mercy Warren's later.
Hubley's in 1805. Bancroft gives to it the 38th
chapter of his seventh volume. It is described
in ch. 20 of the second volume of Elliott's New
England; in the third volume of Barry's Massachusetts; and in ch. 15 of Carrington's Battles of
the American Revolution, with an eclectic map.

In Biographies. — The biographers of Washington, like Marshall and Irving, needed to describe it as leading to the consolidation of the army
of which he took command on the 3d of July next
following. There is a brief account in Tudor's
Life of Otis. The memoirs of Heath have already
been mentioned, and the lives of other observers
and participants will give occasional minor details,
like the Journals of Samuel Shaw, Boston, 1847,

etc.; the lives of General Ward and Colonel
Knowlton, in the New England Historical and
Genealogical Register, July, 1851, and Jan. 1861;
the life of Deborah Sampson, called " The Female
Review," by Herman Mann, 1797, edited in 1866
by J. A. Vinton. A list of officers who were in
the battle, and who are named in Frothingham, is
given in the New England Historical and Genealogical Register, April, 1873; and in the number
for July, 1874, there is an English list of the Yan-
kee officers in the forces about Boston, June, 1775.

New Hampshire Troops. — For the part borne
by them, see the memoirs of Stark by Caleb Stark
and Edward Everett. Stark's report to the New
Hampshire Congress is in the New Hampshire
Historical Society's Collections, vol. ii.; in Ellis's
edition of 1843, etc. The Adjutant-General of New
Hampshire, in his report for 1866, second volume,
rehearses the military history of that State, and
gives some details regarding the troops engaged.
The manuscripts in the Adjutant-General's office
(New Hampshire), containing the rosters of
Stark's and Reed's regiments, have never been
printed in full. C. C. Coffin, in a letter in the
Boston Globe, June 23, 1875, epitomizes the service of New Hampshire troops in the battle; and
details will be found in the New Hampshire Provincial Papers, vol. vii.; in the histories of the
towns of Hollis (see New England Historical and
Genealogical Register, Oct. 1873, and July, 1876,

and History by S. T. Worcester, 1879, p. 146), whence came Captain Dow's company of Prescott's regiment; of Manchester, by Potter, whence came Captain John Moore's company of Stark's regiment; and of New Ipswich. See also the New England Historical and Genealogical Register, vol. xxvii. p. 377, etc.; and the account by E. H. Derby in the number for Jan. 1877.

Connecticut Troops. — For the part borne by them, see lives of Putnam, Stuart's Life of Jonathan Trumbull, histories of Connecticut, by Hollister and others; Hinman's Connecticut in the Revolution.

Who Commanded? — The question of the highest command in the battle has given rise to much controversy. In many of the unofficial contemporary accounts, particularly in the British ones, Warren is represented as the commander. Putnam is known to have been the adviser of the expedition in the Council of War, and in the less authoritative accounts of the time is represented, as also in engravings, as the responsible director. Gordon, in his history in 1788, was the earliest, in print, to give the command to Prescott, following the Committee of Safety's account. The earliest printed direct mention of Putnam as commander is in a note to the sermon preached at his funeral by Rev. Josiah Whitney, in 1790, where he took exception to Humphreys's statement in his Life of Putnam, 1788, published while Putnam was still living, in which no mention is made of Putnam having commanded. Eliot, in his biographical dictionary, in 1809, represents Prescott as commanding in the redoubt, and Stark at the rail fence. The earliest reflection upon the conduct of Putnam in the action appeared in General Wilkinson's Memoirs, which were published in 1816, and were reviewed in the North American Review, Oct. 1817. The Analectic Magazine for Feb. and March, 1818, had articles on the battle, following chiefly the accounts of Thacher and Gordon, but with some important differences, and giving documents in the latter number.

General Henry Dearborn, who was a captain in Stark's regiment at the rail fence, opened a controversy, not yet ended, and which at that time soon got to have a political bearing, when he printed his communication in the Portfolio for March, 1818, in which he aimed to show that during the battle Putnam remained inactive at the rear, and this paper has since been reprinted separately, and twice in the Historical Magazine, Aug. 1864, and June, 1868, p. 402. A summary of this Dearborn controversy is given in G. W. Warren's History of the Bunker Hill Monument Association. Colonel Daniel Putnam, the son of the general, replied to Dearborn in the May number of the Portfolio, and appended numerous depositions, all of which have been reprinted in Dawson's Historical Magazine, June, 1868, p. 407.

4

This reply of Daniel Putnam led General Dearborn to vindicate his former statement by the publication, in the Boston Patriot of June 13, 1818,
of various depositions and confirmations of other
participants, all of which may also be found in
Dawson, p. 414. At this time Daniel Webster,
in the North American Review, July, 1818, vindicated the character of Putnam, but, examining
the evidence judicially, came to the conclusion
that Prescott commanded the fatigue party during
the night, and on the subsequent day exercised a
general command over the field so far as he could,
and should be considered the commanding officer,
and as acting under the orders of General Ward,
at Cambridge, only, and to whom he made report
of the action after it was over. See also the Proceedings of the Massachusetts Historical Society
for June, 1858.

Judge John Lowell next reviewed Dearborn's
defense of his attack on Putnam in the Columbian
Centinel for July 4 and 15, 1818, and strengthened his points with counter-depositions of actors
in the struggle, all of which are again given in
Dawson, p. 423. Colonel Swett now entered into
the controversy in an Historical and Topographical Sketch of Bunker Hill Battle, which, in Oct.
1818, was appended to an edition of Humphreys's
Life of Putnam, and this sketch was subsequently
published separately and with enlargements, derived in part from conversations with the surviv-

ors who attended the semi-centennial jubilee of 1825, and this appeared in 1826, and again in 1827 (see Sparks's notice in the North American review, vol. xxii.). Meanwhile, Colonel Daniel Putnam, in 1825, recapitulated his views in a communication to the Bunker Hill Monument Association, and this document is printed in the Connecticut Historical Collections, vol. i. The account of Swett has been substantially followed in Rand, Avery & Co.'s Bunker Hill Centennial. Swett's first publication was criticised by D. L. Child, in the Boston Patriot, Nov. 17, 1818, who claimed that Putnam was not in the battle, and whose article was reprinted as an Enquiry into the Conduct of General Putnam. On the other hand, Alden Bradford, in his pamphlet in 1825, claimed the command for Putnam.

In 1841 Ellis in his oration, and subsequently in his History of the Battle in 1843, taking advantage of intercourse with Prescott's descendants, made the first extended presentation of Prescott's claims, to which Colonel Swett demurred in the Boston Advertiser, where also can be found Ellis's rejoinder. See Judge Prescott's letter to Dr. Ellis in the Proceedings of the Massachusetts Historical Society, June, 1858. Prescott is assigned the command in the narrative of Major Thompson Maxwell, who was present in the fight, which is printed in the Collections of the Essex Institute, vol. vii. See also the New England Historical and Genealogical Register, Jan. 1868. Cf. the Report to the Massachusetts Legislature on a monument to Colonel Prescott, 1852.

Again, in 1843, John Fellows, in his Veil Removed, animadverted upon Swett's views regarding Putnam, and reproduced Dearborn's statement and many others which aimed to detract from Putnam's fame.

When Frothingham's Siege of Boston appeared in 1849, in which the question of the command was critically examined, p. 159, etc., giving that authority to Prescott, Swett renewed the controversy in a critique on that work in 1850, with a tract, Who was the Commander? etc., to which Frothingham replied in a pamphlet of fifty-six pages, The Command in the Battle of Bunker Hill, substantiating his position, and pointing out the inconsistencies and seeming perversions of Swett. In 1853 Irving in his Life of Washington favored Prescott. In 1855 L. Grosvenor in an address before the descendants of General Putnam "exposed" (as he claimed) "the ungenerous conduct of Colonel Prescott toward General Putnam, *the* commander in the battle." When Bancroft in 1858 published his seventh volume, he took the ground, already foreshadowed in a lecture which he had delivered, that Prescott commanded the Provincials. In 1859 "Selah" of the Hartford Post, favoring Putnam, had a controversy with Dawson, who held Putnam to have been a

" blusterer and swaggerer," and intimates that he
was also treacherous, and this was reprinted in an
unpublished quarto, called Major-General Israel
Putnam. Again, in Putnam's favor, the Hon. H.
C. Deming delivered a discourse before the Connecticut Historical Society on the presentation of
Putnam's sword, and it was repeated, June 18,
1860, at Putnam's grave, at Pomfret, before the
Putnam Phalanx. The argument, as regards the
claims of Putnam, was presented by the Rev. I.
N. Tarbox, in the New York Herald, June 12
and 14, 1875, and in the New Englander, April,
1875, and more at length in his Life of Putnam,
1876. S. A. Drake's General Israel Putnam the
Commander at Bunker Hill argues on the basis of
military rule, and summarizes the authorities.
See also Hollister's History of Connecticut and
Hinman's Connecticut in the Revolution. Judge
Devens's oration at Bunker Hill, 1875, favors
Prescott. Wheildon's New History favors Put-
nam. A pamphlet, entitled Colonel William
Prescott, by Francis J. Parker, issued since 1875,
presents the case anew in favor of Prescott.

Death of Warren.—In 1825, when General W.
H. Sumner was Adjutant-General of Massachusetts, and it devolved upon him to arrange for the
appearance of the veterans in the celebration of
that year, he collected from the recitals of some of
them a few particulars regarding the appearance
and death of Warren, and held some correspond-

ence with Dr. Waterhouse on the subject in the Boston Patriot, in August of that year. This matter he reproduced in a paper in the New England Historical and Genealogical Register, April and July, 1858. See further the accounts in Loring's Boston Orators; in Mrs. J. B. Brown's (Warren's grand-daughter) Stories of General Warren; in Dr. John Jeffries's (son of the royal surgeon on the field) paper in the Boston Medical and Surgical Journal, June 17, 1875; and in the Life of Dr. John Warren, brother of the general. See also the Eulogy on General Warren in 1776, by Perez Morton, and the memorial volume on the occasion of the dedication of the Warren statue, and particularly Frothingham's Life of Warren. The history of Warren's sword is given in the Proceedings of the Massachusetts Historical Society, Sept. 1866.

There is an account of the different celebrations in Charlestown in the New York Herald for June 4, 1875; and of Ralph Farnham, the last survivor of the battle, in the Historical Magazine, iv. 312.

There are other papers on the battle in the New England Historical and Genealogical Register, and Dawson's and Frothingham's notes will indicate additional publications of small importance not mentioned here.

Plans and Maps. — The earliest of the plans of the action seems to have been a slight sketch, after information from Chaplain John Martin, who was in the battle, drawn by Stiles in his diary, which is reproduced in Dawson, who also, as does Frothingham, gives the slight sketch, made with printers' rules, which accompanied the account in Rivington's Gazette, August 3, 1775.

The careful plan made by Page of the British engineers, based upon Captain Montresor's survey (which closely agrees with Felton and Parker's survey of Charlestown in 1848), is much the best, and it shows the laying out of Charlestown, the position of the frigates, and the battery at Copp's Hill. The successive positions of the attacking force are indicated by a superposed sheet. This was issued in London in 1776, and the same plate, with few changes, was used in Stedman's history in 1794. The original impression was reëngraved for Frothingham's Siege of Boston, and is also given in his Centennial Narrative.

The plan by De Berniere, of the Tenth Royal Infantry, on much the same scale as Page's, differs in some points from it, is not so correct in the ground plan, and is the first plan that appeared in an American engraving, in the Analectic Magazine, Feb. 1818, where it is represented as from a sketch found in the captured baggage of a British officer in 1775. General Dearborn made some remarks on this plan in the Portfolio, March, 1818, which are reprinted in Dawson, p. 438. Dearborn's subsequent plan, as altered in red on that of De Berniere, was criticised upon the field in

June, 1818, by Governor Brooks (who acted as messenger from Prescott to Ward in the battle), as detailed by General Sumner in the New England Historical and Genealogical Register, July, 1858. This map was made the basis of one engraved by Smith, and issued in Boston, at the time of the completion of the monument, in 1843.

A map of Boston, showing Charlestown and the field, with Burgoyne's letter attached, was issued in London, and has been reproduced in fac-simile in F. Moore's Ballad History of the Revolution, part 2.

There is also an English map of the eastern part of Massachusetts, dated London, Sept. 2, 1775, in which the lines of march of the troops of the different provinces are designated as they assembled to the relief of Boston. This has been reproduced in smaller size in the Centennial Graphic, and Frothingham styles it "more curious than valuable." In a side-sketch, of this same sheet, there is a semi-pictorial plan of the battle, with the whole of Boston, and this has been fac-similed in Wheildon's, Pulsifer's, and Bugbee's sketches, and in George A. Coolidge's Centennial Memorial. There is a map of New England at this time in Hilliard d'Auberteuil's Essais historiques, 1782.

Colonel Swett made a plan of his own, based on De Berniere's, of about the size of Page's, and it was reproduced full size in Ellis's oration, 1841;

but the reproductions of it in Lossing's Field-Book, in Ellis's New York Herald article, June 8, 1875, and in his History and Centennial History, in Rand, Avery & Co.'s Bunker Hill Centennial, in George A. Coolidge's Brochure, in the Bunker Hill Times, June 17, 1875, and in Bugbee's sketch, are reduced in size. See also Tarbox's Life of Putnam. Little regard is paid in this plan to the laying out of the town of Charlestown. There is a plan in the English translation of Botta's History of the War of Independence; and lesser plans are in Ridpath's United States, and are other popular histories.

Of contemporary plans of Boston, that in the Gentleman's Magazine, Oct. 1775, p. 464, shows the peninsula, with " Charlestown in ruins." This is drawn from the same original as that in the Pennsylvania Magazine, 1775, which in the June number has a plan of Boston Harbor, with only one eminence delineated on the Charlestown peninsula, which is marked " Bunk[s] H." The houses in the town are represented as on fire, and similarly in the plan in Murray's Impartial History of the American War. There is a plan of Boston in the Geschichte der Kriege in und aus Europa, Nuremberg, 1776. The London Magazine, April, 1774, has a chart of the coast of New England, with a plan of Boston in the corner, and this plan was inserted, enlarged, in Jeffery's Map of New England, Nov. 1774, with also a plan of Boston

Harbor, and was again copied in Jeffery's American Atlas, 1776, and a French reproduction of it was published at Paris in 1778, in the Atlas Ameriquain septentrional. Another chart of the harbor and plan of the town is in the Political Magazine, Nov. 1782.

Views, etc. — There are rude contemporary views of the action, one of which appeared in 1775, known as Roman's, representing Putnam on horseback, as in command, and was reduced in the Pennsylvania Magazine, Sept. 1775, and this has been heliotyped in Frothingham's Centennial sketch, in Rand, Avery & Co.'s, and in Coolidge's memorials, and is also reproduced in Moore's Ballad History, and in the Bunker Hill Times, June 17, 1875. In Cocking's poem, The American War, published in London, 1781, is a somewhat extraordinary picture, which, with extracts from the poem, has been reproduced in S. A. Drake's monograph ; and the picture is also given in Bugbee's sketch, and in Coolidge's Brochure. In the Gentleman's Magazine, Feb. 1790, there is a view of Charlestown and Howe's encampment on the hill, taken after the battle ; and in the Massachusetts Magazine, Sept. 1789, is a view of Charles River Bridge, showing the configuration of Bunker's and Breed's hills.

The well-known picture which Colonel Trumbull, in 1786, painted of the battle, and of which a key will be found in the New England Historical and Genealogical Register, vol. xv., and of which there is a description in Trumbull's Autobiography, gave the command in the redoubt to Putnam, and a subordinate position to Prescott, which the painter is said afterwards to have regretted, as indicating views on the question of command at variance with the truth. A picture by D. M. Carter represents Prescott in command, and this is reproduced in Coolidge's Brochure. Chappel's picture of the battle is given in W. L. Stone's History of New York City. There is a curious engraving of a group where an eulogy is being pronounced over Warren's body, in Hilliard d'Auberteuil's Essais historiques, 1782.

The Monument. — For accounts of the monument, see Ellis's ed. of 1843; Frothingham's Siege of Boston, and Wheildon's Life of Solomon Willard. A History of the Bunker Hill Monument Association has been written by G. W. Warren, 1877. See, also, A. S. Packard's account in the Collections of the Maine Historical Society, vol. iii.

In Fiction. — Dr. O. W. Holmes, in his Grandmother's Story of Bunker Hill Battle, rehearses the events of the day in verse; and the battle is described in Cooper's novel of Lionel Lincoln.

The Siege of Boston, June, 1775 — March, 1776.

The siege of Boston began with the return of the British troops from Concord on the evening of April 19, 1775; and Putnam fortified Prospect

Hill (now Somerville) immediately after the battle of Bunker Hill; and after Washington's taking the command, July 3, 1775, the work of completing the lines about the town was begun.

The fullest accounts of the events succeeding the 17th of June will be found in Frothingham's Siege of Boston, and in the memorial volume of the Centennial Celebration, printed by the City of Boston, in 1876, including an historical address by Geo. E. Ellis, to which is appended a chronicle of the siege by the same hand. A general survey of the events will be found in Bancroft's United States, vol. viii.; and Barry's Massachusetts, vol. iii.; in Paige's History of Cambridge; in the Memoirs of Gen. Heath; the Memoirs of Gen. Wilkinson; Greene's Life of Greene, i. 88, and other accounts of the Rhode Island troops in the Rhode Island Historical Society's Collections, vi.

Popular accounts can be followed in Dawson's Battles of the United States; in E. E. Hale's One Hundred Years Ago; in H. E. Scudder's paper on the Siege in the Atlantic Monthly, April, 1876, and in the general histories.

Gordon, vol. ii., gives details from diaries of the times; and illustrative matter of contemporary origin is given in Almon's Remembrancer; in Force's American Archives; in Moore's Diary of the American Revolution; in the Collections of the Essex Institute, vol. iii.; in the diary of General Heath in the camps at Roxbury and Cambridge, in the Proceedings, May, 1859, of the Massachusetts Historical Society, which contains matter not in his Memoirs; and the accounts in Niles's Principles and Acts of the Revolution. Cf. also F. S. Drake's History of Roxbury.

The letters of Washington, in Sparks's edition, vol. iii., during his stay at Cambridge, are of the utmost importance, as are those of Joseph Reed, his military secretary. The Life of Reed contains some of Washington's letters which Sparks did not print; others are in the Rhode Island Colonial Records, vii. Consult the autobiography of Col. John Trumbull, who was at this time of Washington's military family; the Revolutionary Services of Gen. William Hull, ch. 2; and the Life of Dr. John Warren, brother of General Joseph Warren, and of the medical staff. A journal of Knox's expedition in Nov. 1775, to Ticonderoga to get cannon for conducting the siege of Boston, is given in the New England Historical and Genealogical Register, July, 1876. Drake's Life of Knox.

Of the associations of Washington with his head-quarters at Cambridge, see Alexander McKenzie's article in the Atlantic Monthly, July, 1875; and Charles Deane's paper in the Proceedings of the Massachusetts Historical Society, Sept. 1872, — see also June, 1858. In the Harvard Book are chapters on the Old President's House, by Chas. Deane; on the Cragie House, by George

Dexter, and on the Washington Elm, by Alexander McKenzie. Cf. T. C. Amory's Old and New Cambridge. In this connection see the Centennial volume published by the City of Cambridge, 1875, which includes Rev. Dr. Peabody's oration at Cambridge, July 3, 1875. There is a poem, Under the Great Elm, in the Atlantic Monthly, Aug. 1875, by James Russell Lowell. A letter of Washington is in the Magazine of American History, Feb. 1879, p. 113. Much connected with the Cambridge centre, and the left wing can be learned from Drake's Middlesex; and for the whole line, from Lossing's Field-Book.

The Rules and Regulations for the Massachusetts army were published by order at Salem in 1775.

Various orderly books, contemporary letters, and diaries, etc., have been printed, covering the American camp life, and the experiences of the troops and prisoners in Boston : —

American Camp. — Thacher's Military Journal, the author being a surgeon in the forces on Prospect Hill, and in Boston after the evacuation. Dr. Belknap's diary, Oct. 1775, at Cambridge, in the Proceedings of the Massachusetts Historical Society, June, 1858. Paul Lunt's diary, Cambridge, May 10 to Dec. 23, 1775, in the same, Feb. 1872. Ezekiel Price's diary, along the American lines, in the same, Nov. 1863. Crafts's journal, beginning at Cambridge, June 15, 1775,

in Collections of the Essex Institute, vol. iii. p.
51. The letters written by Abigail Adams to her
husband, John Adams. A MS. orderly-book,
Cambridge, July 3 to Sept. 21, 1775, is in the cabinet of the Pennsylvania Historical Society. Daniel McCurlin's journal in Thomas Balch's Maryland Line during the Revolution. David How's
diary, a soldier in Col. Sargent's regiment of the
Massachusetts line, printed with notes by H. B.
Dawson, New York, 1865. William Henshaw's
orderly-book, April to Sept. 1775, with notes by
C. C. Smith, in the Proceedings of the Massachusetts Historical Society, Oct. 1876, and reprinted. Glover's orderly-book, in Collections of
the Essex Institute, vol. v. p. 112. Col. Israel
Hutchinson's orderly-book, Aug. 13, 1775 to July
8, 1776, in Proceedings of Massachusetts Historical Society, Oct. 1878, with notes by C. C. Smith,
and an introduction by Lucius R. Paige, also
printed separately. Jeremiah Fogg's orderly-
book, Winter Hill, Oct. 28, 1775 to Jan. 12,
1776, is preserved in Harvard College library.
Major William Lee's orderly-book is still in MS.
in the cabinet of the Massachusetts Historical
Society. Aaron Wright's diary, in Boston Transcript, April 11, 1862. A Diary in the Historical Magazine, Oct. 1864. Letters during Oct.
1775 of William Thompson of the Pennsylvania
line in Read's Life of George Read, pp. 112,
128. For the camp on Winter Hill see Amory's
Sullivan, p. 15.

In Boston. — The Andrews papers in the Proceedings of the Massachusetts Historical Society, July, 1865. Letters, which had been used by Frothingham, but were not printed in full till they appeared in the New England Historical and Genealogical Register, April, 1857. Letters in the American Historical Record, Dec. 1872. Newell's diary in Boston, in the Collections of the Massachusetts Historical Society, 4th series, vol. i. Letters during the occupation of Boston, edited by W. P. Upham, in the Collections of the Essex Institute, vol. xiii., July, 1876; and see in this connection Mr. Upham's paper on the occupation of Boston, in the Institute's Bulletin, March, 1876. Letters written from Boston, by the Rev. Dr. Eliot, in the Proceedings of the Massachusetts Historical Society, Sept. 1878. Letters written from Boston to Gardiner Greene, in the Proceedings of the Massachusetts Historical Society, June, 1873. Samuel Paine's Letter, Oct. 1775, in the New England Historical and Genealogical Register, July, 1876. John Leach's diary during his confinement in Boston as a prisoner, June 29 to Oct. 4, 1775, in the same, July, 1865, — also see Oct. 1865. Peter Edes's diary during his confinement in Boston, printed at Bangor, 1837. The journal of a British officer in Boston, edited by R. H. Dana, Jr., in the Atlantic Monthly, April, 1877. Fonblanque's Life of Burgoyne, ch. 4. Adjutant Waller's orderly-book, with the

British in Boston, never printed, in the cabinet of the Massachusetts Historical Society. See their Proceedings, i. 481. The log-book of the British ship Preston, in Boston Harbor, April to Sept. 1775, in the Maine Historical Society's Collections, Aug. 1860. An account of the contributions sent by the Friends in Philadelphia to the sufferers in Boston is given in the Pennsylvania Magazine of American History, i. 168.

On the evacuation in March, 1776, there are letters by Eldad Taylor, in the New England Historical and Genealogical Register, July, 1854; and others by Edmund Quincy, in the Proceedings of the Massachusetts Historical Society, April, 1858. Cf. Force's American Archives, 4th series, v. and vi.; Reed's Joseph Reed, i. ch. 8; Hollister's Connecticut, ch. 10. Dawson in his Battles gives Howe's dispatch from Nantasket Roads, March 21, 1776, and Washington's dispatch of March 19, 1776. Washington's instructions to Gen. Ward on leaving Boston for New York, are given in the Heath Papers, Massachusetts Historical Society's Collections, 5th series, iv. 4; and p. 296 there is a letter of John Winthrop to John Adams, after the evacuation.

Landmarks and Memorials. — The appearance of Boston at this time can be judged of from a plate representing the landing of the British troops to garrison the place in 1768, by Paul Revere, which is reproduced in Rand, Avery &

Co.'s Bunker Hill Centennial, and in the Boston
Evacuation Memorial, 1876. There is a view of
the harbor and town in the Pennsylvania Magazine, June, 1773; a description with a view in
the Columbian Magazine, Dec. 1787; and one of
the town from Breed's Hill in the Massachusetts
Magazine, June, 1791, and in July, 1793, a large
view of the Old State House, and for another see
Aug. 1791; in July, 1789, one of the Hancock
House; in March, 1789, one of Faneuil Hall, —
all showing the aspects of revolutionary Boston.
Several of these are reproduced in the Boston
Evacuation Memorial. A view showing Dorches-
ter Heights is in the number for Nov. 1790, and
another of Boston from those heights in 1774, is
copied from a contemporary English print in
Lossing's Field-Book, i. 512; a view of Charlestown, with the north battery in Boston in the
foreground, engraved by Paul Revere, is in the
Proceedings of the Massachusetts Historical Society, Oct. 1877.

Descriptions of the town and its society at a
little later date will be found in the letters of Anburey, who was one of Burgoyne's officers quar-
tered at Cambridge in 1777; in Abbé Robin, a
chaplain of Rochambeau in 1781, whose account
is quoted by Shurtleff, and translated in the Historical Magazine, Aug. 1862; and in Chastellux,
1782, vol. ii., also quoted in Shurtleff's Description of Boston.

There is a view of Gage's lines on Boston Neck in Frothingham, from a print published in 1777, and a plan of them in Force's American Archives, vol. iii.; another original plan is reproduced in the Centennial Graphic. An original plan of the Neck defenses of the British, made within the American lines, largely from information of a deserter, with all the guns marked, their calibre and quantity of shot given, is preserved among the Lee papers in the library of the American Philosophical Society in Philadelphia. See also Pennsylvania Magazine, Aug. 1775, for Gage's lines. A plan of the fort erected by the British on Bunker Hill proper is given in Frothingham's Siege, from one published in London in 1781. William Carter's Genuine Detail of the Several Engagements, etc., London, 1784, gives a plan of these works at the time of their evacuation.

A gold medal given by Congress to Washington to commemorate the Siege of Boston is preserved in the Boston Public Library, and an account of it is given in the Boston Evacuation Memorial, 1876. See also Snowden's Medals of Washington and Loubat's Medallic History of the United States. Washington's letter to Congress is given in fac-simile in Force's American Archives, 4th series, v. 977.

Fiction. — The events of the siege are worked into the story of Cooper's Lionel Lincoln, and of Scribe's play La Bohémienne.

Maps, Plans, etc. — Shurtleff, in his Description of Boston, ch. 6, gives a section to the enumeration of maps of the town and its harbor, some of which are of interest in understanding the circuit of fortifications erected by the provincial forces at this time. The best for ordinary consultation is the eclectic map given by Frothingham in his Siege of Boston, p. 91. See also that in Force, vol. iii., and the military maps in Marshall's Washington, Sparks's Washington, repeated in the Evacuation Memorial, and reproduced by Guizot, in his Washington; Carrington's Battles of the American Revolution, p. 155; Lossing's Field-Book, etc.

For contemporary maps, that in vol. i. of Almon's Remembrancer, drawn at Boston in June, 1775, and published in London, Aug. 28, 1775, shows for the field of battle the words " Breed's pasture," which accords with the belief that that eminence was not known as Breed's *Hill* till after the battle. It is not otherwise very accurate.

The Gentleman's Magazine, Jan. 1775, gave a chart of the town and harbor.

The Pennsylvania Magazine, July, 1775, gave a plan of Boston, with a side-sketch of the lines about the town, which has been reproduced in Moore's Ballad History, and in the Centennial Memorials of Rand, Avery & Co., of George A. Coolidge, etc. Col. Trumbull, in his autobiography, gave a map of the lines made by himself in Sept. 1775. A plan of the works on Winter Hill is among the Washington maps in the Sparks Collection.

A large map of the town, with surrounding country and harbor, after Samuel Holland's surveys, was published by Des Barres in London, Aug. 5, 1775. It shows no fortifications except those at Copp's Hill and on the Neck. A colored copy of this is in the Boston Public Library, as is also a French map, 1780, Carte particulière du Havre de Boston, réduite de la carte anglaise de Des Barres. The 1775 plate of Des Barres, without change of date, but nevertheless with changes in some parts, and with the various fortifications of the siege delineated, was published again in 1780–83 in the Atlantic Neptune, and it was from Frothingham's copy of this that the reproduction in Shurtleff's Description of Boston was made in 1870.

Faden's map of Boston, with the intrenchments of 1775, based on the observations of Page in 1775, was published, London, Oct. 1, 1777, and in a later edition, Oct. 1778, and it has been facsimiled in Frothingham's Siege.

Roman's map of The Seat of Civil War in America, 1775, has a rude view of the lines on Boston Neck, and a plan of Boston and its environs.

In 1776 there was published by Beaurain, at Paris, a Carte du Porte et Havre de Boston,

which is copied from a British plan, and has in a
vignette the earliest known printed representation
of the Pine-tree banner (this vignette is copied
by Frothingham, who calls the map "curious but
not correct "). There is also a German edition
of the same, published in the first part of the
Geographische Belustigungen, Leipsic, 1776, by
J. C. Müller, " von dem Cheval. de Beaurin nach
dem Pariser original von 1776."

Henry Pelham's map of Boston and environs,
which is called " the most accurate " of all, was
published in London, June 2, 1777, shows the
military lines, and has been reproduced, much reduced, in Moore's Diary of the Revolution and in
Drake's Landmarks, but is fac-similed full size in
the Evacuation Memorial of the City of Boston,
1876.

In 1777 Faden published in London a plan of
Boston and vicinity, showing the " Rebel works,"
and based on Page's and Montresor's observations.

The Impartial History of the War in America,
published in Boston, 1781–1785, has a plan of Boston with Charlestown (represented in flames) and
the attack on Bunker Hill. The engraving is
marked " J. Norman, Sc."

The earliest of the eclectic maps, and the one
followed by later authorities in assigning the lo-
cation of the military lines, was that given by
Gordon in his History, vol. ii., who took Page's
for the town, and Pelham's for the country.

The contemporary American Atlas, London, contains various maps of interest in this connection, namely: Plan of Boston and vicinity, made by English engineers, Oct. 1775 (No. 16); maps of New England (Nos. 13 and 14), and small plans of Boston (Nos. 13 and 15).

See Josiah Quincy's descriptions of a map of Boston and harbor, 1775, in the Proceedings of the Massachusetts Historical Society, May, 1860, and other accounts in the Proceedings for 1864, pp. 361, 474.

Burning of Falmouth, Maine, October, 1775.

Contemporary accounts are given in the Gentleman's Magazine, London; in the Historical Magazine, March, 1869; in Bailey's letter printed in the Maine Historical Society's Collections, vol. v. p. 437. See also Williamson's, ii. 422, and other histories of Maine, Willis's Portland, ch. 19 and App. 17 to 20, Sparks's Washington, iii. App., and the New England Historical and Genealogical Register, July, 1873. The act was disowned by the British government. Stanhope's England, vi. 75, and Sparks's Washington, iii. 520.

A plan of Falmouth is given in a Boston edition of the Impartial History, vol. ii.; and in Smith and Deane's Journal of Portland, showing the burnt section.

The Second Continental Congress, 1775.

This assembly came together at Philadelphia May 10th, and their proceedings are given in Journals of Congress, ii.

Illustrative accounts will be found in histories of the United States, by Bancroft, vii. 353, viii. 25, 51; by Grahame, iv. 407; by Pitkin, i. ch. 9; by Hildreth, iii. ch. 31; in Frothingham's Rise of the Republic, p. 419; in Thaddeus Allen's Origination of the American Union; in histories of states, like Barry's Massachusetts, Mulford's New Jersey, etc.; in Gordon's Revolution. Documents are in Force's Archives.

Compare the lives of its members, etc., like those of Franklin by Sparks, i. 393, by Bigelow and by Parton; of Washington by Marshall, Sparks, and Irving; of Samuel Adams by Wells, ii. ch. 37; of John Adams by C. F. Adams, i., with Adams's diary in vol. ii. p. 408; of Richard H. Lee, i. 140; of Schuyler by Lossing, i. 316; of Jefferson, by Randall, i. ch. 4, and by Parton, ch. 19; of Jay by Jay; of Rutledge by Flanders, ch. 8; of George Read by Read, p. 105.

For commentary on events see the letters of John Adams to Abigail Adams; the letters of Silas Deane in the Connecticut Historical Society's Collections, ii. 129; the Diary of Christopher Marshall; Frothingham's Rise of the Republic, ch. ii.; and, for the composition of parties, the Life of John Adams, i. 212; also Magazine of American History, April, 1878.

John Hancock was chosen President May 24th. For the character of Hancock, not favorably drawn, see Wells's Samuel Adams; also compare Sanderson's Lives of the Signers of the Declaration of Independence, Loring's Hundred Boston Orators, and C. W. Upham's Speech in the Massachusetts Legislature, March 17, 1859, on the bill for preserving the Hancock House. Sparks's Washington, iii. 37. For Hancock's correspondence as President of Congress, see Force's American Archives, 4th series, v., and 5th series, i., ii., and iii. An account of the Hancock Papers in the cabinet of the Massachusetts Historical Society is given in their Proceedings, i. 271.

The address to the inhabitants of Great Britain was drafted by R. H. Lee. Cf. his Life, i. 143.

For action on the nomination of Washington to the command of the army, see Bancroft, vii. ch. 37; J. C. Hamilton's Alexander Hamilton, i. 110; John Adams's Diary, in Works ii. 415; Frothingham's Rise of the Republic, p. 430. Cf. also C. F. Adams's paper in the Massachusetts Historical Society's Proceedings, June, 1858.

The petition to the King, which was adopted July 8th, is given in Force's American Archives, 4th series, iv. 607.

November 9th an agreement to keep all the proceedings secret was signed by the members, and a fac-simile of this paper is given in Force's American Archives, 4th series, iii. 1918.

November 29th Congress established a Committee of Secret Correspondence for keeping up intercourse with sympathizers in Europe. Cf. C. W. F. Dumas's letters in Diplomatic Correspondence, ix.; and Force's American Archives, 5th series, ii. and iii., *index*, under Dumas and Secret.

Political Effects, 1775.

Sabine in his American Loyalists, i. ch. 2, 3, and 4, gives the condition of parties, as does Frothingham in his Rise of the Republic. The effect of the Lexington fight is traced in the general histories, and for distant responses in feeling see Lossing's Schuyler, i. 307 ; W. B. Stevens's Georgia, ii. 100 ; and other local histories and biographies.

In Massachusetts, Warren's oration on the anniversary of the Massacre in March shows the strong patriotic impulses of the time. Cf. Frothingham's Warren, ch. 13 ; Magoon's Orators of the Revolution ; Loring's Hundred Boston Orators. The Provincial Congress met at Watertown, in February (see Force's Archives, 4th series, iii., for proceedings, and Amory's James Sullivan, ch. 3), and President Langdon's sermon before it in May was the first public commemoration of the Lexington fight. Cf. Thornton's Pulpit of the Revolution.

The Proceedings of the New York Provincial Congress are also given in Force; but compare J. C. Hamilton's Republic of the United States, i. ch. 3; and the letters of Joseph Reed in his Life by W. B. Reed, i. 93.

As indicative of Southern feeling, see the progress of events in Virginia as given in Girardin's continuation of Burk's Virginia, written with the cognizance of Jefferson; 'Rives's Madison, i. ch. 4; and Wirt's Patrick Henry, which shows the somewhat exuberant pride of an ardent Virginian. Cf. also under Dunmore and Virginia in the *index* of Force's American Archives, 4th series, iii.–vi.

Late in the year the feelings engendered by the refusal of the King to recognize the petitions of Congress, and the burning of Falmouth, wrought changes which are depicted in Frothingham's Rise of the Republic, p. 447, and in Wells's Samuel Adams.

Relations with the Indians, 1768–1776.

In 1768 a treaty had been made at Fort Stanwix, defining the line between the settlements and the Indian territory. Accounts, with map, may be found in the Documentary History of New York, i. 587; in Documents relative to the Colonial History of New York, viii. 136. A map of 1771, showing the country of the Six Nations, is in the Documentary History of New York, iv. 661.

In April, 1775, the Provincial Congress of Massachusetts had sought to establish friendly relations with the Indians of the Mohawk Valley. Stone's Life of Brant, i. 55. Amory's Life of James Sullivan, p. 48, gives the letter to the Indians to induce enlistments under an order of the Provincial Congress, May 12, 1775. In May and June Congress had passed orders for the employment of Indians in certain ways. Secret Journals, i. 44–46. Adolphus thinks that Ramsay (ii. ch. 18) gives a candid account of the efforts made by both sides to secure the assistance of the Indians. Cf. Stone's Life of Brant, ch. 9. Sparks (Washington, iii. 494) thinks the Americans equally culpable in intentions, though in effect the British caused most misery to ensue from the policy. See also v. 274.

Congress also arranged (Journals, 1775, p. 162) for commissioners to meet the chiefs of the Six Nations, to fix, by treaty, their neutrality. They met at German Flats Aug. 15th. Cf. Force's Archives, 4th series, iii. 473, and 5th series, i. ; Massachusetts Historical Society's Collections, 3d series, v. 75 ; Colonial History of New York, viii. 605. A loyalist's view is given in Jones's New York in the Revolutionary War, i. 71.

This was followed by a conference at Albany. Cf. Lossing's Schuyler, i. ch. 22.

Force's American Archives contain many documents. Cf. 4th series, iv., under Indians and Six Nations in the *index ;* v., under Indians ; vi., under Six Nations and Indians; 5th series, i. and ii., under Indians.

Sir John Johnson's leaguing with the Indians against the Americans is set forth in Force, 4th series, vi.; 5th series, ii. and iii.; and in Lossing's Schuyler, i.

In January, 1776, Schuyler led an expedition to Johnstown to disarm the tories and intimidate the Indians. Cf. Lossing's Schuyler, ii. ch. 1; Dunlap's New York, ii. ch. 2; Stone's Life of Brant, i.; Documents relative to the Colonial History of New York, viii.; and a tory view in Jones's New York in the Revolutionary War, i. 71, 578, 583. Accounts of Indian and tory alliances in Central New York are given in Simms's Schoharie County and in Campbell's Tryon County.

Accounts of the expedition against the Cherokees beyond the Blue Ridge are given in a paper by D. L. Swain in the Historical Magazine, Nov. 1867; in the Chapel Hill University Magazine, May, 1852; and in a journal in the Historical Magazine, Oct. 1867.

Loyalists.

The chief contemporary authorities for the condition and vicissitudes of the loyalists are these: —

New York in the Revolutionary War, by Judge Jones of Long Island, who was at one time a prisoner in Connecticut, and who wrote his history in England, just after the close of the war. He is equally severe, both upon the British Ministry, their generals, and upon the Congress and its generals. The MS. was printed for the first time in 1879, edited by De Lancey, and issued by the New York Historical Society.

The posthumous volume of Hutchinson's History of Massachusett's Bay.

The examination of Joseph Galloway before the House of Commons was printed, and has been edited by Thomas Balch for the Seventy-Six Society.

The Life of Peter van Schaack has been written by H. C. van Schaack.

Curwen's Journal is that of a refugee in England, 1775–1784, recording current news and passing judgment on it, and there are reviews of it in the Southern Review, July, 1843; North American Review, Jan. 1843, and Oct. 1844.

Much of contemporary record will be found by the *index* under Disaffected or Suspected persons and Tories, in Force's American Archives, 4th series, iv., v., and vi.; 5th series, i., ii., and iii.

The most important of later works is Sabine's American Loyalists, which has an historical introduction, and consists of an alphabetical list of such persons, with brief accounts of them individually. It was reviewed by C. C. Smith in the North American Review, xcix. Winthrop Sargent made a collection of Loyalist Poetry. Long Island was a stronghold of this class, and there is illustrative matter in the histories of Long Island by Silas Wood, 1826; by B. T. Thompson, 1843; by N. S. Prime, 1845; and in Onderdonk's Queens and Suffolk County. Sabine in ch. 8 of his introduction gives an account of the loyalists in arms, and Sparks's Washington, iv. 519, has a note on their service in the British army. See also Massachusetts Historical Society's Proceedings, 1878; Ellis's Life of Count Rumford, p. 112; Huntington's Stamford, Connecticut, ch. 17; and other local histories.

Capture of Ticonderoga, May 10, 1775.

This expedition, planned in Connecticut (J. H. Trumbull's paper in the Hartford Daily Courant, Jan. 9, 1869, subsequently privately reprinted; the documents, including the diary of Mott, edited by Trumbull in the Connecticut Historical Collections, i. 163, and Mott's letter to the Provincial Congress of Massachusetts, printed in their journal, with other papers), was strengthened in Berkshire (Holland's Western Massachusetts; Barry's Massachusetts; Smith's History of Pittsfield, i. ch. 12), and at Bennington was joined by Ethan Allen and his Green Mountain Boys, and the whole placed under Allen's command.

Meanwhile Benedict Arnold, with a commission from Massachusetts, went to Berkshire to raise a force for the same purpose, but finding the other expedition afoot, joined it, and after some dispute about the command, went on as a volunteer. Lossing's Schuyler, i. 310; De Lancey's notes to Jones's New York in the Revolutionary War, i. 546, for Allen's commission, and a letter, May 14th; Force's American Archives, 4th series, iii.

Details of the capture and of events closely following will be found in the following works : —

Sparks's Life of Benedict Arnold. Schuyler's letters in Sparks's Correspondence of the American Revolution. Sparks's Life of Gouverneur Morris, i. ch. 4. The Lives of Ethan Allen by Sparks and Hugh Moore, with De Puy's Ethan Allen and the Green Mountain Heroes. Lossing's Life of Schuyler, i. 311; his Field-Book, and his article in Harper's Monthly, vol. xvii. Irving's Washington. Historical Magazine, Feb. 1869, p. 126. Watson's Essex County, N. Y., ch. 9. Palmer's Lake Champlain, ch. 6. De Costa in the Galaxy, Dec. 1868, and his Fort George, with Hiland Hall's pamphlet in reply to De Costa, Montpelier, 1869. Hollister's History of Connecticut, ii. ch. 7. Connecticut Historical Collections, vol. i. Elmer's journal of the Expedition, in the New Jersey Historical Society's Proceedings, ii. and iii. Force's American Archives, ii. Beman's questionable account in the Historical Magazine, May, 1868; and Col. Caldwell's narrative in the number for Aug. 1867. L. E. Chittenden's address, 1872, at the unveiling of Allen's statue at Burlington, Vt., July 4, 1873.

A loyalist view of these transactions is given in Judge Jones's New York in the Revolutionary War, i. 47.

A plan of Ticonderoga, with its dependencies, is given in John Trumbull's Memoirs, p. 33. For the ruins of the fort see Harper's Monthly, vii. 170, and Lossing's Field-Book.

Allen figures in Thompson's Green Mountain Boys, a fiction.

The Advance into Canada, 1775.

Washington in New York, June 25th, intrusted Schuyler with the command in the North. Lossing's Schuyler, i. 330. Notes of the preparations Schuyler made are in Jones's New York in the Revolutionary War, p. 58.

Congress put forth an Address to the Canadians. Journals of Congress, and Pitkin's United States, i. App. 19.

The movements of Benedict Arnold and Ethan Allen, and the action of Connecticut in dispatching more troops (Lives of Arnold, Allen, Gov. Trumbull; Hollister's Connecticut, Lossing's Schuyler), took place before Schuyler reached Ticonderoga, July 18th, after which events can be followed in Lossing's Schuyler, i. ch. 21; Palmer's Lake Champlain, ch. 6; Irving's Washington, ii.

A Journal by Gen. Irvine, beginning in May, is in the Historical Magazine, April, 1862; a plan of coöperation in the New York State Calendar, i.

Schuyler and Montgomery pushed to the foot of Lake Champlain in Sept. Lossing's Schuyler, i. ch. 23. Montgomery, Sept. 18th, advanced to the siege of St. John's.

Meanwhile Ethan Allen, instead of joining Montgomery, started to capture Montreal by a surprise, but was himself taken prisoner Sept. 25th. Moore's Diary of the American Revolution, pp. 152–159; Allen's Narrative of his Captivity; Lossing in Harper's Monthly, xvii. 721.

The juncture of Gen. Wooster and his Connecticut troops with the invading army perplexed Schuyler with the question of Wooster's ranking officers already in the field. Cf. Lossing's Schuyler and Hollister's Connecticut. Much about the proceedings of Wooster in Canada will be found in Force's American Archives, 4th series, iv., v., vi.; 5th series, i.

St. John's surrendered to Montgomery Nov. 2d. Lossing's Schuyler, i. 444; Sargent's Major André, p. 79; Armstrong's Life of Montgomery.

The Advance by the Kennebec, September, 1775.

Arnold, having returned to Cambridge, was put in command of a force, and Washington instructed him (Sparks's Washington, iii. 86) to proceed by the Kennebec valley, and effect a junction with Montgomery before Quebec. Arnold's reports to Washington are in Sparks's Correspondence of the Revolution, i.

Accounts are given in Lossing's Field-Book of the Revolution, i.; his Schuyler, i. ch. 26 ; Bancroft, viii. ; Sparks's Arnold, ch. 3 and 4 ; Quebec Literary and Historical Society's Transactions, 1871–1872, 1872–1873, 1876–1877; Historical Magazine, ii. ; New England Historical and Genealogical Register, April, 1857 ; Graham's Life of Gen. Morgan, ch. 4 ; Potter's American Monthly, Dec. 1875.

The following journals of this march and the sequel have been printed : —

Melvin's, separately, and in part in the Appendix to Parton's Aaron Burr. Henry's, 1812, also reprinted in 1877. Ware's, in the New England Historical and Genealogical Register, April, 1852. Allen's, in the Maine Historical Society's Collections, 1831, pp. 341, 387, where are given Arnold's letters and Montresor's journal of the survey of the route in 1760, which suggested this present expedition. Meigs's, separately, and in the Massachusetts Historical Society's Collections, 2d series, vol. ii. See Jones's account of Meigs in his New York in the Revolutionary War, i. 180, and the correction in note, p. 668. Senter's, in Bulletin No. 1, 1845–1847, of the Pennsylvania Historical Society. Thayer's, in E. M. Stone's Invasion of Canada in 1775, privately printed with introduction and notes, Providence, 1867. This book contains a full bibliography of the subject. The volume makes part of the Rhode Island Historical Collections, vi. See B. Cowell's Spirit of Seventy-Six in Rhode Island. A contemporary map of the Kennebec region is given in the Atlantic Neptune.

Montreal and Quebec, November and December, 1775.

Montgomery reached Montreal Nov. 12th, and sent a letter to the inhabitants, which is fac-similed in Force's American Archives, 4th series, iii. 1596 ; and another for the surrender, v. 312. Montgomery's letters to Schuyler as the campaign went on are given in Sparks's Correspondence of the Revolution, i. App., and in the same volume are Schuyler's letters to Washington, repeating the intelligence. The diligence and coöperation of Schuyler is shown in Lossing's Life of Schuyler, and in Force's American Archives, 4th series, iii. and iv. and subsequent volumes, *index.*

Arnold crossed the St. Lawrence on Nov. 13th, and finally retired up the river to await Montgomery. The two, joining, advanced to Quebec Dec. 5th ; and on the 30th attempted to carry the place by storm. Cf. Force's American Archives, 4th series, iv., v., vi. ; Remembrancer, ii. 368 ; Documents relative to the Colonial History of New York, viii. 663 ; Lossing's Schuyler, i. ch. 28, 29 ; Leake's Life of Gen. Lamb, ch. 7 and 8 ; Bancroft's United States, viii. ch. 52–54 ; Irving's Washington, ii. ch. 12 and 13.

For the death of Montgomery, see Moore's Diary of the American Revolution, i. 185 ; Force's Archives, 4th series, iv., *index ;* Marshall's Washington, i. 329 ; Read's Life of George Read, p. 141; Bisset's George the Third, i. ch. 15 ; Armstrong's Life of Montgomery; Geo. W. Cullum's Sketch of Montgomery, 1876 ; Wm. Smith's oration before Congress, Feb. 19, 1776 ; Miss L. L. Hunt's Notes on Montgomery; Historical Magazine, Nov. 1873. An account of the sword taken from his body is given in the Living Age, No. 1017, p. 428.

Arnold's letter describing the attack is in Sparks's Correspondence of the Revolution, i. 116. Force, 4th series, v. and vi., gives reference under Arnold in the *index.* For other accounts of these events, see the letters in the Appendix of Sparks's Correspondence of the Revolution, i. ; Sparks's Life of Arnold ; Lossing on Arnold in Harper's Monthly, xxiii. 721 ; Ramsay's American Revolution, where the insubordinate spirit of the Americans is emphasized; Irving's Washington, ii. ch. 8 and 23 ; Graham's Life of Morgan, ch. 5 ; Dawson's Battles of the United States, ch. 7 ; Carrington's Battles of the Revolution, ch. 20–21 ; Hollister's History of Connecticut, ii. ch. 9 ; Garneau's Histoire du Canada, and Bell's translation of the same, iii.

A journal of Col. Ritzema is in the Magazine of American History, Feb. 1877. A paper on Quebec, by Lossing, is in Harper's Monthly, xviii. 176.

Gen. Carleton had arrived in Canada in Sept. 1774, and his movements in contesting the American advance can be followed in Force's Archives. His account of the repulse of Montgomery and Arnold, as gazetted in London, is given in the Gentleman's Magazine, June, 1776.

See, further, Stedman's American War, ch. 2 and 10; Andrews's Late War, ch. 19 and 20; Annual Register, xix. ch. 1 and 5, and xx. ch. 1; a Journal of the Siege, London, 1824, with notes by W. T. P. Short; histories of England, by Adolphus, ii. 237, and Stanhope, vi. 76.

There are deposited with the Literary and Historical Society of Quebec the following MS. : —

1. Le témoin oculaire de la guerre des Bastonnais durant les années 1775 et 1776, par M. Simon Sanguinet.

2. Journal contenant le récit de l'invasion du Canada en 1775–1776, redigé par M. Jean B. Badeaux, printed in their Historical Documents, 3d series.

3. Journal of the siege of Quebec, kept by Hugh Finlay, printed in their Historical Documents, 4th series.

4. Journal tenu pendant le siège du fort St. Jean en 1776 par M. Antoine Foucher.

5. Letter from Col. Henry Caldwell, 15 June, 1776, on the Siege of Quebec, 1775–1776.

Maps and Plans. — Contemporary maps of Canada are in the American Atlas, Carver's map, with plan of Quebec, No. 4 ; and in Hilliard d'Auberteuil's Essais historiques, 1782. Carver's map was reëngraved in Paris, 1777.

Plans of the attack on Quebec are in Stone's Invasion of Canada; in Lamb's Life and Times, by Leake; in the Atlas to Marshall's Washington; in Carrington's Battles. A manuscript plan, by a British officer, is in the Faden Collection in the Library of Congress, and a plan engraved by Faden was published in London. Another plan is in the Sparks Collection in Harvard College Library.

Commission to Canada, Spring of 1776.

Franklin, Samuel Chase, Charles Carroll, and the Rev. John Carroll were sent by Congress to secure, if possible, the sympathy of the Canadians. See Lives of Franklin by Sparks, Parton, and Bigelow. Charles Carroll's Diary is given in the Maryland Historical Society's Transactions, i. Sparks's Washington, iii. 390. Sparks's Correspondence of the American Revolution, i. App. Lossing's Schuyler, ii. Their instructions are in the Journals of Congress, 1776, p. 100. Cf. papers in Force's Archives, 4th series, iv. and v.

Beginnings of the Navy.

Most of the early documentary evidence will be found in the several volumes of Force's American Archives, under the *index* heads of Armed Vessels, Biddle, Fleet, Hopkins, Jones (Paul), Manley, Massachusetts Armed Vessels, Marine Committee, Navy, Privateers, Prizes, Row Galleys, Seamen, Vessels.

Sabine's Report on the Fisheries of the United States, p. 198, represents the fisheries as a school for the navy. Cf. Babson's Gloucester.

John Adams (Works, iii. 7) names the proceedings in Congress, Nov. 25, 1775, as "the true origin and formation of the American navy." Cf. Journals of Congress. The Act of Massachusetts authorizing the fitting out of armed vessels will be found in the Provincial laws, and in the Gentleman's Magazine, Jan. 1776. See Massachusetts Historical Society's Proceedings, Jan. 1809, p. 203, and Austin's Gerry, ch. 9.

The most considerable of the histories of the navy is Cooper's. Consult also the lives of the early naval heroes, like H. T. Tuckerman's Life of Talbot; Mary Barney's Memoirs of Com. Barney; Life of Capt. Manly; Sheppard's Life of Samuel Tucker, etc.

Incidental accounts of the early naval operations will be found in Sparks's Washington, iii. App. 516; Arnold's Rhode Island, ii. 351, 363, 369, etc.; Letters in the Revolutionary Correspondence, Rhode Island Historical Collections, vi.; Gammel's Life of Samuel Ward; Stevens's History of Georgia, ii. 134, and the histories of Massachusetts. Particulars of private armed ships are

given in Lossing's Field-Book, i. ; Caulkin's New
London ; Mrs. E. V. Smith's History of New-
buryport ; Felt's Annals of Salem; life of E. H.
Derby in Hunt's American Merchants, ii.

Com. Hopkins's likeness is more common in contemporary engravings than those of the other officers. A portrait of him engraved in 1776 is reproduced in Preble's History of the Flag of the
United States. Cf. An Important History of the
War, London, 1780 ; Geschichte der Kriege in
und aus Europa, Nuremberg, 1776.

Maps of the coast are given in the Atlantic
Neptune.

Ithiel Town's Particular Services, etc., gives
the journal of a British naval officer.

EVENTS OF 1776.

The Retreat from Canada.

ARNOLD continued for a while before Quebec, and was joined by Wooster, from Montreal, April 1st, who took command, while Arnold retired to Montreal. Cf. Force's Archives, 5th series, i.; Lossing's Schuyler, ii. ch. 1 and 2; Read's Life of George Read, 150.

Gen. Thomas had been appointed to the command in Canada, and reached the camp before Quebec May 1st, but a British fleet with reinforcements arriving, Carleton attacked the American camp, and Thomas began his retreat. Lossing's Schuyler, ii. 60; Force's American Archives, 4th series, iv., vi.; 5th, i.; Bancroft's United States, viii. ch. 67; Irving's Washington, ii. ch. 20, 22.

Carleton's account of the retreat is in the Gentleman's Magazine, July, 1776. Burgoyne with the Brunswick troops reached Quebec in June. Cf. Fonblanque's Burgoyne, p. 211.

Subsequent events are best followed in Lossing's Schuyler and Stone's Life of Brant, i. 154; with illustrative documents, particularly for the affair at the Cedars, in Force, 4th series, vi., and 5th series, i.

Gen. Thomas having retreated to Chamblée, died there June 2d, and was succeeded by Sullivan. Cf. Amory's Sullivan; Lossing's Schuyler, ii.

For the failure of Gen. Thompson at Three Rivers in June, see Force's Archives, 4th series, vi.; Lossing's Schuyler, ii. 85; Read's George Read, p. 155; Marshall's Washington, ii. 362.

In July Sullivan had reached Crown Point. Cf. Force, 4th series, vi., and 5th, i. and ii.

In general on the campaign, see Schuyler's, Sullivan's, and Arnold's letters on the retreat in Sparks's Correspondence of the American Revolution, i.; Watson's Essex County, ch. 10; Dunlap's New York, ii. ch. 1, 4; Mrs. Bonney's Historical Gleanings, i.; Marshall's Washington, ii. ch. 5; Irving's Washington, ii. ch. 23; Davis's Life of Burr, i.; Sparks's Life of Arnold; Smith's History of Pittsfield, Mass., i. ch. 15; Temple and Sheldon's History of Northfield, Mass.; and other local histories.

In July Gates was sent to command the troops "in Canada," and as the retreat had brought the forces into New York State, there arose a question of command between him and Schuyler. Cf. Lossing's Schuyler, ii.; Life of Gates; Force's Archives, 4th series, vi., 5th series, i., ii., iii.

The Campaign for the Hudson, 1776.

The Americans had early been warned of the British plan to secure the line of the Hudson and Lake Champlain. Journal of Provincial Congress of New York, p. 172; Lossing's Schuyler, ii. 16.

As early as Sept. 1775, plans of intended fortifications in the river passes had been made. Force's American Archives, 4th series, iii. 735. Washington had intrusted an examination of plans to Stirling. Force, vi. 672; Boynton's West Point, p. 29. Many documents can be found referred to under Highlands and Hudson River in the *index* of Force, 4th series, iv., and subsequent volumes. See also for the efforts at different times to place obstructions in the river, Lossing's Schuyler, ii. 150; Boynton's West Point, ch. i.; and Ruttenber's Obstructions of the Hudson River.

There is an account of the attempts to destroy the British frigates threatening the ascent in July, 1776, in the Historical Magazine, 1866, supplement, p. 84.

Washington, after the evacuation of Boston, had suspected that New York would be the next point of attack, and sent Putnam ahead to take the command there, with instructions, given in Sparks's Washington, iii. 337. Putnam reached New York April 2d. For the period of his control, before the arrival of Washington, see Force,

4th series, v., *index ;* the Lives of Putnam; Heath's Memoirs, 44; Sparks's Gouverneur Morris, i. ch. 5; Histories of New York; Almon's Remembrancer.

Jones (New York in the Revolutionary War, i. ch. 6, and notes) depicts the trials of the tories.

Washington arrived April 13th. Cf. Irving's Washington, ii. ch. 24; Quincy's Journals of S. Shaw; Joseph Reed's letters during the summer, in Reed's Reed, i.

For details of the tory plot in June, see Eustis's letter in the New England Historical and Genealogical Register, 1869, and papers in Force, 4th series, vi.

On the campaign which ensued from the battle on Long Island to the retreat of Washington through the Jerseys, there is an elaborate monograph, Campaign of 1776 around New York and Brooklyn, by H. P. Johnston, which enters into details, and prints original documents. Other works, covering with more or less fullness all the military events of this interval, are Dunlap's New York, ii. ch. 6; the histories of the City of New York; Stiles's History of Brooklyn; J. C. Hamilton's Republic of the United States, i. ch. 5, and other general histories like Gordon, Botta, Bancroft, etc.; Allen's Origination of the American Union; Sparks's Washington, iv., and the Lives by Marshall, Sparks, and Irving; Greene's Life of Greene; Memoirs of Colonel B. Talmadge; Quincy's Shaw; Read's Life of George Read, p. 170; histories of states for the part borne by their troops, like McSherry's Maryland, ch. 9.

There are maps in Gordon, ii., Stiles's Brooklyn, and in Johnston's work.

North Carolina, 1776.

The British invasion of this year is the subject of a lecture by Swain, which is included in W. D. Cooke's Revolutionary History of North Carolina. Cf. Frothingham's Rise of the Republic, p. 502; Sparks's Correspondence of the Revolution, ii. App., as well as for other southern movements during the spring and summer of 1776.

Fort Moultrie, Sullivan's Island, June 28, 1776.

This was an attempt by the British fleet and troops, under Sir Peter Parker and Sir Henry Clinton, respectively, to force an entrance to Charleston harbor, and reduce South Carolina.

Various contemporary documents will be found in Force's American Archives, 4th series, iv., v., vi.; 5th, i., ii., iii., under Charleston, Fort Moultrie, Lee, and Sullivan's Island in the *index*. Gen. Lee's report to Washington is in Sparks's Correspondence of the Revolution, i. 244. A letter of Gen. Morris in the New York Historical Society's Collections, 1875, p. 435. Moultrie's Memoirs of the American War; Bancroft's United States, viii. ch. 66; Irving's Washington, ii. ch.

29; Simms's South Carolina; Garden's Anecdotes of the Revolution; Lossing's Field-Book, ii.; Dawson's Battles, ch. 10; Carrington's Battles, ch. 28; Memoirs of Elkanah Watson; Harper's Monthly, xxi. 70, by T. D. English; Flander's Life of Rutledge, in his Chief Justices; Wm. Crafts's Address in 1825, reprinted in his Miscellanies; C. C. Jones's Address on Sergeant William Jasper, 1876, and an account of the Fort Moultrie Centennial Celebration, Charleston, 1876.

For British accounts, see Gentleman's Magazine, Oct. 1776; Annual Register; History of the Civil War in America, Dublin, 1779; Adolphus (History of England, ii. 346) bases his narrative in part on unpublished documents. A loyalist view is given in Jones's New York in the Revolutionary War, i. 98.

Maps. — American plans of the attack are in Johnson's Traditions and Reminiscences of the American Revolution in the South, and in Drayton's Memoirs of the American Revolution in the South, ii. 290.

A British plan was published by Wm. Faden, Aug. 10, 1776, and is No. 37 in the American Atlas. Col. James's MS. plan is in the Faden Collection, Library of Congress. The Political Magazine, London, 1780, has a map.

In England, 1775–1776.

Bancroft (United States, viii.) follows the political aspects, and traces the movements of the opposition in Parliament, before they became estranged by the declaration of independence. Smyth, Modern History, lectures 31 and 32, sets forth the condition of parties, and in 33 he compares the American and English views as exemplified in Ramsay's American Revolution, and in the Annual Register, whose successive volumes were " the very mirror of public sentiment."

For the movements in Parliament, see the Parliamentary History, and Force's American Archives. Lord North had introduced a conciliatory plan, Feb. 20, 1775. Force, 4th series, i. 1597, and later, vi. March 22d Burke brought forward a plan, and again in Nov. His March speech is in his works, Boston edition, ii. 99. Force, 4th series, i. 1745, and vi. 178. MacKnight's Life of Burke, ii. 127. The *index* to Force, vi., will show the debates of Barré, Fox, Camden, and Chatham; and later debates, Oct. and Nov. 1776, are in Force, 5th series, iii. 961–1020. Stanhope says that " in the reports of Chatham's speeches in Almon's Register, the whole spirit evaporates." Cf. Russell's Memoir, and Correspondence of Fox, i. 157; Walpole's Last Journals, ii. 7, 22; Campbell's Lives of the Chancellors.   ·   \

Political Movements, 1776.

We have the doings of Congress in the Journals and in Force's Archives, 4th series, iv. 1625. Events can also be followed in the Correspondence of John Adams, Works, ix. 372; Frothingham's Rise of the Republic; Lee's Life of R. H. Lee, i. 161; Wells's Samuel Adams; Bancroft's United States, viii. ch. 60, 63; letters in W. B. Reed's Life of Joseph Reed, i. 241, 271; Flanders's Life of Rutledge, ch. 7, in his Chief Justices. In Greene's Life of Nathanael Greene we see the weakness of Congress in its executive work.

Sir William Howe, on his arrival off Sandy Hook, July 12th, issued a declaration of pardon for such as would return to their allegiance. For its failure, see Parton's Franklin, ii. 136. He also sent a letter which he had brought from an English friend to Joseph Reed, and made other advances in the character of a commissioner to restore harmony. Reed sent the letter to Congress. Cf. Reed's Joseph Reed, i. 197; Sparks's Washington.

The feeling in Massachusetts can be traced in Perez Morton's Eulogy over Warren's body, April 8th (Loring's Boston Orators, p. 127); in Samuel West's Election Sermon May 29th (Thornton's Pulpit of the Revolution); in the statement of the principles of the Revolution as given in a letter of John Adams to Mercy Warren, in 1807

7

(Massachusetts Historical Society's Collections, 5th series, iv. 338) ; in the records of the Boston Committee of Correspondence, May to Nov. (in the New England Historical and Genealogical Register, July, 1876). Cf. Dawson's paper on the act of Massachusetts assuming sovereign power May 1st, in the Historical Magazine, May, 1862, and Barry's Massachusetts.

Bancroft devotes a chapter (ix. ch. 15) to the Constitutions which the states severally adopted, beginning in 1776. On the Constitution of New York, see the histories of that state, and Flanders's Life of Jay, ch. 8, and Sparks's Life of Gouverneur Morris. The movements for political consolidation in 1776 in Pennsylvania are described in Reed's Joseph Reed, i. ch. 7. For the Declaration of Rights in Virginia in 1776, see Rives's Madison, i. ch. 5 ; Madison's Writings, i. 21. Randall's Jefferson, i. ch. 6, gives an account of the convention, and so does Grigby's commemorative discourse in 1855.

Thomas Paine's Common Sense, published in Jan. 1776, affected sensibly the current of political feeling through the year. Cf. Frothingham's Rise of the Republic, pp. 476, 479; Barry's Massachusetts, iii. 89; Life of John Adams, i. 204; Randall's Jefferson, i. 137 ; Bancroft's United States, ch. 56 ; Parton's Franklin, iii. 108 ; and the papers in Force's American Archives, 4th series, iv. *index.* For an English view, see

Smyth's Modern History, 33d lecture ; and for a tory one, Jones's New York in the Revolutionary War, i. 63.

Foreign Relations, 1776.

As early as Feb. 1776, an agent of the French government was secretly communing with Congress.   Cf. Bancroft's United States, viii. ch. 61 ; De Witt's Jefferson and the American Democracy ; and documents in Force's Archives, 4th series, vi., and 5th, i., ii., iii.

Arthur Lee was now in London, having been appointed agent of Congress, and was holding correspondence with the Secret Committee of Congress.   Sparks's Diplomatic Correspondence, ii., gives his instructions, Dec. 12, 1775, and letters ; also in Force's Archives, 4th series, iv. Cf. Lee's Life of Arthur Lee.

The correspondence of William Carmichael is in the Diplomatic Correspondence, ix.

Silas Deane had been a member from Connecticut of this and the 1774 Congress.   (See his Correspondence, in the Connecticut Historical Collections, ii. 129.)   He was now sent to Paris.   His instructions, dated March 3, 1776, are in the Diplomatic Correspondence, i. 5, and in Pitkin's United States, App. 23.   He reached there in June.   See Pitkin's United States, i. 384, and App. 24, for Deane's first letter.   It was arranged that the secret dispatches should be written in invisible ink. Jay's Life of Jay, 64. Deane's letters are in the Diplomatic Correspondence, i.: Force's Archives, 5th series, ii.

For Deane's proceedings in Paris see Papers in Relation to the Case of Silas Deane, published in 1855 by the Seventy-Six Society, in which he goes over his doings from March, 1776 to March, 1778. His quarrel with Arthur Lee is set forth in the Life of Lee; and Lee's counter narrative is given in the Papers, etc., already mentioned. Cf. Parton's Franklin, ii. 189; and later references under 1778.

Bancroft (viii. ch. 61) goes over the whole story of these French negotiations at this time.

For Beaumarchais' connection with the agents, see Lomenie's Life of Beaumarchais; Parton's Franklin, ii. 167, 203; Pitkin's United States, i. ch. 10; Quarterly Review, 1873; Lossing, in Harper's Monthly, xiv.; Hours at Home, June, 1870; Magazine of American History, Nov. 1878; and various documents in the Diplomatic Correspondence, i. and xii. 162, 167; and Force's Archives, 5th series, i. Later relations are given in John Bigelow's Beaumarchais, the Merchant, — Letters of Theveneau de Francey, 1777–1780, an address before the New York Historical Society, 1870.

In Sept. three commissioners to France were appointed by Congress — Lee, Deane, and Franklin; and the latter proceeded to join the others in Dec. Their instructions from Congress are in the Diplomatic Correspondence, i. See Lives of Franklin and Lee; Deane's Narrative; Journals of Congress, iii.; Force's Archives, 5th series, ii. Franklin, Dec. 8, 1776, announces his arrival. Diplomatic Correspondence, iii. 5. Letters. of Congress to the agents, Dec. 1776 to Feb. 1777, are given in Lee's R. H. Lee, App. 8.

For views upon the mission at the time, see Mercy Warren's History of the Revolution; Wells's Life of Samuel Adams.

Parton, in his Franklin, ii. 248, goes into a history of the different agents of Congress in Europe at this time, beginning with Franklin, and enlarges upon the difficulties engendered by Arthur Lee's conduct; but compare Lee's Life of Arthur Lee, and the Calendar of the Lee Manuscripts in Harvard College Library. Also see the references under 1778.

Dec. 6, 1776, an agreement was entered into with Lafayette and De Kalb to serve the states. Diplomatic Correspondence, i., and p. 291 for the Commissioners' letter, May 25, 1777, on the subject. The Memoirs of Lafayette touch upon the feelings rife in France when he determined to go to America; and for his arrival see Sparks's Washington, v. App. Cf. Hilliard d'Auberteuil's Essais historiques, ii.

The Spirit of Independence.

The growth of this spirit is traced carefully in Frothingham's Rise of the Republic, pp. 245, 291, 315, 369, 428, 438, 449, 452, 453, 469, 483, 489, 499, 506, 509. Botta, in his History of the Revolution, had represented it as rife long before the outbreak, — a statement that John Jay and John Adams take exception to in letters printed by Jeremiah Colburn in the New England Historical and Genealogical Register, July, 1876, and published separately as American Independence: Did the colonists desire it? Cf. John Adams's Works, iii. 45; his Letters in Massachusetts Historical Society's Collections, 5th series, iv. 300, 465, addressed to Mercy Warren.

For intimations of the existence of the spirit before it became an organized force, see Hutchinson's Massachusetts Bay, iii. 134, 264, 265; Bancroft's United States, viii. ch. 64, 65, 68; Grahame's United States, iv. 315; J. C. Hamilton's Republic of the United States, i. 110; Barry's Massachusetts, iii. ch. 3, noting articles in favor of it in Boston Gazette, April 15 and 29, 1776; Jefferson's Notes on Virginia; Galloway's Examination before Parliament; Wells's Samuel Adams, ii. 352, etc.; Randall's Jefferson, i. 124; Sparks's Washington, ii. App. p. 496; Greene's Life of N. Greene, i. 122; Austin's Gerry, ch. 13; Sparks's Franklin, i. 379, 380; Rives's Madison, i.

108, 124; Matthew Thornton's letter in Force's Archives, 4th series, ii. 696; also see vi. *index*, under Independence.

Independence declared, July 4, 1776.

On the 7th of June, 1776, a resolution was offered in Congress that these United Colonies are, and of right ought to be, free and independent states. A fac-simile of this paper is given in Force's American Archives, 4th series, vi. 1700.

Frothingham (Rise of the Republic) traces the culmination of the various influences, resulting in the agreement of independence; and he shows how the several colonies instructed their representatives to provide for local interests. Bancroft (ch. 69 and 70) follows these events. A showing of the parties in Congress at this time is given in Randall's Jefferson, i. 153; Read's Life of George Read; John Adams's Life and Works, i. 220, 517; ii. 31–75, 93; Pitkin's United States, i. 362.

Very scant records of the debates previous to the passage of the Declaration are preserved. John Adams claimed that from 1774 to 1778, covering his period in Congress, there were no records of speeches, except some by Dr. Witherspoon, delivered *memoriter*, which he printed, and one by Dickinson against the Declaration, which was afterwards printed, and seemed very different to Adams from the one actually delivered. Some slight notes and accounts of the debates, however, have been printed in John Adams's works, i. 227; iii. 55; ix. 418; in the Madison Papers, i. 12, by Jefferson — reprinted in Read's George Read, p. 226; in Wells's Samuel Adams, ii. 413, 432.

General accounts will be found in the biographies of the signers and principal political characters of the day. Wells's Life of Samuel Adams, ii., shows his strenuous efforts at thwarting all plans of conciliation. Stanhope (History of England, vi. 121) takes a low view of Samuel Adams's character. Loring (Hundred Boston Orators) prints a letter of Hancock. C. F. Adams's Life of John Adams, ch. 4 and 5, and McKean's letter to Adams, in Massachusetts Historical Society's Collections, 5th series, iv. 506. Lives of Jefferson by Tucker, i. ch. 4; by Randall, i. 142, 164; by Parton; Jefferson's autobiography in Writings, i. 12, 96, and App. p. 117. Rives's Madison, i. 130; Lee's Life of R. H. Lee, i. ch. 7; Read's George Read, p. 162; Austin's Life of Gerry, ch. 13; the sketches of Robert Morris, who opposed the Declaration. Lives of Franklin by Sparks, ch. 9; by Parton and by Bigelow. Reed's Life of Joseph Reed, i. ch. 8 and 9. Lives of Washington by Marshall, ii. ch. 6, and by Irving.

There are contemporary notes in the Journals of Congress; in Force's American Archives, 4th se-

ries, iv., 5th, i., ii., iii. *index;* in Niles's Principles
and Acts of the Revolution; and in Sparks's Correspondence of the Revolution. The early historians, Mercy Warren, Gordon, and Ramsay, give a
reflex of contemporary views. The famous letter
of John Adams to his wife, prophesying the continued observance of the anniversary, is in the
Familiar Letters of John and Abigail Adams,
p. 190, dated July 3d, with a note explaining the
change of date to 5th when first printed. For
Philadelphia life at this time, see Historical
Magazine, Nov. 1868, and the Diary of Christopher Marshall.

Jefferson's original draft of the Declaration is
given in Randall's Jefferson, p. 172; in Niles's
Weekly Register, July 3, 1813; in Timothy
Pickering's Review of the Cunningham Correspondence, 1824; in Papers of James Madison,
1840, — not always agreeing, as different autograph drafts were followed. It is given with the
changes indicated as adopted in Congress, in Jefferson's Works, i.; Russell's Life and Times of
Fox; Lee's Life of R. H. Lee, i. 275. Cf. John
Adams's Works, i. 233; Parton's Jefferson, ch.
21; Parton's Franklin, ii. 126.

The Declaration as adopted is given in Frothingham's Rise of the Republic, p. 539, and in
various general histories and manuals.

A fac-simile of the original draft, with Adams's
and Franklin's changes, is given in Jefferson's

Writings, i. 26; in Randall's Jefferson; in the Declaration of Independence, quarto, issued by the City of Boston, 1876, where is also a reduced fac-simile of the engrossed document, as signed Aug. 2d ; and a full-size fac-simile of the latter is in Force's American Archives, 5th series, i. 1595. Cf. also the Atlas of Guizot's Washington. Facsimiles of the signatures are in many places. Reproductions of autograph letters of the signers are given in Sanderson's Lives of the Signers, and in Brotherhead's Centennial Book of the Signers.

There is an account of the Declaration by B. J. Lossing in Harper's Monthly, iii. and vii.; and Col. T. W. Higginson tells the Story of the signing in Scribner's Monthly, July, 1876.

For the question of the observance of the 2d or 4th of July, see Potter's American Monthly, Dec. 1875.

There are accounts of Independence Hall, by John Savage, in Harper's Monthly, xxxv.; Potter's American Monthly, July, 1875; Belisle's History of Independence Hall; Col. Etting's Memorials of 1776. Cf. Etting's Historical Account of the Old State House, 1876, of which there is a contemporary print in the Columbian Magazine, July, 1787, taken in 1778.

The desk upon which Jefferson wrote the Declaration is now in Boston. Cf. Randall's Jefferson, i. 177; Massachusetts Historical Society's Proceedings, 1855–1858, p. 151.

For the immediate effects of the Declaration, see Frothingham's Rise of the Republic, p. 548; Reed's Life of Joseph Reed, i. 195.

The Declaration was reprinted at once in London in the Gentleman's Magazine, Aug. 1776; Annual Register, 1776, p. 261; Almon's Remembrancer, iii. 258. It occasioned comments and rejoinders in the Gentleman's, in Almon, and in other publications. Gov. Hutchinson's strictures on it, after circulating in manuscript, were printed in Almon, iv. 25. Adolphus (History of England) says that An Answer to the Declaration of the American Congress, which appeared in London the same year, is " worthy the perusal of those who wish to have the means of thinking rightly on the origin of the American dispute." Lord Camden's views are given in Campbell's Lives of the Chancellors, v. 301. Lord John Russell, in his Memoirs and Correspondence of Fox, i. 152, thinks the truth was warped in charging all upon the King, while the fact was " the sovereign and his people were alike prejudiced, angry, and wilful." Earl Stanhope's view, in his History of England, was criticised by Col. Peter Force in a privately printed pamphlet, 1855. Morley, in his Edmund Burke, p. 125, has a chapter on the significance of the American passage to Independence.

The Hessians.

Bancroft, viii. ch. 50 and 57, narrates the efforts of the British Ministry to secure the aid of Russian troops, and subsequently of the Hessians. See results in vol. ix. ch. 18; x. ch. 3. The preliminaries of the negotiations are given in Donne's Letters of George III. to Lord North, i. 293, 297. The treaties with the German princes are given in Force's American Archives, 4th series, vi. 356–358. Debates, Nov. 1775, on the employment of mercenaries are in the Parliamentary History, and in Force, vi. 88, 107, 271. See, further, in Force, 5th series, i., ii., iii. *index.*

Eelking's Die Deutsche Hülfstruppen in Nord Amerika, gives a list of the MS. journals of the officers to which he had access. Of Eelking's Life of Riedesel, the German commander, there is an English translation. Ewald's Feldzug der Hessen nach Amerika, and Kapp's Der Soldatenhandel deutscher Fürsten nach Amerika, 2d ed. 1874, are epitomized in G. W. Greene's German Element in the War for Independence. Cf. Gen. Von Ochs's Neuere Kriegskunst, 1817.   •

See also a review of Eelking in the Historical Magazine, Feb. 1864 and Jan. 1866, and G. W. Greene's paper in the Atlantic, Feb. 1875; Sparks's article on Riedesel in the North American Review, xxvi.; Fonblanque's Life of Burgoyne, 213.

Battle of Long Island, August 27, 1776.

An elaborate study of the battle fought at Brooklyn has been made by Thomas W. Field, and published in the Memoirs of the Long Island Historical Society, ii. He gives many contemporary documents. He had previously made it the subject of a lecture. Historical Magazine, Nov. 1866.

Howe landed his troops at Gravesend Aug. 22d. Sir George Collier commanded the fleet, covering the landing. Naval Chronicle, xxxii.

Greene had done the work on the lines of defense. Greene's Greene, i. 158.

Howe's army in effective strength was double that under Washington. Cf. Force's American Archives, 5th series, i.; Beatson's Naval and Military Memoirs of Great Britain, vi.; De Lancey's note, in Jones's History of New York in the Revolutionary War, i. 600.

Contemporary Accounts. — Washington's dispatches are given in Sparks and in Field; also his letters in Sparks, iv. and App. Graydon's Memoirs, ch. 6, are important. Documents in Onderdonk's Revolutionary Incidents in Queens County. Almon's Remembrancer, iii. Force's American Archives, 5th series, i., ii., iii. Brodhead's Letters in Pennsylvania Archives, v. 21. Atlee's Journal in App. of Reed's Life of Joseph Reed; and in Pennsylvania Archives, 2d series,

i. 509; and p. 517 is the Journal of Col. Samuel
Miles. President Stiles's diary is given in Johnston.

Death of Gen. Woodhull. — Force's Archives,
5th series, ii., iii. *index.* Jones's New York in the
Revolutionary War, ii. 593. Luther R. Marsh's
Oration. J. Fenimore Cooper and Henry Onder-
donk, Jr., had a newspaper controversy about
Woodhull's capture and death. See Historical
Magazine, 1861.

Later Accounts. — Mercy Warren's and Gor-
don's Histories of the Revolution. Marshall's
Washington, ii. ch. 7. Irving's Washington, ii.
ch. 31 and 32. Samuel Ward's Lecture, 1839.
Johnston's Campaign of 1776, ch. 4. Dunlap's
New York, ii. 64. Reed's Joseph Reed, i. 222.
Amory's Gen. Sullivan, p. 25. Hollister's Con-
necticut, ii. ch. 11. Parton's Burr, i. ch. 6. Los-
sing's Field-Book. Dawson's Battles of the United
States, i. Stiles's History of Brooklyn. Williams's
Life of Olney. Harper's Monthly, Aug. 1876.
Knickerbocker's Magazine, xiii. Personal Recol-
lections of the American Revolution, edited by
S. Barclay, for family experiences in the neigh-
borhood. Thompson's Long Island.

Bancroft, ix. ch. 4, commented adversely on the
conduct of General Greene in the battle, and
Geo. W. Greene has examined that historian's
statements in a pamphlet, which he has reprinted
in his Life of General Greene, ii. In his first vol-

ume, book ii. ch. 7, Greene gives his own version of
the battle. Greene's arraignment of Bancroft is
examined in the Historical Magazine, Feb. 1867.
See also Aug. 1867. Bancroft also in a note, ix.
105, controverts the statements of President Reed
on the question of the retreat from the island, as
given in W. B. Reed's Life of Reed, ch. 11.

British Accounts. — Sir Wm. Howe's dispatch
to his government was printed in a Gazette extraordinary, Oct. 10th, and is given in Field's monograph. It elicited a pamphlet of Remarks, with
the Gazette account annexed. The evidence before Parliament is also given in Field; and
Howe's Narrative of his Conduct in America
before the Committee of the Commons was separately printed. Cf. Parliamentary Register, xi.
340, and Almon's Debates, xiii. Howe's Narrative is commented upon in the Detail and Conduct of the American War.

Stedman's American War, ch. 6. Andrews's
History of the Late War, ch. 21, with a portrait
of Howe. Annual Register, xix. ch. 5. An Impartial History of the late War. Stanhope's
England. The Popular History of England, by
C. Knight. Lushington's Life of Lord Harris,
p. 76.

A loyalist view of the opportunity lost in not
forcing the American lines after Howe had gained
his victory, is taken in Jones's New York in the
Revolutionary War, i. 112.

German Accounts. — Eelking's Deutsche Hülfs-truppen, ch. 1; and other accounts in the Appendix of Field's Battle of Long Island.

French Account. — Hilliard d'Auberteuil's Essais historiques, ii.

Political Effects. — John Adams's Works, ix. 438, etc. Stuart's Life of Jonathan Trumbull. Sedgwick's William Livingston, p. 201.

In England: Donne's Corrrespondence of George III. and Lord North, ii.; Rockingham and his Contemporaries, ii. 297; Russell's Life of Fox, and his Memorials and Correspondence of Fox, i. 145; Horace Walpole's Last Journals, ii. 70.

Maps. — A contemporary *American* plan of Brooklyn, showing the American lines, is in the New York City Manual, 1858.

One of New York and parts adjacent is given in Gordon's History, ii.

In the large and small atlases to Marshall's Washington, in Sparks's Washington, iv. 68, showing the island; and in Guizot's Washington.

Field in his monograph gives a large plan, showing the projection of the modern streets overlying the ancient landmarks. Full plans are given in Johnston's Campaign of 1776.

Others are in Ward's Lecture, 1839; in Duer's Life of Lord Stirling, ii. 162; in Carrington's Battles, ch. 14; in W. L. Stone's History of New York City, p. 246; in Onderdonk's Queens County; in Ridpath's United States; in Harper's Monthly, Aug. 1876.

There are *British* plans, as follows: Faden's engraved plan, 1776, with Gen. Howe's Letter to Lord George Germain, being No. 22 of The American Atlas. Various MS. maps, made by British officers, of the operations of this campaign, are in the Faden collection, Library of Congress, of which E. E. Hale printed a list in 1862.

In Gentleman's Magazine, Oct. and Dec. 1776.

A map, 15 × 17 in., published in London, 1776, by Sayer and Bennett.

In Stedman's American War, which is reproduced with additions in the large illustrated edition of Irving's Washington, ii. 308. In Mackinnon's Coldstream Guards, and a large map for the Campaign in Hamilton's Grenadier Guards, ii.

A Hessian officer's map is fac-similed in Field's monograph; and a contemporary map of Long Island is given in the Geographische Belustigungen, Leipsic, 1776.

Cf. further titles of maps in the Bibliography of Long Island in the American Bibliopolist, Oct. 1872, and in the Appendix to Furman's Antiquities of Long Island.

Howe as a Commissioner, September, 1776.

Gen. Sullivan, taken a prisoner in the battle of Long Island, was paroled by Howe, and was sent to Congress with a message of conciliation.

Franklin, John Adams, and Rutledge were sent to confer with Howe, and they met at Amboy.

An account of the interview is given in Franklin's Works, v. 97; viii. 187; also in Parton's Franklin, ii. 141.

Journals of Congress, Sept. 1776; and Force's American Archives, 4th series, vi.; 5th, i., ii.

John Adams's Works, i. 237; iii. 73; ix. 440. Wells's Samuel Adams, ii. 443. Amory's Sullivan, 30. Reed's Joseph Reed, i. ch. 12. Read's George Read, pp. 174, 189, 190. Lossing's Schuyler, ii. 37.

Howe's report to his government is in Almon's Remembrancer, viii. 250; Parliamentary Register, viii. 249.

Washington withdraws to New York.

Washington withdrew his army from Long Island by night without loss.

Gordon indicates the contemporary recognition of the mistake Howe made through his inertness and his failure at once to gain the rear of the Americans either by the river or by the Sound. See also Putnam's letter to Gov. Trumbull, Sept. 12, 1776.

What was done for the maintenance of a position in New York itself is narrated in the Correspondence of the Provincial Congress of New York; in General Lee's Memoirs; in Booth's New York, p. 493; in New York during the Revolution, p. 82 ; in Johnston's Campaign of 1776, ch. 5; in Irving's Washington, ii. ch. 33, etc.

There is a journal of the American occupation in the Historical Magazine, Dec. 1868 ; and an American orderly-book, Sept. 1–13, 1776, captured in New York, is among the Percy MSS., according to the Third Report of the English Commission on Historical MSS. H. B. Dawson gives an account of the town at this time, in New York during the Revolution.

Nathan Hale. — This young Connecticut officer was sent into the British camp on Long Island, and being detected, was executed as a spy, Sept. 22, 1776. See the Histories of Connecticut, and I. W. Stuart's Life of Nathan Hale.

The British occupy New York, September 15, 1776.

Washington was acting warily to avoid being inclosed by the British occupying the island to the north of him. Howe landed his troops at Turtle Bay. Connecticut troops stationed there fled precipitately. Washington's letter to Congress in his Official Letters, i. 246 ; and in Sparks, iv. 94. Greene to Gov. Cooke of Rhode Island, in Force's Archives, 5th series, ii. 370. Bancroft, ix. 122, cites a letter of Cæsar Rodney, and shows how the story has grown. Gordon's American Revolution, ii. 327. Heath's Memoirs, p. 60. Davis's Life of Burr, i. 100. Read's George Read, p. 193. Col. N. Fish's letter in Historical Magazine, 2d

series, iii. 33.   Baumeister's Narrative, a MS. in
Bancroft's possession, translated in the Magazine
of American History, Jan. 1877.

A considerable section of the city was burned,
the British charging the act upon the retiring
Americans as a part of a concerted plan to destroy the town.   Force's Archives, 5th series, ii.;
Journals of Congress, and Washington's Letters
(see Sparks's note in iv. 101) show that the act
was not authorized by the American leaders.
Howe's report to Lord George Germain is given
in Force and in Jones's New York in the Revolutionary War, with note, i. 611.   Cf. J. C.
Hamilton's Republic of the United States, i.
127 ; Henry's Campaign against Quebec ; Reed's
Life of Joseph Reed, i. 213.

In general, on the British occupation, see
Fish's Letter in the Historical Magazine, Jan.
1869; Gentleman's Magazine, Nov. and Dec.
1776; a Diary in the Pennsylvania Magazine
of American History, i. 133; and the histories
of New York City.   Cf. the papers on New York
in the Revolution in Harper's Monthly, xxxvii. ;
Scribner's Monthly, Jan. 1876.

Maps and Plans. — The map used in the
campaign by the American leaders is now in the
Library of the New York Historical Society, and
is engraved in the large illustrated edition of
Irving's Washington, ii. 276.   There are other
reproductions of contemporary plans of the city

and of the military movements in the New York City Manual for 1863, 1864, and 1866; and, in connection with Dawson's account, New York in the Revolution. An old view of the city is reproduced in Moore's Diary of the American Revolution, p. 311.

There are other maps in Gordon's History; in Marshall's Washington; in Sparks's Washington, iv. 96.

A German map is given in the Geschichte der Kriege in und aus Europa, Nuremberg, 1776.

British maps will be found in Stedman's American War; in Hall's Civil War in America, 2d ed., London, 1780; in the Gentleman's Magazine, Dec. 1776; in the Political Magazine, London, Nov. 1781. Major Holland's surveys are given in a contemporary map covering the country from Sandy Hook to Haverstraw; a chart of the harbor from Sandy Hook to New York was published in London, 1776, by Sayer and Bennett. Montresor's plan of New York in 1775 is No. 25 in the American Atlas, and No. 20 is the same officer's plan of the vicinity of the town. A plan of the city as surveyed by Bernard Ratzen, 1767, was engraved by T. Kitchin, and reissued in 1776 and 1777, and is given on a reduced scale in Jones's New York in the Revolutionary War. Faden of London published in 1777 a map of the northern part of the island, drawn by Saulthier.

The American Retreat, September—November, 1776.

Washington withdrew up the island as the British advanced. The campaign in general can be followed in Johnston's Campaign of 1776; in Bancroft, ix.; Irving's Washington, ii.; Greene's Life of Greene, i. Washington's letters are in Sparks, and in the Heath Papers, printed in the Massachusetts Historical Society's Collections, 5th series, iv. The Historical Magazine, Dec. 1863, gives a military journal.

British Accounts. — Stedman's American War; Conduct of the American War; and the general histories.

German Accounts. — Eelking's Deutsche Hülfstruppen; Schlözer's Briefwechsel, ii. 99.

The following sections give details of the retreat :—

Harlem Plains, September 16, 1776.

Howe landed his troops at Frog Neck, in an endeavor to cut off Washington's retreat. Irving's Washington. Heath's Memoirs.

For contemporary accounts of the action, see Washington's letters in Sparks; those in the Life of Greene by Greene; Reed's in the Life of Joseph Reed, i. 237 ; Gen. Silliman's in the notes of Jones's New York in the Revolutionary War, i. 606; Gen. Clinton's letter in New York in the Revolution ; and Documents in Force, 5th series, ii.

Later Accounts. — In the general histories; Johnston's Campaign of 1776; Lossing's Field-Book; Dawson's Battles, and his paper in the New York City Manual, 1868; the Centennial Oration of John Jay before the New York Historical Society, 1876; Lushington's Lord Harris, p. 79; and the histories of New York City.

Map. — Johnston's Campaign of 1776, ch. 6.

Bancroft, ix. 175, gives a note collating the authorities on the origin of the retirement of the Americans from the island of New York.

White Plains, October 28, 1776.

Heath's Memoirs gives a daily chronicle of events during October.

Washington's Letters, iv., gives his daily observations. See also Force's Archives, 5th series, ii., iii.; Marshall's Washington, ii. ch. 8; Irving's Washington, ii. ch. 37; Hamilton's Republic of the United States, i. 132; Bancroft, ix. ch. 10; Reed's Life of Joseph Reed, i. ch. 12; General Hull's Revolutionary Services, ch. 4; Lossing's Field-Book, ii.; Dawson's Battles, ch. 14; Johnston's Campaign of 1776, ch. 7; De Lancey's note to Jones's New York in the Revolutionary War, i. 621. A diary by Allen is in Smith's History of Pittsfield, Massachusetts, i. 252.

British Accounts. — In Stedman, ch. 7, and in a Gazette of Dec. 30, 1776, which gave the first intelligence in London, and prompted a pamphlet by Israel Maudit, entitled Observations on the Conduct of Sir William Howe at Whiteplains, London, 1779.

There is a German account in Eelking's Hülfstruppen, ch. 2.

Maps. — The Lives of Washington, by Marshall and by Sparks; Hamilton's Republic of the United States, i. 132. A plan by Saulthier, engraved by Faden, 1777, is in the American Atlas, No. 23; and there is another British plan in Stedman.

Fort Washington, November 16, 1776.

While evacuating the island of New York with his main body, Washington had left, contrary to his own judgment, a force to maintain this post. It fell before an attack of the combined fleet and army of the enemy.

Washington's letters are in Sparks's edition of his writings, iv.; but compare the Lives of Washington by Marshall and Irving. Heath's Memoirs, p. 86. G. W. Greene's Life of Nathanael Greene, book ii. ch. 11, gives that general's share in the affair, and in a separate tract the biographer controverts the view taken in Bancroft, ix. ch. 11. See documents in Force's Archives, 5th series, iii.

Reed's Life of Joseph Reed, ch. 13; Dawson's Battles, ch. 15; Lossing's Field-Book, ii.; Magazine of American History, i.

Graydon's Memoirs, ch. 7, had intimated that the success of Howe was perhaps due to information of an officer of the fort who deserted to the enemy. De Lancey, in his notes to Jones's New York in the Revolutionary War, i. 630, prints a letter of William Demont, adjutant of the commander, dated 1792, which states that he bore plans of the fort to the enemy, "by which plans that fortress was taken." Howe's intention of attacking Washington's main force was changed by this information.

Maps. — Washington's Writings by Sparks, iv. 96, and the Atlas to Guizot's Washington and Carrington's Battles, ch. 37. A large contemporary map is reproduced in the New York City Manual for 1861. An account of the capture in the Magazine of American History, Feb. 1877, is accompanied by a fac-simile of an original map.

There is a British plan in Stedman's American War. An English plan of the attack was given to the New York Historical Society, in 1861, by R. L. Stewart. A fac-simile of Faden's plan of the attack is in the New York Calendar of Historical MSS. i. 533.

There is a German map in the Geschichte der Kriege in und aus Europa, Nuremberg, 1776.

General Charles Lee, 1776.

The conduct of Lee began to incite observation during the movements of Washington after the

fall of Fort Washington, when he moved with his
army into New Jersey to cover Philadelphia.
Cf. Geo. H. Moore's Treason of Charles Lee;
Heath's Memoirs, p. 88; Reed's Life of Joseph
Reed, i. 253; Drake's Life of Henry Knox; J.
C. Hamilton's Republic of the United States, i.
ch. 6.

Lee was taken prisoner in his quarters, Dec.
13th. Cf. Sparks's Washington, iv., App. 8;
Irving's Washington; Moore's Treason of Lee,
p. 60; Charles Lee's Memoirs; Memoirs of Mrs.
E. S. M. Quincy, privately printed, 1861; Jones's
New York in the Revolutionary War, i. 173;
Force's Archives, 5th series, iii.

Washington in the Jerseys, December, 1776—January, 1777.

The letters of the commander-in-chief are in
Sparks's Washington's Writings, iv. Various
original papers are in Force's Archives, 5th series, iii. Bancroft, ix. ch. 12, and Irving's Washington, ii., are still the best to follow. Geo. W.
Greene gives a separate chapter to this retreat in
his Life of General Greene, and controverts Bancroft on special points. See also Read's George
Read, p. 216; Reed's Life of Joseph Reed, ch.
14; Gordon's History, ii. ; Johnston's Campaign
of 1776, ch. 8. There is a series of minor monographs by C. C. Haven, namely, Washington and
his Army in New Jersey, 1856; Thirty Days in
New Jersey Ninety Years Ago, 1867; Historical
Manual concerning Trenton and Princeton.

See, further, J. F. Tuttle's Washington in Morris County, in the Historical Magazine, June, 1871; Washington at Morristown, in Harper's Monthly, xviii. 289, and in the Magazine of American History, Feb. 1879, p. 118; Glimpse of '76 in New Jersey, in Harper's Monthly, July, 1874; Washington at Trenton and Princeton, in Potter's American Monthly, Jan. 1877, and a little tract by T. White, published at Charlestown, Mass.

The State of New Jersey has printed the correspondence of its executive, 1776–1786.

The political aspects of the campaign can be traced in Mercy Warren's History; in Ellery's letters to the Governor of Rhode Island, in Rhode Island Colonial Records, viii.; and in Wells's Life of Samuel Adams, ii. The state of affairs in Philadelphia is shown in R. Morris's letters to the President of Congress in Pennsylvania Historical Society's Memoirs, i. 50. A loyalist's view of the unmilitary management of the British general is in Jones's New York in the Revolutionary War, i.

The British view is given in the general histories of Stedman and Andrews; in the Annual Register, xx. ch. 1; in General Howe's Narrative; in the Detail and Conduct of the American War for the evidence of Cornwallis, etc.; in Letters to a Nobleman on the Conduct of the War in the Middle Colonies, London, 1779.

A contemporary tabular view of Howe's losses,

Aug. – Dec. 1776, is given on a folded sheet in the History of the War in America, Dublin, 1779.

Maps of the Campaign. — A reproduction of that used by the American commander is given in Irving's Washington, large illustrated edition, ii. 430. Others are in Gordon, ii. p. 524; Lives of Washington, by Sparks, iv. 266, and by Marshall; in Carrington's Battles, p. 302; in Lossing's Field-Book, ii.

The British maps are in Gentleman's Magazine, Sept. 1776; Stedman's American War. Faden's map of New Jersey, Dec. 26, 1776 – Jan. 3, 1777, is in the American Atlas.

Holland's map of New York and New Jersey was engraved by Jefferys in 1775, and reappeared as improved by Pownall in 1776. Saulthier's plan of Howe's operations was published by Faden in 1777; and another of the seat of war in New York, New Jersey, and Pennsylvania was published by Almon in 1777. Faden again published Ratzer and Banker's map of New Jersey in 1777, and the same year a plan of the operations of Washington against the King's troops, in 1776–1777.

Trenton, December 26, 1776.

Washington unexpectedly crossed the Delaware and surprised a camp of the Hessians. Cf. Eelking's Deutsche Hülfstruppen, and papers in Force's Archives, 5th series, iii.

Washington's Letters, iv. 242–246, and App. 541, and his account to Heath, in Massachusetts Historical Society's Collections, 5th series, iv. 32; and Lives of Washington, by Marshall, ii. ch. 8, and Irving.

The representations by the Committee of Congress to the Commissioners in France are in Sparks's Diplomatic Correspondence, i. 246.

Bancroft, ix. ch. 13.   Greene's Life of Greene, book ii. ch. 13.   Wilkinson's Memoirs, ch. 3. Reed's Joseph Reed, i. 270.   An account by Major Morris in the Sparks MSS. in Harvard College Library.   Letter of R. H. Lee in the Massachusetts Historical Society's Proceedings, 1878, p. 109.   Drake's Life of Knox.   Hull's Revolutionary Services, ch. 5.   Dawson's Battles, ch. 16.   Lossing's Field-Book, ii., and his article in Harper's Monthly, vii. 445.   Carrington's Battles, ch. 39 and 40.   Raum's History of Trenton. C. C. Haven's Annals of Trenton, 1866.   Hilliard d'Auberteuil's Essais historiques, ii.   H. K. How's Poem on the battle, 1856.

The English historians, Adolphus, ii. 385, and Stanhope, vi. 130, assign the credit of this surprise to Arnold.   Gov. Tryon's letters to Lord George Germain, in Documents relative to the Colonial History of New York, viii. 694.

Maps. — Washington's Writings by Sparks, iv. 258, and the atlases to Marshall's and Guizot's Lives of Washington; Lossing's Field-Book, ii. ; Raum's Trenton.

Princeton, January 3, 1777.

The Letters and Life of Washington by Sparks. Irving's Washington, ii. ch. 14. Custis's Recollections of Washington, ch. 3. Wilkinson's Memoirs, ch. 3. St. Clair's Narrative. Hull's Revolutionary Services. Bancroft, ix. ch. 14. Lossing's Field-Book, ii. and his paper in Harper's Monthly, vii. 447. Dawson's Battles, ch. 17. Stone's Life of John Howland. Reed's Joseph Reed, i. 287. W. B. Reed's oration on General Mercer. J. F. Hageman's History of Princeton. Hollister's Connecticut, ii. ch. 13. An account by a sergeant in Newark Daily Advertiser is reprinted in E. S. Thomas's Reminiscences, i. 283.

Bancroft, ix. 247, has a note on the authorities for giving Washington the credit of the plan of a roundabout march to Princeton.

Maps. — Sparks's Washington, ii. 258, and Lossing's Field-Book.

Arnold on Lake Champlain, October, 1776.

This was an attempt by Arnold to drive back the British flotilla advancing up the lake. Cooper's Naval History of the United States. Wilkinson's Memoirs, ch. ii. Marshall's Washington, iii. ch. 1. Irving's Washington, ii. ch. 39. Sparks's Life of Arnold. John Trumbull's Memoirs, p. 34. Lossing's Schuyler, ii. 116, 137, and his Field-Book, i. Dawson's Battles, ch. 13.

Palmer's Lake Champlain, ch. 7.   Battle of Valcour, a pamphlet, 1876.

Arnold's naval tactics are examined in the introduction to General Wayne's Orderly-Book of the Northern Army, Oct. 17, 1776 – Jan. 8, 1777. A new view of Arnold's escape is given in Winslow C. Watson's Naval Campaign on Lake Champlain, in the American Historical Record, iii. 438–501. A contemporary sketch of the action is in the Sparks MSS. in Harvard College Library. Arnold's letters are in Sparks's Correspondence of the American Revolution, i. Appendix. Various contemporary reports will be found in Force's American Archives, 5th series, i., ii., iii. *index*, under Arnold, Fleet, and Lake Champlain.

Maps. — A map of Lake George and the southern end of Lake Champlain is in Wayne's Orderly-Book; and another map is in Palmer's Lake Champlain. A map of Hudson River and the communication with Canada by the lakes, by Saulthier, was published by Faden, in 1776; and the original plan by a British officer, of the action, subsequently engraved, is in the Faden Collection in the Library of Congress. An earlier survey of the region by Brassier, made for Amherst in 1762, was published by Sayer and Bennett in 1776, who also engraved the map which is given in the Military Pocket Atlas, 1776. See also American Atlas, No. 21.

EVENTS OF 1777.

Political Aspects.

THE journals of Congress are always meagre. "It is impossible to touch upon any interesting incident in the history of the Congress of the Revolution, and not regret," says G. W. Greene, "the meagreness of the journals." Events are followed in the lives of the principal members, like Samuel Adams, ii. ch. 44; R. H. Lee, John Adams, etc.

The insufficiency of Congress, and its needless interference with military matters, are pointed out in Lossing's Schuyler, ii. ch. 19, and in Greene's Life of Greene, i. ch. 18, etc.

July 1st, Congress instructed William Lee as Commissioner to Berlin and Vienna. Diplomatic Correspondence, ii. 289. Pitkin's United States, i. App. 25. Ralph Izard was commissioned to Italy. Diplomatic Correspondence, ii. 367. Arthur Lee's Life, and Life of Samuel Adams, shows Lee's proceedings in Paris; but the negotiations prompted by the surrender of Burgoyne, leading to an alliance with France, will be referred to under 1778. Bancroft, ix. ch. 17, traces the progress of negotiations with Spain. A set of diplomatic papers, beginning in 1777, and relating to their negotiations with the United States and Great Britain, has been printed by the States General of the Netherlands.

Nov. 15th, articles of confederation were adopted. Bancroft, ix. ch. 26; Life of John Adams, i. 269; ix. 467; Life of Samuel Adams; Pitkin's United States.

The national flag of thirteen stars and thirteen stripes was adopted by Congress this year. Preble's Flag of the United States, p. 182, where will also be found an account of the flags used from 1766 to 1777. Cf. Lossing's Schuyler, ii. 113; Schuyler Hamilton's History of the National Flag; J. F. Reigart's History of the First United States Flag, and the patriotism of Betsey Ross, Harrisburg, 1878; and documents in Force's Archives, 4th series, iv.

The views of the Opposition in England may be drawn from Burke's Letter to the Sheriffs of Bristol, in his works, Boston edition, ii. 189.

British Plans for the Campaign, 1777.

The British army, under Sir William Howe, were in possession of New York, and documents relating to their rule in the city will be found in Valentine's New York City Manual for 1868. See a picture of life in New York under British rule in the Unitarian Review, Nov. 1876, by Samuel Osgood, D. D.

March 29th, Gen. Charles Lee, then a prisoner in British hands, presented a plan of campaign to Gen. Howe, as calculated to thwart the American purposes. George H. Moore first brought this to the attention of students in his Treason of Charles Lee, in which he gave a fac-simile of the document in Lee's handwriting, and in which he traces the influence of it on the plan of the campaign as carried out by Howe. Cf. Bancroft, ix. 330; Howe's Narrative; Greene's Life of Greene, i. 385; Lossing in Magazine of American History, July, 1879, p. 450.

This plan of Lee seems to account in part for the mistake, recognized by Gordon and others, by which Howe, failing to coöperate with Burgoyne up the Hudson, subjected his troops to the confinement and danger of a sea voyage in order to approach Philadelphia from the Chesapeake.

Stedman (American War, i.) considers Howe responsible for the failure of the British arms in this campaign. A copy of this book, annotated by Sir Henry Clinton, is in the Carter-Brown Library at Providence, and a transcript of Clinton's notes is among the Sparks MSS. in Harvard College Library. De Lancey used these notes in his Jones's New York in the Revolutionary War, where a loyalist's criticism upon Howe will be found. A pamphlet of Observations by Clinton on Stedman's History was printed in London, 1794, and privately reprinted in New York, 1864.

Howe defended himself in a Narrative, and this drew out Galloway's Letters to a Nobleman, London, 1779. Howe again replied in Observations, to which Galloway gave a Reply in 1781. Papers relating to the campaign are appended to a View of the Evidence relative to the Conduct of the American War under Sir William Howe, Lord Viscount Howe, and General Burgoyne, as given before a Committee of the House of Commons, London, 1779.

Sparks wrote in his copy of the third edition of the Detail and Conduct of the American War, that " its principal object was to attack and injure the characters of Sir William Howe, Lord Howe, and General Burgoyne, and that the facts are everywhere distorted, opinions perverted by prejudice and a vindictive spirit, and the representations extravagant and often false."

Further examination of these charges against Howe and of the conduct of the campaign at large will be found in Smyth's Modern History, lecture 34; Gordon's American Revolution, ii.; Andrews's Late War, ii. ch. 26; Murray's War in America; Adolphus's England, ii. ch. 31; Lives of Washington by Marshall and Irving; Histories of the United States by Bancroft, ix. ch. 23, and Hildreth, iii. ch. 37; Lossing's Field-Book; Sargent's Life of André, ch. 7.

Bancroft, ix. ch. 16 and 18, gives an account of the preparations made in England for the campaign of 1777. Arthur Lee writes to Congress of the British plans. Diplomatic Correspondence, ii. 85.

Maps. — American Atlas, No. 12, dated 1771, and John Andrews's Map of the Colonies for 1777 in the same. Hall's American War has a map of the campaign, 1776–1777. Mellish and Tanner's Seat of War in America. Montresor's Province of New York, Pennsylvania, etc., 1777. Evans's Middle British Colonies, extended by Pownall, 1776. Saulthier's Province of New York, made for Gov. Tryon, 1777, published by Faden, 1779, is reproduced in Documentary History of New York, i. Faden's Map of New Jersey, Dec. 1, 1777. The Gentleman's Magazine, Dec. 1777, has a map of the approaches to Philadelphia. Barber engraved a map showing a circuit of twenty - five miles about New York, in 1777. There is a map in Howe's Narrative.

Of the French maps may be named : Du Chesnoy's Théatre de la Guerre, 1775–1778. Beaurain's Carte pour servir à l'intelligence de la Guerre, Paris, 1777. Brion de la Tour's Théatre de la Guerre, Paris, 1777, with one by Phelippeaux, 1778, pour servir de suite. Bourgoin's Théatre de la Guerre, Paris.

There is a contemporary German map in the Geschichte der Kriege in und aus Europa, Nuremberg, 1776.

Howe evacuates Jersey, 1777.

After the spring opened, the British commander endeavored, without success, to draw Washington into a battle, and finally withdrew all his forces from the Jerseys. Irving's Washington, iii. ch. 8; Graydon's Memoirs; Bancroft, ix. ch. 20; Greene's Life of Greene, i.; Graham's Life of Morgan; Life of Timothy Pickering, i.; Eelking's Die Deutsche Hülfstruppen.

In Connecticut and Rhode Island, 1777.

In April an expedition under Gov. Tryon invaded Connecticut from the Sound to destroy the American stores at Danbury. This object was accomplished, but the British were vigorously pursued to their ships. Leake's Life of General Lamb, ch. 11, with a plan; Teller's History of Ridgefield; Deming's Oration at the Dedication of the Wooster Monument in 1854; Stuart's Life of Jonathan Trumbull, ch. 27; Hollister's Connecticut, ii. ch. 12; Dwight's Travels in New England, iii.; Hinman's Historical Collections; Marshall's Washington, which account is examined by E. D. Whittlesey in the New York Historical Society's Collections, ii.; Irving's Washington, iii. ch. 5; Sparks's Washington, iv. 404; Lossing's Field-Book, p. 407. The English account will be found in Stedman, ch. 14, and a loyalist one in Jones's New York in the Revolutionary War, i. Dawson, in his Battles of the United States, ch. 18, gives the authorities and illustrative documents.

In July the British General Prescott was captured in Rhode Island by a party led by Lieut. Col. Barton. Cf. the histories of Rhode Island; Force's American Archives, 4th series, iv. ; Diman's Address, with a map, on the centennial observance of the event.

Burgoyne's Advance from Canada, May and June, 1777.

In the campaign of 1776, the British had advanced up Lake Champlain to Crown Point, which they held till, on the approach of winter, they returned to Canada. It was already expected that Burgoyne would conduct the next campaign over the same ground. Cf. Force's American Archives, *index* of the various volumes, under Burgoyne, Canada, and Carleton. Burgoyne returned to England, and drew up a plan of operations, which is in the Gentleman's Magazine, April, 1778 ; and in the Appendix of Fonblanque's Burgoyne, with the King's comments on it, which are also printed from a manuscript in the royal hand, in Albemarle's Rockingham and his Contemporaries, ii. 330. Lord George Germain's instructions to Gen. Carleton relative to Burgoyne's movements are in the Gentleman's Magazine, Feb. 1778.

Burgoyne arrived at Quebec May 6th. Los-

sing's Schuyler, ii. 194. What of preparation
had taken place or was made up to the time of the
advance, is shown in the lives of Baron Riedesel
and the Baroness Riedesel; Anburey's Travels;
Hilliard d'Auberteuil's Essais historiques, ii.;
Schlözer's Briefwechsel, Th. iii. pp. 27, 321; Th.
iv. p. 288, etc. Also see Bancroft, ix. ch. 21, who
gives much information regarding the German
material among the troops, and the recruiting of
them in Germany, ch. 18. This matter has special treatment in Kapp's Der Soldatenhandel
Deutscher Fürsten nach Amerika; and in Eelking's Die Deutsche Hülfstruppen in Nord Amerika, where is a list of manuscript journals, to
which access was had; and in ch. 4 there is an
account of these preparations in Canada.

The proclamation issued by Burgoyne June
23d, to induce the adhesion of the country people,
is given in the Appendix to Fonblanque's Burgoyne; in the Gentleman's Magazine, Aug. 1777;
in F. Moore's Diary of the Revolution; in Riedesel's Memoirs; in Niles's Principles and Acts; in
the Proceedings of the New York Historical Society, Jan. 1872; and there are accounts of it in
Anburey's Travels; in Lossing's Schuyler, ii.;
and in Thacher's Military Journal.

June 26th, Burgoyne reached Crown Point,
and, generally, for the early stages of the advance, see Fonblanque's Burgoyne; Riedesel's
Memoirs; Lossing's Schuyler, ii.; Bancroft, ix.

ch. 21; Irving's Washington, iii. ch. 9; Palmer's Lake Champlain, ch. 8; De Costa's Lake George, and his Narrative of Events at Lake George, 1868.

The fight at Diamond Island is described in the New England Historical and Genealogical Register, April, 1872, p. 150.

In the meanwhile the preparations which Schuyler was making to oppose Burgoyne are detailed in Lossing's Schuyler, ii. ch. 7. The dispute of command with Gates had finally resulted in Schuyler's being confirmed in the charge of military operations in the northern department, May 22d, and Gates journeyed to Philadelphia to lay his grievances before Congress. Irving's Washington, iii. ch. 3.

Ticonderoga evacuated, July 6, 1777. •

For the arrangements which had been made for the defense, see Force's American Archives, 5th series, i., ii., and iii., and Lossing's Schuyler. St. Clair was in command. Burgoyne seized and fortified the summit of Mount Defiance, which had been thought inaccessible to artillery, and this movement rendering the post untenable, Ticonderoga was evacuated in the night.

Burgoyne's letter on the capture was printed in the Gentleman's Magazine, Aug. 1777. Fonblanque's Burgoyne, p. 248, and Dawson's Battles of the United States. Cf. Anburey's Travels, letter 30.

St. Clair explained the necessity he was under in a letter to Washington, in Sparks's Correspondence of the Revolution, i. 400, and in ii. App. 2, there are various letters from St. Clair and others. Dawson also gives St. Clair's account. The disheartenment through the colonies was general. Wells's Samuel Adams, ii. ch. 45, and the letter, Aug. 7th, of the Committee of Congress to the Commissioners in France, in the Diplomatic Correspondence, i. 315. St. Clair was tried by court-martial and acquitted. The papers used are among the Sparks MSS. in Harvard College Library.

In general, on this event, see Sparks's Washington, v.; Heath Papers in Massachusetts Historical Society's Collections, 5th series, iv. 65; Wilkinson's Memoirs, ch. 4 and 5; Gen. Hull's Revolutionary Services, ch. 7; Orderly-Book of the Northern Army at Ticonderoga, with Notes, published by Munsell, 1859; Dawson's Battles, ch. 20; Lossing's Field-Book, and his Schuyler; Van Rensselaer's Essays; Jay's Life of Jay, i. 74; Sparks's Gouverneur Morris, i. ch. 8; J. C. Hamilton's Life of Hamilton, i. 79, 91, and Hamilton's Works, i. 31; Sedgwick's Livingston, p. 233; Palmer's Lake Champlain; De Costa's Fort George; Watson's Essex County, ch. 11; Smith's History of Pittsfield, Massachusetts, i. 282; Historical Magazine, Dec. 1862, July, 1867, Aug. 1869; Rev. Lewis Kellogg's Historical Discourse, Whitehall, 1847.

Maps. — A large plan of the works and topography of the neighboring ground, at the time of Abercrombie's attack, nineteen years before, is given in the Documents relative to the Colonial History of New York, x. 726. A copy of the map used at St. Clair's trial is in the Sparks Collection, Cornell University. Palmer's Lake Champlain has a map dated Aug. 1776.

Hubbardton, Vermont, July 7, 1777.

A part of the Americans, retreating from Ticonderoga, was overtaken by Generals Fraser and Riedesel, and defeated. Wilkinson's Memoirs, ch. 5; Lossing's Schuyler, ii. 223, and his Field-Book, i. 145; Dawson's Battles, i. ch. 20, giving the authorities; Carrington's Battles, ch. 45; Amos Churchill's History of Hubbardton, 1855; Henry Clark's Historical Address, 1859; and the histories of Vermont.

A journal by Enos Stone is in the New England Historical and Genealogical Register, Oct. 1861. Ebenezer Fletcher was wounded and taken prisoner, and he printed at Windsor, 1813, a Narrative of his Captivity.

Burgoyne's Narrative gives the British account.
Maps. — In Burgoyne and Carrington.

Murder of Miss McCrea, July 27, 1777.

This event, as evincing the untrustworthy alliance of the Indians, whom Burgoyne had joined to his army, and as being the subject of much agitation in England and America, was of importance in the progress of the war. A Life of Jane McCrea, by D. Wilson, was privately printed in New York, 1853, and there is an account of her in Mrs. Ellet's Women of the American Revolution, ii. Cf. Lossing's Schuyler, ii. 250, and his Field-Book, i. ; Stone's Life of Brant, i. 203 ; Irving's Washington, iii. ch. 14 ; Asa Fitch's account in the New Jersey Historical Society's Proceedings, reprinted in the Revolutionary Memorials, edited by Stephen Dodd ; W. L. Stone in Historical Magazine, April, 1867 ; in Galaxy, Jan. 1867, the last reprinted in Beach's Indian Miscellany ; and the Appendix to Stone's Burgoyne's Campaign. See also Ruttenber's Hudson River Indians, p. 273.

Her fate is the subject of a story, Miss Mac Rea, by Hilliard d'Auberteuil.

The opposition in England to the employment of Indians by Burgoyne showed itself in Burke's speech, Feb. 6, 1778. Cf. Parliamentary History ; Gentleman's Magazine, March, 1778 ; McKnight's Burke, ii. 213 ; Walpole and Mason Correspondence, i. 335 ; Fonblanque's Burgoyne.

Fort Stanwix and Oriskany, August, 1777.

A part of the British plan of the northern campaign was to send a force of British, Hessians, and Indians, under St. Leger, by way of Oswego, to

capture Fort Stanwix (or Fort Schuyler, as sometimes called), and then to follow down the Mohawk valley, hoping to unite with Burgoyne at
Albany. For the preliminaries, see Stone's Life
of Brant, i.; and for condition of affairs, see
Force's American Archives, 5th series, i., ii., iii.
Col. Gansevoort commanded at Stanwix, and St.
Leger laid siege to it Aug. 3d. Gen. Herkimer,
with the militia, advanced to raise the siege, and
the somewhat doubtful conflict which ensued is
known as the Battle of Oriskany, fought Aug.
7th.

American Accounts. — Gordon gives some details from eye-witnesses. Dwight picked up various anecdotes about the field in 1799, which are
given in his Travels, iii. The best of the later
accounts are in the elder W. L. Stone's Life of
Brant, i. ch. 10 and 11, and in the younger Stone's
Campaign of Burgoyne and Expedition of St.
Leger, 1877. Other narratives are in Lossing's
Schuyler, ii. 273, and Field-Book, i.; Hull's Revolutionary Services, ch. 8; Irving's Washington,
iii. ch. 15; Bancroft's United States, ix. 378;
Dawson's Battles, ch. 21, where various contemporary documents will be found; Benton's Herkimer County, ch. 5; Campbell's Tryon County,
ch. 4; Harper's Monthly, xxiii. 327, by T. D.
English; Magazine of American History, Nov.
1877; E. H. Roberts's Address, 1877.

British Accounts. — St. Leger's account is in

the Gentleman's Magazine, March, 1778, in the
Appendix to Burgoyne's State of the Expedition,
and in the Appendix to Roberts's Address. The
Annual Register, 1777, is followed in Andrews's
History. Almon's Parliamentary Debates, viii.,
gives some details. Beatson's Naval and Military
Memoirs, vi. 69.

St. Leger still continued the siege, but retreated
on the approach of Arnold, Aug. 22d, with a force
dispatched by Schuyler. Lossing's Schuyler, ii. ;
Irving's Washington, iii. ch. 16 and 17 ; Journals
of the Provincial Congress, i. ; Sparks's Correspondence of the Revolution, ii. 518.

Maps. — Fort Stanwix, with a topographical
map of the surrounding country, in 1758, is in
the Documentary History of New York, iv. 325,
326. A plan of the fort, in its relation to the
modern town of Rome, is given in the English
translation of Pouchot's Late War in North America, edited by F. B. Hough, p. 207. Plans of the
siege will be found in Lossing's Field-Book, i.
249 ; Campbell's Tryon County ; Stone's Life of
Brant, i. 230. A copy of Lieutenant Fleury's
plan is in the Sparks Collection at Cornell University.

Bennington, August 16, 1777.

Burgoyne, in order to secure forage and destroy
the stores which the Americans had accumulated
at Bennington, as well as to encourage the loyalists, sent a force of Hessians, under Col. Baum,

towards that place.   He was met by Stark with a
force of Green Mountain, New Hampshire, and
Massachusetts troops, and routed.   The British
supports under Breyman were likewise driven
back.

Burgoyne's original instructions to Baum are
preserved in the cabinet of the Massachusetts
Historical Society, and are printed in their Collections, ii., and in W. L. Stone's Burgoyne's
Campaign, App. 3.

American Accounts. — Lincoln communicated
the first accounts to Schuyler, who transmitted
them to Washington.   Sparks's Correspondence
of the Revolution, i. 425.   Stark's dispatch is
given in Dawson's Battles.   An account, by the
Rev. Mr. Allen, was printed in the Connecticut
Courant, Aug. 25, 1777, and is reprinted in App.
F of Smith's History of Pittsfield, Mass.

In 1848 there was delivered before the legislature of Vermont an address on the battle of
Bennington, by James D. Butler, which was
printed in 1849, together with an account of the
life and services of Col. Warner, by George
Frederick Houghton.   Professor Butler's address,
says the author, " contains original testimonies of
witnesses now long dead, and notes from papers
since burned in the Vermont State House."

Reminiscences by participants are given in the
App. of W. L. Stone's Burgoyne's Campaign.
Documents illustrating the part taken by Ver-

mont in resisting Burgoyne's invasion are in the Vermont Historical Society's Collections, 1870, p. 161. Wilkinson's Memoirs, i. ch. 5.

Later Accounts.—Bancroft, ix. ch. 22. Irving's Washington, iii. ch. 16. Lossing's Schuyler, ii. ch. 14; his Field-Book, i., and article in Harper's Monthly, v. Dawson's Battles, ch. 22, and his account in the Historical Magazine, May, 1870. Carrington's Battles, p. 334. Hall's and other histories of Vermont. Holland's Western Massachusetts, ch. 15. Smith's History of Pittsfield, Mass., i. 293. Lives of Stark, by Caleb Stark, Edward Everett, and others. Jennings's Memorials of a Century. Letters in the New England Historical and Genealogical Register, April, 1860. Chipman's Life of Seth Warner, and the account of Warner's share in the battle, in Historical Magazine, iv. 268. Harper's Monthly, xxi. 325, also Aug. 1877. Albert Tyler's address on Bennington before the Worcester Society of Antiquity. Noah Smith's speech at Bennington, in the Vermont Historical Society's Collections, 1870. F. W. Coburn's Centennial History of Bennington.

De Lancey (Jones's New York in the Revolutionary War, i. 685) has a note on the forces engaged.

A Bennington Historical Society was formed in 1876 for the purpose of commemorating the battle.

British and Hessian Accounts. — Burgoyne's dispatch is given in Dawson. Cf. Fonblanque's Burgoyne, p. 271, and his Narrative, with evidence as laid before Parliament. Riedesel in part controverts Burgoyne's statement in his Memoirs, i. 259, and in the App. p. 299, there are some Recollections of Bennington. Schlözer's Briefwechsel. Stedman's American War, i. ch. 17.

Maps. — In Burgoyne's Narrative; in Jennings's Memorials; in Lossing's Field-Book; in Carrington's Battles. There is a MS. plan among the Sparks MSS. in Harvard College Library.

The Change in Command, August 19, 1777.

A check had been given to the enemy at Oriskany in the west, and he had been defeated at Bennington in the east. At this juncture, when Burgoyne felt the toils tightening about him, a change in the command allowed Gates to reap the fruits of victory. Schuyler has long since been acquitted of blame for his conduct of the campaign; but a certain imperious manner and incautiousness of tongue had created a prejudice against him among the New England troops, and the change was perhaps a necessary one. The movement in behalf of Gates was assuming a political significance. Wells's Samuel Adams, ii. ch. 45; Sparks's Washington, v. 14; Sparks's Gouverneur Morris, i. 138. Bancroft, ix., holds

Schuyler in some measure responsible for the misfortunes of the early part of the campaign. Schuyler, however, has earnest defenders in George L. Schuyler's Correspondence and Remarks upon Bancroft's History of the Northern Campaign, 1777 ; and in Lossing's Schuyler, ii. 325. Cf. Sparks's Washington, iii. 535 ; Headley's Washington and his Generals ; American Historical Record, April, 1873 ; Magazine of American History, Feb. 1877, by J. W. De Peyster.

W. L. Stone has a paper on Schuyler's faithful spy in the Magazine of American History, July, 1878.

Gates reached headquarters Aug. 19th, and communicated with Washington Aug. 22d. Sparks's Correspondence of the Revolution, i. 427. Cf. Irving's Washington, iii. ch. 12 ; Hamilton's Republic of the United States, i. 306.

A portrait of Gates, after a pencil-sketch by Trumbull, is given in the Orderly-Book of the Northern Army at Ticonderoga. Other contemporary likenesses are in Murray's War in America, ii., and in An Impartial History of the War, London, 1780.

Freeman's Farm, September 19, 1777.

(Sometimes called the first battle of Bemis's Heights, or the battle of Stillwater.)

This was an effectual defense of the left wing of the American army. General Wilkinson's Memoirs, i. ch. 6, gives the best account of the action by any participant. Also see Headley's Washington and his Generals, and Lossing's Schuyler, ii. ch. 19. Morgan, who, with his riflemen, had been sent by Washington to join Gates, did much to increase the power of the American army during the rest of this campaign, and his career can be examined in Graham's Life of Morgan, ch. 7–9.

See the account in Burgoyne's Narrative; in Fonblanque's Burgoyne; in Col. Carrington's Battles of the American Revolution, ch. 46. Dawson, ch. 25, treats this and the action of Oct. 7th in one continuous narrative, with copious references and illustrations of official dispatches, etc. Cf. Lossing's Field-Book.

A panoramic view of the position of Burgoyne's army after this battle is given in Anburey's Travels.

Bancroft, ix. 410, cites the authorities to show that Arnold was not present, as often represented.

Robert Lowell read a poem, Burgoyne's Last March, at the centennial celebration of this battle, Sept. 19, 1877.

Maps. — In Burgoyne's Narrative; in Carrington's Battles.

Sept. 27th, Burgoyne sent Captain Scott to open communication with Sir Henry Clinton, who was now ascending the Hudson to coöperate. Scott's journal is given in Fonblanque's Burgoyne, p. 287.

Bemis's Heights, or Saratoga, October 7, 1777.

Burgoyne advanced with a strong force to cover foraging parties and to reconnoitre the American position. He was attacked sharply and driven back. The Lives of Arnold indicate his important share in this success. Cf. Magazine of American History, May, 1879, p. 310. There is a monograph on the battle by Neilson, and in his Appendix is the story of Woodruff, an eye-witness. Cf. Wilkinson's Memoirs; Stone's Burgoyne's Campaign; Hull's Revolutionary Services, ch. 10; Bowen's Life of Gen. Lincoln; Creasy's Decisive Battles of the World; Irving's Washington, iii. ch. 22; Lossing's Schuyler, ii. ch. 20, and his Field-Book; A. B. Street in the Historical Magazine, March, 1858.

Silliman's account of his visit to the battlefield, is given in an Appendix to Stone's Burgoyne's Campaign.

Maps. — In Burgoyne's Narrative; in Fonblanque's Burgoyne; in Stedman's American War; in the Analectic Magazine, 1818; in Carrington's Battles.

In the night Burgoyne withdrew across the Fishkill and intrenched himself. Wilkinson's Memoirs, i. ch. 8, gives fac-similes of Burgoyne's letters to Gates, commending to the care of the victorious general his abandoned hospital and Lady Ackland, who sought her husband, Major

Ackland, wounded, and in the American camp.
The devotion of Lady Ackland is a pleasing episode in all the accounts of this battle. See, concerning her, the Historical Magazine, ii. 121;
Ellet's Women of the American Revolution; and
the portraits of her in Burgoyne's Orderly-Book,
and in Bloodgood's Sexagenary.

Burgoyne's Surrender, October 17, 1777.

With his retreat cut off, his supplies exhausted,
and an enemy much superior in numbers surrounding him, Burgoyne opened negotiations for
a surrender. The council of war is described in
Riedesel's Memoirs. The correspondence and
convention papers are given by O'Callaghan in
Burgoyne's Orderly-Book, and they are also in
Stedman's American War, and in Dawson's Battles, ch. 25. The original MS. of the Convention
is in the New York Historical Society's Cabinet,
and fac-similes of the signatures are given in
Lossing's Field-Book, i. 79.

General accounts of the surrender are in Wilkinson's Memoirs, ch. 8; Bancroft, ix. ch. 24;
Lossing's Schuyler, ii. ch. 21; Irving's Washington, iii. 22; Blackwood's Magazine, lxiii.; Bloodgood's Sexagenary; Pennsylvania Archives, v.

Loubat (Medallic History of the United States)
describes the medal given to Gates.

Burgoyne, while the guest of Schuyler in Albany, Oct. 20th, wrote a dispatch to his govern-

ment, which is given in the Gentleman's Magazine, Dec. 1777; in Fonblanque's Life of Burgoyne, p. 313, with other letters; in the Brief
Examination of the Plan and Conduct of the
Northern Expedition in America, 1777, London,
1779; and in Dawson's Battles. Cf. Stanhope's
History, vi. 207. Riedesel in his Memoirs comments on Burgoyne's dispatch.

Maps. — The position of Burgoyne's army is
shown in Burgoyne's Narrative; Fonblanque's
Burgoyne, p. 302; Carrington's Battles of the
Revolution, p. 354.

Strength of the Armies. — De Lancey, in his
notes to Jones's New York in the Revolutionary
War, i. 674, examines the question of the relative
strength of the British and American armies in
this campaign, with references to the authorities.
The return of Gates's army, given in the Gates
MSS. in the New York Historical Society, at the
time of the Convention, shows a total of 11,098.
Burgoyne printed in the Appendix of his Narrative a return, which he said Gates gave him, and
it foots up 18,624. The difference may be explained by the sick and furloughed men. Gordon (American Revolution, ii. 578) gives 5,791 as
the number of the British at the surrender; but
there are diversities in the statements, as De
Lancey shows.

The Convention Troops. — The captured army
became known by this designation during their
subsequent detention till the close of the war.

They were marched to Cambridge, Mass., under escort; and in Anburey's Travels there is a map showing their line of march. At Cambridge the officers gave their parole to keep within defined limits, the English and Germans signing separate papers. The originals of these are now in the Public Library of Boston. They are printed in Burgoyne's Orderly-Book. For the reception of the troops, see Heath's Memoirs, p. 134. Of their stay in Cambridge, there are particulars in Schlözer's Briefwechsel, Th. iv. 341, etc.; in Riedesel's Memoirs, ii.; in Madame Riedesel's Memoirs; in Lossing's Field-Book; in Drake's Middlesex; in Eelking's Deutsche Hülfstruppen, ch. 9. Nathan Bowen's Book of General Orders during the sojourn of the troops in Cambridge was copied in part by S. G. Drake, and his copy is in the Public Library of Boston.

Col. Henley, an American officer of the guard, was accused by Burgoyne of ill-treatment of the Convention troops; and the account of Henley's trial, London, 1778, shows glimpses of the camp life and traits of Burgoyne's character. This trial is epitomized in P. W. Chandler's American Criminal Trials, ii. Various letters relating to the Convention troops at this time will be found in Sparks's Washington, v., and in Heath's Memoirs.

Burgoyne returned to England on parole, and sat in Parliament while still unexchanged. Fonblanque's Burgoyne and Macknight's Burke, ii. ch. 30.

The difficulties of provisioning the troops in Cambridge, and the apprehension lest the British should attempt their rescue, induced Congress to order their removal to Virginia. Anburey gives a map of their route in Nov. 1778. Accounts of their sojourn in Virginia are given in Anburey, Riedesel, and Eelking; the Bland papers, edited by Campbell; Jefferson's Writings, i. 212; Lives of Jefferson by Tucker, i. ch. 5; by Randall, i. 232, 285; and by Parton, p. 222. Howison's History of Virginia, ii. 250. Cf. Pennsylvania Archives, ix.; and in vi. 162, the Report of Congress, Jan. 8, 1778, on the breach of the Convention by the British.

Charles Deane, in the Council Report of the American Antiquarian Society, Oct. 1877, examined the tortuous course of Congress in carrying out the provisions of the Convention of Surrender; and this question is further discussed by G. W. Greene in the Magazine of American History, April, 1879. Cf. also Stanhope's History of England, vi. 194; Jones's New York in the Revolutionary War, i., with De Lancey's note, p. 698.

General Views of Burgoyne's Campaign, 1777.

American Accounts. — Gen. Lincoln gives an account of his experiences in a letter in Sparks's Correspondence of the Revolution, ii. 533. Cf. Bowen's Life of Lincoln, and the account in Headley's Washington and his Generals. Dr. Thacher was with the army, and his Military Journal gives frequent records. The reminiscences of Col. Seth Warner are in the Historical Magazine, July, 1860. The part borne by Col. Brooks of Massachusetts is shown in the Massachusetts Historical Society's Proceedings, Sept. 1864; and there are other details under Feb. 1858. F. Kidder's First New Hampshire Regiment follows that regiment through the campaign. Gates's own papers are in the New York Historical Society's Cabinet. Wilkinson was selected to carry the news of the surrender to Congress, and his Memoirs give the experiences and observations of a staff officer. Bloodgood's Sexagenary details the experiences of the country people on the line of Burgoyne's march. Various papers, including Armstrong's letters, are in the Sparks MSS. in Harvard College Library.

The correspondence of the Committee of Congress with the Commissioners in France regarding the effects of the surrender, is in the Diplomatic Correspondence,.i. 338, 355. Cf. Stuart's Life of Jonathan Trumbull.

There are accounts, more or less full, in Gordon; Ramsay; Bancroft, ix.; Hildreth, iii. ch. 36; J. C. Hamilton's Republic of the United States, i.; Marshall's Washington, iii. ch. 5; Irving's Washington, iii.; Thaddeus Allen's Origination of the American Union; Hollister's Connecticut, ii. ch. 14; Dunlap's New York, ii. ch. 8;

McAlpine's Memoirs, 1788 ; Stone's Life of Brant; Mrs. Bonney's Historical Gleanings, i. 58 ; and the Lives of Gates, Schuyler, Lincoln, and Arnold.

Samuel Woodruff, a participant, gave Stone some reminiscences, which are included in the Life of Brant, i. 475.

Neilson, son of an old resident of Saratoga, contemporary with the events, and himself familiar with the ground on which the battles of Sept. 19th and Oct. 7th were fought, published a monograph, Burgoyne's Campaign.

The younger W. L. Stone published, 1877, a new study on The Campaign of Lieutenant-General Burgoyne, in which he gives a bibliography of the subject. He has also printed a short history of the Saratoga Monument Association.

Magazine Papers. — Harper's Monthly, lv. ; Historical Magazine, Jan. 1869, by J. Watts De Peyster ; Magazine of American History, May, 1877, by E. H. Walworth ; Galaxy, Nov. 1876, by J. T. Headley, on Burgoyne's Orderly-Book.

Commemorative Addresses. — N. B. Sylvester's Saratoga and Hay-ad-ros-se-ra, July 4, 1876 ; George G. Scott's Saratoga County ; J. S. L'Amoreaux's at Ballston Spa, July, 1876 ; Edward F. Bullard's at Schuylerville, July 4, 1876 ; J. A. Stevens's Burgoyne's Campaign ; Geo. W. Curtis's Address ; H. C. Maine's Burgoyne Campaign.

Landmarks. — Lossing's Field-Book, and his Book of the Hudson.

British Accounts. — The Gentleman's Magazine, Oct. 1777, p. 472, warned the public of the difficulties Burgoyne must expect to encounter. Lord Shelburne (Fitzmaurice's Shelburne, i. 358) intimates that Burgoyne's disaster arose from Lord George Sackville's dilatoriness in not sending instructions to Howe to coöperate up the Hudson. Fonblanque's Burgoyne, p. 233.

Burgoyne underwent examination, and produced his witnesses before Parliament, May, 1779, and the documents are given in the Parliamentary Register. The Gentleman's Magazine chronicled the progress of the examination from month to month. Cf. Annual Register, xxi. 168 ; Russell's Life of Fox, and his Memoirs and Correspondence of Fox, i. 176. Burgoyne printed his statement in Parliament, with the evidence, in his State of the Expedition from Canada, London, 1780. Some copies have a supplement of the Orders issued by Burgoyne, and these Orders were privately reprinted in New York in 1865. This account is substantially followed in Fonblanque's Life of Burgoyne, ch. 6.

Burgoyne had already defended himself in a Letter to his Constituents, London, 1779, which elicited a Reply, the same year.

Portraits of Burgoyne are given in the Political Magazine, Dec. 1780 ; Fonblanque's Burgoyne (painted 1750) ; Andrews's Late War, ii. 382 ; Murray's War in America, ii. ; Burgoyne's Orderly-Book ; Bloodgood's Sexagenary.

The testimony of the Earl of Balcarras and other officers is in the Conduct of the American War.

Burgoyne charged the loyalists and Indians with failure to support him, and this charge is answered in a paper printed by De Lancey in the App. of Jones's New York in the Revolutionary War, i. 683 ; and pp. 198–218 will be found a very good account of the campaign, with loyalist sympathies, and deprecatory criticism of the military conduct of it on the part of the British general.

Contemporary Narratives. — Sergeant Lamb's Journal of Occurrences, the record of a subaltern of the Fusiliers. An English diary in the Magazine of American History, Feb. 1878. A MS. journal of Lieutenant Hadden is in the possession of General Horatio Rogers of Providence.

General Histories. — Stedman, i. ch. 16 ; Stanhope, ch. 56 ; Pictorial History of England.

The effect of the surrender upon parties in England is shown in the Debates in Parliament ; Macknight's Burke, ii. 202 ; Donne's Correspondence of George the Third and Lord North, ii. 93, ·111 ; the excerpts in Moore's Diary of the American Revolution, i. 525 ; Russell's Memoirs and Correspondence of Fox, i. 161 ; Fitzmaurice's

Shelburne, iii. 12; Walpole's Last Journals, ii.
70; Fonblanque's Burgoyne, ch. 8; Madison's
Writings, i. 31; Curwen's Journal, p. 175; Bancroft, ix. 478.

German Accounts. — Baron Riedesel, the German general accompanying Burgoyne, took excep-
tions to the English commander's narrative as not
doing justice to the auxiliary troops; and the Leben
und Wirken of General Riedesel, by Max von
Eelking, translated by W. L. Stone, contains letters and reports. In Madame Riedesel's Memoirs,
also translated by Stone, there is an abstract of
her husband's account of the campaign, p. 94, etc.
Eelking, in his Die Deutsche Hülfstruppen, devotes two chapters to this campaign, ch. 7 and 8.
See also Remer's Amerikanisches Archiv. Kapp's
Soldatenhandel covers the organization of the
German auxiliaries, and George W. Greene's
German Element in the War for Independence,
epitomizes Kapp's investigations in part.

The Effect in France. — Jonathan Loring Austin, dispatched by the Massachusetts authorities,
carried the first intelligence. Cf. Boston Monthly Magazine, July, 1826; Loring's Hundred Boston Orators, p. 174; Parton's Franklin, ii. 283.
The Baron de Schulenberg congratulated the
Commissioners, writing from Berlin. Diplomatic
Correspondence, ii. 120; and for Izard's letter,
ii. 370. Robin's New Travels, letter 12, gives the
general hearsay accounts prevalent during the
few following years.

In Fiction. — Gleig's Saratoga, in his Chelsea
Pensioners ; D. P. Thompson's Rangers.

General Maps of the Campaign. — Burgoyne's
Narrative, and also in his Orderly-Book. An-
burey's Travels. Gordon's American Revolution.
Neilson's Burgoyne's Campaign, whose map is
reproduced as revised in W. L. Stone's Lieut.
Gen. Burgoyne. Carrington's Battles, p. 312.
Magazine of American History, May, 1877.

Saulthier's survey of the inhabited part of
Canada, with the frontiers of New York, was published in London by Faden in 1777. A map,
after Saulthier's survey, showing the province of
New York, with the old divisions of counties,
manors, etc., covering the present Vermont, together with New Jersey, was published at Augs-
burg in 1777, and is reproduced in Jones's New
York in the Revolution, i. Medcalfe's map of the
country in which Burgoyne acted was engraved by
Faden. Montresor's map, made in 1775, is in the
American Atlas. The Faden Collection, in the
Library of Congress, has various contemporary
maps. There are maps also in Hilliard d'Auberteuil's Essais historiques, ii.

Clinton's Advance up the Hudson, October, 1777.

Sir Henry Clinton moved up the Hudson with
troops and vessels to open the navigation of it
and to effect a junction with Burgoyne at Albany.
He deceived Putnam by his strategy, and fell

upon and took Forts Clinton and Montgomery, Oct. 6th.

American Accounts. — Letters of Putnam and George Clinton in Sparks's Washington, v., App. p. 471 ; Correspondence of the Revolution, i. 438 ; ii. 536. Leake's Life of Samuel Lamb, who was a participant. Lossing's Schuyler, ii. ch. 20, and his Field-Book, ii. 165. Irving's Washington, iii. ch. 21. Sargent's Life of André, p. 102. Hamilton's Republic of the United States, i. 321. Lives of Putnam by Humphreys and Tarbox. Dawson's Battles, i. ch. 28, who gives the dispatches, and his paper in the National Repository, ii. Carrington's Battles.

There is an account of the burning of Esopus, as the British pushed up the river, in the Ulster County Historical Society's Collections, i. 109.

British Accounts. — Sir Henry Clinton's dispatches are in Almon's Remembrancer, v., and in Dawson. A letter of his is in Rockingham and his Contemporaries, ii. 334. His annotations on the account in Stedman's American War, ch. 18, are printed by De Lancey in Jones's New York in the Revolutionary War, i. 704.

Fonblanque, in his Life of Burgoyne, and other defenders of that general, trace his ill-success to the tardiness of this diversion.

Maps. — Col. Palmer's plan of Fort Montgomery, 1776, in the New York Calendar of Historical Manuscripts, i. 474, and a sketch of the river obstructions, p. 616 ; and ii. 298, a plan of the attack on the two forts, after Faden's plan. MS. plans are in the Sparks Collection at Cornell and at Harvard. Stedman's American War, ch. 1, follows the plan by John Hills, which was first published by Faden, June 1, 1784. Sparks's Washington, v. 92. Leake's Life of Lamb. Boynton's History of West Point, with drawings of the river obstructions. Lossing's Field-Book. Carrington's Battles.

Howe's Campaign, 1777.

Howe's obvious movement was to proceed up the Hudson and coöperate with Burgoyne; but the spring and early summer wore away, and Washington was not satisfied of his intentions. See his letters in Sparks's edition of his Writings, iv. 442, 453, 501, 505 ; v. 42 ; and in the Heath Correspondence, Massachusetts Historical Society's Collection, 5th series, iv. In August, embarking 18,000 troops on transports, Howe sailed for the Chesapeake, and, landing them at the Head of Elk, he began to advance towards Philadelphia. Jones's New York in the Revolutionary War, ii. 431.

General accounts of the campaign which ensued for the possession of Philadelphia, will be found in Gordon, Bancroft, Hamilton's Republic, i. ch. 10; in Lives of Washington by Marshall, iii. ch. 3, and Irving; Histories of Pennsylvania; McSherry's Maryland, ch. 11; and various biographies, like Greene's Greene, Quincy's Shaw, ch. 3, etc. The Minutes of the Pennsylvania Board of War, March to August, are in Pennsylvania Archives, 2d series, i.

Brandywine, September 11, 1777.

Washington had hastily marched his army through Philadelphia to the Brandywine, where he encountered Howe, Sept. 11th, but was driven back.

American Accounts. — Washington's letters are in Sparks, v. 58, and in Dawson. Marshall is full on this part of Washington's career. Irving's Washington, iii. ch. 18. Gordon's American Revolution. Bancroft, ix. charges Sullivan with defeating Washington's plans, and Sullivan is defended in Amory's Military Services of Gen. Sullivan, p. 45. For charges against and defence of Sullivan, see Pennsylvania Historical Society, Bulletin, i. Cf. also Sparks's Washington, v. 108 and App. Johnson's Life of Nathanael Greene ; Greene's Greene, i. ch. 19. Muhlenberg's Life of Gen. Muhlenberg, ch. 3. Pennsylvania Historical Society's Proceedings, Sept. and Dec. 1846, and Memoirs, i. A letter written in 1820 by C. C. Pinckney, who was in Washington's military family at this time, is in the Historical Magazine, July, 1866. J. C. Hamilton's Life of Alexander Hamilton, who was at the time on Washington's staff. Pickering's Life of Timothy Pickering, i.

ch. 10. Reed's Life of Joseph Reed, i. ch. 15.
Lafayette's Memoirs. Read's Life of George
Read. Dawson's Battles, ch. 24. Carrington's
Battles. Lossing's Field-Book. Hollister's Connecticut, ii. ch. 16. Thaddeus Allen's Origination of the American Union. Smith's Delaware
County, p. 305. Lewis's History of Chester
County. H. M. Jenkins in Lippincott's Magazine, xx. A pamphlet account by J. Townshend,
1836. Some particulars of events following the
battle are given in Read's George Read, p. 319.

British and Hessian Accounts. — Howe's dispatches are in Almon's Remembrancer, v. 409;
and in Dawson. The evidence before Parliament
regarding this battle is in The Conduct of the
American War. Stedman gives a clear account.
For a statement of the breech-loading rifles used
by the British, see Bisset's History of George the
Third, ch. 19 and 25.

Eelking's Deutsche Hülfstruppen, ch. 6. Bancroft quotes Ewald's Beyspiele Grosser Helden,
as the story of an eye-witness to the well-guarded
retreat of Washington; but see, on the other hand,
Du Portail in Stanhope's England, vi. App. 27.

Maps. — Faden published, 1778, a map of the
battle. MS. plans are in the Faden Collection in
the Library of Congress, and one is in the Sparks
Collection at Cornell. A large map of Pennsylvania, chiefly after Scull, 1770, was published by
Sayer and Bennett, 1775, and the next year they

issued a chart of the Chesapeake, after surveys of Anthony Smith.

Later Plans of the Field. — Sparks's Washington, v. 58; Marshall's Washington, v.; Duer's Lord Stirling, ii.; Lossing's Field-Book, ii. 377; Irving's Washington, iii.; Hamilton's Grenadier Guards, ii.; Carrington's Battles, 382; Bowen and Futhey's Sketch of the Battle. A large plan, with topography as surveyed in 1846, is in Pennsylvania Historical Society's Memoirs, i.

Paoli, September 20, 1777.

Washington, on his retreat, detached Wayne with a force to fall upon the enemy's rear. Howe sent, as a counter-movement, Gen. Grey, who surprised Wayne's camp at Paoli, and routed his detachment. Irving's Washington, iii. ch. 19; Lives of Wayne by Sparks and Moore; Pennsylvania Magazine of History, i. 285.

Map. — Faden published, July 1, 1778, a Plan of the British Camp at Trudruffrin, Sept. 18–21, 1777, with Grey's attack near White Horse Tavern, Sept. 20th.

Philadelphia taken, September 27, 1777.

Washington was unable to impede Howe's advance, and the British general entered Philadelphia.

American Accounts. — Bancroft, ix. ch. 23. Hildreth, iii. ch. 37. Lossing's Field-Book, ii.

p. 302.   Greene's Life of Greene, i. ch. 21.
Drake's Life of Knox.   Letter of Thomas Paine
to Franklin, in the Pennsylvania Magazine of
History, ii. 283.   Memoirs of Col. Benj. Talmadge.

Papers relating to the War, 1777–1781, in the
Pennsylvania Archives, 1st series, v., and 2d series, iii., for affairs in Philadelphia during Howe's
advance.

British Accounts. — Sir William Howe's Narrative.   The Conduct of the American War.   Ross's
Life of Cornwallis.

The catalogue of the Philadelphia Library
shows, p. 1553, numerous proclamations of Howe.

For the events of the British occupation, see
Christopher Marshall's Diary ; Robert Morton's
Diary, in the Pennsylvania Magazine of History,
No. 1 ; Sargent's Life of André.   W. B. Reed's
Life of Esther Reed, p. 278.   United Service
Journal, 1852.

The relations of the Quakers to Congress, and
the arrest of some of them in Philadelphia, and
their removal before the Americans left the city,
are told in Gilpin's Exiles in Virginia.   Cf. Pennsylvania Archives, *passim.*

Maps. — Sparks's Washington, v. 66, gives a
map to show all the movements of this campaign.
See also Pennsylvania Archives, 2d series, iii. ;
Hall's History of the Civil War, 1780 ; Gentleman's Magazine, 1776 and 1777, and July, 1779,

for Fisher's Chart of Delaware River, made in 1776 ; Moore's Diary of the Revolution; History of the Coldstream Guards; Moorsom's Fifty-Second Regiment.

A plan of the city following the surveys of Scull and Heap was engraved by Faden in 1777; another after Eastburn's survey of 1776, and one after Hill's survey, were issued in Philadelphia in 1777.

There are various MS. maps in the Faden Collection in the Library of Congress.

Germantown, October 4, 1777.

While a part of Howe's force was operating on the river below Philadelphia, Washington made a vigorous attack on that part of it encamped at Germantown, and was nearly successful.

American Accounts. — Washington's letters are in Sparks, v. 86, 463 ; and in the Heath Papers, Massachusetts Historical Society's Collections, 5th series, iv. 76. Marshall was in the fight, and gives a good account in his Washington, and so do Sparks, i., and Irving, iii. ch. 23. Custis's Recollections of Washington, ch. 4. Gordon used original authorities. Bancroft, ix. ch. 25, is controverted by Amory in his Military Services of Gen. Sullivan, p. 57, where a letter of Sullivan's is given. Lives of Greene by Johnson and Greene, i. ch. 21. Life of Timothy Pickering, i. ch. 11. A controversy, participated in by Johnson, Pickering, and Sparks, can be followed in the North American Review, April, 1825, and October, 1826, and in National Intelligencer, Dec. 5, 1826, and Jan. 27 and Feb. 24, 1827. Wilkinson's Memoirs, ch. 11. Life of Gen. Muhlenberg, ch. 4. Armstrong's Life of Wayne. Reed's Life of Joseph Reed, i. 319. Sargent's André, p. 112. Lossing's Field-Book, and his article in Harper's Monthly, i. 448. Dawson's Battles, i. ch. 27.

Jones in his New York in the Revolutionary War gives a loyalist's view. Col. John E. Howard's Narrative is among the Sparks MSS. in Harvard College Library. Cf. Pennsylvania Archives, v. 646.

The centennial observance produced two addresses: Judge Thayer's in the Weekly Times and separately, and Lambdin's in the Pennsylvania Magazine of History, i. 361.

British Accounts. — Stedman's American War, i. ch. 15; Hamilton's Grenadier Guards, ii.

Maps. — By John Hills, published March 12, 1784, by Faden in London. A MS. plan by Montresor is in Harvard College Library. Sparks's Washington, iv. 86. Guizot's Washington, atlas. Johnson's Greene, 4to edition, i. Duer's Life of Stirling, ii. 177. Lossing's Field-Book, ii. 314. Carrington's Battles, p. 392.

Forts on the Delaware, October and November, 1777.

Howe detached a force to coöperate with the fleet in reducing these forts and opening a passage to the sea.

American Accounts. — Sparks's Washington, v. 112, 115, 151; Correspondence of the Revolution, ii. 12, 20; Marshall's Washington, i. 178; Irving's Washington, iii. ch. 24, 25, and 26. Gordon's American Revolution. Ramsay's American Revolution. Bancroft, ix. ch. 25. Life of Pickering, i. 174. Greene's Greene, i. ch. 22. Leake's Life of Lamb, including Knox's letter. Lee's Memoirs. Williams's Life of Olney. Reed's Reed, i. ch. 16. Lossing's Field-Book. Dawson's Battles, i. ch. 29 and 30. Carrington's Battles. Stone's Invasion of Canada, p. 75. Historical Magazine, Feb. 1872. The Minutes of the Pennsylvania Navy Board, Feb. – Sept. 1777, are given in Pennsylvania Archives, 2d series, i. 73.

British Accounts. — Howe's dispatches are in Almon's Remembrancer, v. 499.

Particular narratives of the separate attacks will be found as follows: —

Red Bank, or Fort Mercer, Oct. 22, 1777. — Reed's Reed, i.; Pennsylvania Archives, v.; Smith's Delaware County, p. 321; and the Hessian authorities, Count Donop being killed at the time.

Mud Island, or Fort Mifflin, Nov. 10–16, 1777. — Bancroft, ix. 434, cites as the principal authorities Fleury's Journal in Marshall, and in Sparks, v. 154; Varnum's and Col. Angell's letters in Cowell's Spirit of 1776 in Rhode Island. Pennsylvania Archives, v. 699, vi. Lieut. Col. Laurens's account in Frank Moore's Materials for History, 1861. Life of Pickering, i. 174. Tuckerman's Com. Talbot. J. C. Hamilton's Republic of the United States, i. 297. Potter's American Monthly, Feb. 1877, with a view of the fortifications.

Chastellux's Travels, English translation, i. 260, gives an account.

Maps. — Fisher's chart of the river below Philadelphia, 1776, printed by Sayer and Bennett, is reproduced in Pennsylvania Archives, 2d series, iii., and is also given in Gentleman's Magazine, 1778; also see 1779. Faden published a river chart showing the works in 1778. Sparks's Washington, v. 156. Lossing's Field-Book, ii. 296. Carrington's Battles. Plans of Red Bank are in Smith's Delaware County, p. 321, and Pennsylvania Archives, v.

MS. plans of Fort Mifflin are in the Sparks Collection, Cornell University. Plans for obstructing the river are given in the Pennsylvania Archives, 2d series, i. 749.

The Conway Cabal, 1777.

When the surrender at Saratoga had encouraged the partisans of Gates to claim for him a still higher command, his alienation from Washington showed itself in his hesitancy to return to the commander-in-chief some of the troops which had been sent to him in the season of his necessity. Hamilton was sent by Washington to urge these reinforcements. Hamilton's Works, i. 37; Hamilton's Life of Hamilton, i. 100–113; Hamilton's Republic, i. 339; Irving's Washington, iii. ch. 25.

The movement to prejudice the public mind against Washington soon attracted attention, and Gates, Mifflin, and Conway, together with abettors in Congress, seemed to be the chief spirits at work. Gordon implicates Samuel Adams in the conspiracy; and J. C. Hamilton (Republic of the United States, i. ch. 13 and 14) is very severe on the Adamses in this connection. Mrs. Warren, however, held there was no sufficient ground to connect Samuel Adams with it; and Wells (Life of Samuel Adams, ii. ch. 46) argues against the connection. Sparks (Washington, v. and App.) gives a series of documents elucidating the cabal; and Stanhope (History of England, vi. 243) thinks Sparks "glides over too gently the participation of New Englanders."

Lives of Washington by Marshall, iii. ch. 6, and Irving, iii. ch. 25, 28, 29, and 30. Bancroft, ix. ch. 27. Sparks's Gouverneur Morris, i. ch. 10. Greene's Life of Greene, i. 22; ii. 26 and 27. Kapp's De Kalb. Hamilton's Life of Hamilton,

i. 128–163.   Wirt's Patrick Henry, p. 208.
Austin's Gerry, ch. 16.   Reed's Joseph Reed, i.
342.   Wilkinson's Memoirs.   Lossing's Schuyler,
and his Field-Book, ii. 336.   Dunlap's New York,
ii. ch. 9.

Col. Robert Troup's account is among the
Sparks MSS. in Harvard College Library.

WINTER OF ˙1777–1778.

Washington at Valley Forge, 1777–1778.

AFTER some desultory movements, which can be followed in Simcoe's Journal of the Queen's Rangers and Reed's Life of Joseph Reed, i., Washington hutted his army in winter quarters at Valley Forge in December. The winter's manœuvres were wholly for foraging. Greene's Greene, i. ch. 24. Graham's Morgan, p. 191.

For the trials and incidents of the camp life in general, see the following: Sparks's Washington, v., and the narrative in the App. Irving's Washington, iii. ch. 27 and 31. Custis's Recollections of Washington, ch. 9. Sparks's Correspondence of the American Revolution, ii.; Sparks's Gou- verneur Morris, i. ch. 9. Greene's Greene, i. ch. 24 and 25. Life of Timothy Pickering, i. 200. Reed's Joseph Reed, ch. 17. Read's George Read, p. 326. Bancroft's United States, ix. ch. 27. T. Allen's Origination of the American Union, ii. Lossing's Field-Book, ii. 331. Mrs. Ellet's Domestic History of the Revolution. General Hull's Revolutionary Services, ch. 12. Col. T. W. Bean's Washington and Valley Forge. Col. Brooks's letter in Massachusetts Historical Society's Proceedings, Feb. 1874. Surgeon Waldo's Diary in Historical Magazine, May, 1861, and Letters, April, 1867. Potter's American Monthly, May, 1875, and July, 1878.

In January Washington addressed Congress as to the organization of the army. Hamilton's Works, ii. 139. Bancroft, ix. ch. 27, discloses the relations of Congress to the army. Congress instituted a Board of War, and its operations are followed in the Life of Timothy Pickering. Steuben, who had landed in Dec., was, May 5th, made inspector-general, and his influence in disciplining the army is dwelt upon in Kapp's Life of Steuben; and in ch. 8 Kapp examines the position of foreign officers in the Continental army. For Steuben, see Sparks's Washington, v. 526; Irving's Washington, iii.; Wells's Samuel Adams, iii. 2; Bowen's Steuben; Greene's German Element.

Stuart's Life of Jonathan Trumbull throws light on the sending of supplies to the army; and Greene's Life of Greene, ii. 48, shows the beginning of that general's services as quartermaster-general, having entered upon his duties in March.

. A scheme of sending an expedition to Canada under Lafayette is examined in Sparks's Washington, v. 530; vi. 106, 114, 149; Marshall's Washington, iii. 568; Irving's Washington, iii. 334; Life of John Jay, i. 83; Stone's Life of Brant, ch. 14.

While at Valley Forge, Washington received

a letter from the Rev. Jacob Duché, then in Philadelphia, making representation to induce him to lead the country back to dependence on Great Britain. Washington transmitted the letter to Congress, but Sparks could not find the original in the government archives, and printed it from Rivington's Gazette, in his Correspondence of the American Revolution, i. 448. See also Sparks's Washington, v. App. p. 477; a separate publication, entitled Washington at Valley Forge and the Duché Correspondence; Wilson's Memoirs of Bishop White.

Maps. — Sparks's Washington, v. 196. Guizot's Washington, atlas. Lossing's Field-Book, ii. Carrington's Battles. Harper's Monthly, xii. 307. Plans are in the Sparks Collection at Cornell University.

For the landmarks of Valley Forge, see Lossing's Field-Book and the account from the Ohio State Journal, in Read's George Read, p. 326.

Howe in Philadelphia, 1777-1778.

Details of the winter life of the British in Philadelphia will be found in Sargent's André, ch. 7, 8, and 9; Irving's Washington, iii. The account of the impressions of the Hessian Captain Henrick, as shown in Prof. Schlözer's Correspondence, iii., is translated in the Pennsylvania Magazine of History, No. 1.

In Jan. the Americans sent down the river

some torpedoes in the shape of kegs to destroy the British shipping. They failed of their purpose, but gave rise to a humorous poem by Hopkinson, The Battle of the Kegs. See Lossing's Field-Book, ii., and Moore's Songs and Ballads of the Revolution.

In the spring various foraging parties scoured the surrounding country. Cf. Simcoe's Journal of the Queen's Rangers, with a map of the affair at Quintin's Bridge, March 18th. Dawson's Battles, ch. 33, etc. Lossing's Field-Book, ii. 344, etc. Stedman's American War, ii. Johnson's History of Salem, New Jersey.

Washington in the spring had advanced Lafayette with a corps of observation to Barren Hill, and Howe endeavored to cut him off. Irving's Washington, iii. ch. 33. Sparks's Washington, v. 378, 545, with a map.

In May Sir William Howe returned to England, leaving Sir Henry Clinton in command. Tory arraignments of Howe's conduct in America are given in Jones's New York in the Revolutionary War, i. 252, 714; in the Life of Peter van Schaack, p. 167; and also in Galloway's Examination before Parliament. Cf. Bancroft, x. 120.

The Mischianza. — This was a festival, May 18th, given in honor of Howe on his departure. André described it. Cf. Gentleman's Magazine, Aug. 1778; Lady's Magazine, Philadelphia, Aug. 1792; Sargent's André, 165; Jones's New York in the Revolutionary War, i. 242, 718; Annual Register, 1778, p. 264; F. Moore's Diary of the American Revolution, p. 52; Bland Papers, i. 90; Watson's Annals of Philadelphia; Lossing's Field-Book, ii. 303; Mrs. Ellet's Domestic History of the Revolution; Smith and Watson's American Historical and Literary Curiosities.

Israel Mauduit published Strictures on the Mischianza, London, 1779.

Major Clark communicated to Washington intelligence of the enemy in Philadelphia, during the occupation, Oct. – Dec. 1777, and his letters are in the Pennsylvania Historical Society's Memoirs, i.

EVENTS OF 1778.

American Diplomacy in Continental Europe.

BENJAMIN FRANKLIN was the central figure of the American Commissioners in Paris, who were awaiting the development of events to press an alliance upon the French government. Franklin's Works, i. 434; viii. 229. Sparks's Franklin, ch. 10, and ch. 11 for the efforts of the British emissaries to win him; and on this latter point see also Parton's Franklin, ii. 321, and John Adams's Works, iii. 178, 220. Bigelow's Life of Franklin. Diplomatic Correspondence of the Revolution, iii. Elkanah Watson's Memoirs. Thomas Hughes on the English estimate of Franklin in Lippincott's Magazine, July, 1879. John Adams gives an equivocal estimate of Franklin's fitness for his position. Adams's Works, ix. 486.

The name and fame of Franklin, however, did not preserve harmony among the Commissioners, and there is a sad story of their disagreements. Diplomatic Correspondence of the Revolution, i. John Adams's Works, iii. 123, 129, 138; ix. 477; and in iii. 130, 139, Adams gives descriptions of the several American commissioners and their agents. Arthur Lee headed the opposition to

Franklin. Sparks's Franklin, i. 447; viii. 57, 257, 444. Parton's Franklin takes an extremely adverse view of Lee; and on the other side his position is explained in Lee's Life of Arthur Lee; also in John Adams's Works, vii. 79, 96.

Ralph Izard had been appointed Commissioner to Tuscany, but had never been received at his post, and lived in Paris, siding with Lee. Sparks's Franklin, i. 451; viii. 250, 308, 388. Mrs. Deas's Life of Izard. Diplomatic Correspondence of the Revolution, ii. 367.

Silas Deane had stood by Franklin, but making contracts with foreign officers for service in the United States, which embarrassed Congress, he had been recalled, but was still in Paris at the opening of the year. On his return to the United States, he in vain besought Congress for a settlement of his accounts; and Lee's enmity toward him led to public recriminations. Getting no satisfaction from Congress, Deane resorted to an Address to the People in the Philadelphia Gazette, Dec. 1778, thus making public the extent of the differences among the Commissioners, and this was answered by Thomas Paine in the Philadelphia Packet, Jan. 2, 1779. Cf. John Adams's Diary, Works, iii. 187; vii. 79. Wells's Samuel Adams, iii. 60. Deane's own narrative was printed by the Seventy-Six Society, in 1855, and the story was revived in the Memorial of his heirs to Congress in 1835. Loménie's Life of Beaumarchais at a later day threw such light upon Deane's transactions as lifted the cloud under which he had fallen. His hard fate is traced in the Diplomatic Correspondence; in Parton's Franklin, ii. ch. 9; and reference to the papers of the quarrel with Lee will be found in the Calendar of the Lee MSS. in Harvard College Library Bulletin. Some of Deane's manuscripts were No. 2138 in the Brinley sale, 1879.

Congress had appointed John Adams to succeed Deane. Diplomatic Correspondence, iv. 241. John Adams's Works, i. 277; iii. 91, 121; vii. 5; ix. 472; and his Familiar Letters to his wife. Parton's Franklin, ii. 369. He afterwards expressed his discouragement at the want of harmony which he discovered on his arrival. Letters to Mrs. Mercy Warren, in Massachusetts Historical Society's Collections, 5th series, iv. 368.

Bancroft's United States, x., thoroughly surveys the varied relations of the American Congress to the several European powers, and the relations with Frederick the Great are particularly set forth in ch. 3. A letter of John Adams gives a contemporary view. Works, vii. 99. Cf. Hildreth's United States, iii. ch. 38; Lyman's Diplomacy of the United States, ch. i.; Trescot's Diplomacy of the Revolution; Journals of Congress; G. W. Greene's Historical View of the American Revolution; Stanhope's History of England, vi. 149.

The relations with Spain, involving the question

of the navigation of the Mississippi, are particularly set forth in Bancroft, x. ch. 6 and 8; Madison Papers, i. 64, 74; Pitkin's United States, ii. ch. 13 and 14, and App. No. 8, for Jay's instructions as commissioner; Jay's Life of Jay, i. ch. 4 and 5; Flanders's Life of Jay in his Chief Justices; George Sumner's Fourth of July Oration at Boston, 1859.

The relations to Holland are explained in Bancroft's United States, x. ch. 12. John Adams's Works; Correspondence of Adams and Mrs. Warren, in Massachusetts Historical Society's Collection, 5th series, iv. Muller, in his 1872 Catalogue, Amsterdam, Nos. 1637–1725, gives the bibliography of the subject.

Condorcet in his Works has an essay on the influence of the American Revolution on Europe.

The Treaty with France, February 6, 1778.

On the 6th of Feb. a treaty of alliance and a treaty of commerce were signed at Paris. The negotiations had begun after the reception of the news of Burgoyne's surrender. Sparks's Franklin, i. 430.

French views of the situation can be found in Chotteau's La Guerre de l'Indépendance; Count Segur's Memoirs; Guizot's France, v. ch. 5. Bancroft, ix. ch. 29, and x. ch. 5, claimed that America had substantially gained her independence before the treaty with France; and Count Circourt translated Bancroft's account as Histoire de l'action commune de la France et de l'Amérique pour l'Indépendance des États Unis, adding an Historical Review, which is translated in the Massachusetts Historical Society's Proceedings, Oct. 1876.

The treaty was printed in 4to in Philadelphia in 1778, and it will be found in Gentleman's Magazine, Feb. 1779; Bancroft Davis's Notes on the Treaties of the United States; Treaties and Conventions of the United States, 1871 ; Receuil de Traités par Martens, ii. 587; Lyman's Diplomacy of the United States, i. ch. 2.

The Commissioners notified Congress of the signing of the treaty. Parton's Franklin, ii. 303. Diplomatic Correspondence, i. 364 ; and for the official papers appertaining, i. and ii.; and iv. 250, for John Adams on the Treaty. Cf. Pitkin's United States, ii. ch. 12 ; Marshall's Washington, iii. ch. 7.

Bancroft, ix. ch. 38, describes the effect of the alliance in England.

For the reception of the news of the alliance in the camp at Valley Forge in May, and for the effect upon the country, see Sparks's Washington, v. 355; Irving's Washington; Parton's Franklin, ii. 317 ; Greene's Life of Greene, ii. 72 ; Wells's Samuel Adams, iii. ch. 47.

In July, 1778, Gerard arrived at Philadelphia as the first French minister to the United States.

Diplomatic Correspondence, x. 235. John Adams's Works, i. 235. The introduction to the French translation of Botta's History. Lyman's Diplomacy of the United States, i. 57. Hazard's Pennsylvania Archives, vii.

The British Government.

The reign of George the Third in all its phases is treated elaborately in the Pictorial History of England, v. to viii., with a strong tory leaning. This section is not included in the American reprint of that work. Other general histories covering that part of the reign which spanned the American Revolution are, Adolphus, likewise tory, and compendious ; Stanhope, generally fair ; Massey, liberal ; May's Constitutional History, showing the influence of the Crown, and, of less importance, Belsham and Bisset. Wright traces the humors of the time in his Caricature History of the Georges. Knight's Popular History of England is perhaps the best general account of the more comprehensive narratives. Buckle's History of Civilization, ch. 7, dwells on the political degeneracy of the times.

Contemporary estimates can be found in Walpole's Last Journals, inimical to the court party, and in Wraxall's Historical Memoirs, 1772–1783. The Bedford, Chatham, and Rockingham Correspondence respectively show the three phases of the great Whig Party. Cf. Cooke's History of

Party; G. C. Lewis's Administrations of Great
Britain, 16; Almon's Debates; Bancroft's United
States; Brougham's Statesmen of George III.;
and ch. 30 of Smyth's Lectures on Modern History.

The letters which passed between George III.
and Lord North, 1768–1783, were used by
Brougham and Bancroft, and Sparks summarizes
them; but the originals were published in 1867
as Correspondence of George III. with Lord North,
ably edited by W. B. Donne, who manifests liberal views in his introduction, but lays the blame
of the wrong-headed policy rather on the cabinet and the people than upon the King. This
work is reviewed in the Edinburgh Review, 1867;
in the North American Review, Oct. 1867, by C.
C. Hazewell; in Blackwood, June, 1867, in an article, " Was George III. a Constitutional King ? "
and in the Quarterly Review, 1867, on " The Character of George III."

The personal character of the King was amusingly set forth with views favorable to America,
by Jesse, in 1867, epitomized in the Eclectic Review, 1867, or No. 1186 of Living Age. See in
this connection Thackeray's lecture, or Harper's
Monthly, vol. xxi.; also see vol. xxvi., and Walpole's Letters. Scott takes a favorable view of the
King. Buckle (History of Civilization, i. ch. 7)
has a low estimate. Southey's Vision of Judgment
is a tribute to his memory, while Byron's answer
is the whig view. Brougham's sketch is brief.

Some of the above authorities also portray the social life of this era, for which, further, see chapters in the Pictorial History, Stanhope's History, and Blackwood's Magazine, 1867, or No. 1220 of Living Age.

For the character of North, see the general histories above enumerated; Earle's English Premiers; Jesse's Etonians; Brougham's Statesmen; Macaulay's Chatham; Smyth's 33d lecture; Correspondence of Fox, i. 195; Adolphus's Reign of George the Third, iii. 845; Walpole's George III., ed. by Le Marchant, iv. 78.

The Conciliatory Bills, 1778.

Lord North brought forward his plans of conciliation on the 17th of Feb., and the bills passed March 3d, and were signed by the King March 11th. The minister's speech proposing them is given in the Gentleman's Magazine, Feb. 1778. Parliamentary History. The account of the debates in the Annual Register, xxi. 133, is probably by Burke. Gibbon refers to the proceedings in his letter of Feb. 23, 1778. Walpole's Last Journals, ii. 200, 215. Russell abridged Walpole's account in his Memoirs and Correspondence of Fox, i. 172. Life and Times of Fox, i. ch. 9 and 10. Fitzmaurice's Shelburne, iii. ch. 1. Donne's Correspondence of George III. with Lord North, ii. 135. Rockingham and his Contemporaries, ii. 346. J. E. T. Rogers's Protests of the Lords, ii. 174, 178.

For the debates in March, see Parliamentary
History; Gentleman's Magazine, March, 1778;
Walpole's Last Journals; and a note in Donne, ii.
151, on the difficulties of framing a new ministry.

The American Commissioners in Paris reported
on the conciliatory bills to Congress. Diplomatic
Correspondence, i. 369, and Pitkin's United
States, ii. App. 2. Franklin wrote upon them
to David Hartley. Diplomatic Correspondence,
iii. 34.

The bills were received in the United States
in advance of the arrival of the Commissioners.
Wells's Samuel Adams, iii. 14. Lives of Washington by Marshall, iv. ch. 1, and by Irving, iii.
ch. 32. Reed's Joseph Reed, ch. 18 and App.
Sparks's Life of Gouverneur Morris, p. 182.
Pitkin's United States, ii. ch. 11.

The Commissioners reached America in June,
under instructions from Lord North, printed in
Documents relative to the Colonial History of
New York, viii. 738. They landed in Philadelphia just as Clinton was evacuating that city.
Their letters reached Congress June 13th. Almon's Remembrancer, 1778, p. 11, and p. 127 for
their manifesto, and various other papers about
them are scattered in Almon, vi., vii., and viii.
Gouverneur Morris's reply on behalf of Congress
is in the Journals and in Almon, viii. 40.

The Commissioners threatened a greater feroc-
ity in the conduct of the war. Cf. the letter of

the Commissioners in Paris to Vergennes. John
Adams's Works, vii. 72. Buckle (History of
Civilization, ch. 7) cites, for evidences of the feroc-
ity with which the English conducted the war,
the following : Tucker's Life of Jefferson, i. 138,
139, 160 ; Jefferson's Memoirs and Correspondence, i. 352, 429 ; ii. 336, 337 ; Almon's Correspondence of Wilkes, v. 229 ; Adolphus's George
III., ii. 362, 391 ; Parliamentary History, xix.
371, 403, 423, 424, 432, 438, 440, 447, 487, 488,
489, 567, 578, 579, 695, 972, 1393, 1394 ; xx. 43 ;
Mémoires de Lafayette, i. 23, 25, 99. Jones (New
York in the Revolutionary War) is not reticent
concerning the excesses, particularly in plundering, of the British troops.

A later counter manifesto on the part of Congress was prepared, Oct. 30th, by Samuel Adams,
Cf. Wells's Adams, iii. 46.

Other Accounts. — Marshall's Washington, iii.
ch. 10. Sparks's Washington, v. 344, 397, 401 ;
vi. 16, 79, 96. Sparks's Gouverneur Morris, i.
ch. 11. Bancroft, x. 122. Reed's Joseph Reed,
i. ch. 18 and App. 4. Howison's Virginia, ii.
230. A loyalist account in Jones's New York in
the Revolutionary War.

British Accounts of their Failure. — Massey's
England, ii. 295 ; Stanhope's England, vi. 246 ;
Donne's Correspondence of George III. with Lord
North, ii. 208 ; and letters of Carlisle, one of the
Commissioners, in Jesse's Selwyn and his Contem-
poraries, iii. 280, 339, etc.

Political Movements in England, 1778.

It was thought that if Chatham could have abated his opposition to American independence, a union with the Rockingham whigs might have unseated the North cabinet, and restored peace. Cf. Chatham Correspondence, iv. 484; Donne's Correspondence of George III. with North, ii. 127.

The death of Chatham in May seemingly put off the fall of the North ministry. Cf. Massey's History of England, ii. ch. 22; Fitzmaurice's Shelburne, iii. 40. Chatham, in his relations to the American war, must be studied in Thackeray's heavy and laudatory life of him; but a brilliant account of his political action will be found in Macaulay's two essays. Cf. the Chatham Correspondence; Fitzmaurice's Shelburne, iii. ch. 1; Campbell's Lives of the Chancellors; Stanhope's England; Massey's England, ii. 279; Brougham's Statesmen; Bancroft's United States; Parton's Franklin; Earle's English Premiers; Davenport Adams's English Party Leaders; and the note in Donne's Correspondence of George III. with Lord North, ii. 185.

For illustrations of the hatred which the King bore towards Chatham for his liberal views, see Brougham's Statesmen; Russell's Memoirs of Fox, i. 129; Adolphus's History, ii. 568; Stanhope's England, vi. App.; Grenville Papers, ii. 386; Bancroft's United States.

The death of Chatham afforded a chance of a coalition of the tories with some part of the opposition. See on this point the Rockingham Memoirs; Life and Memorials of Fox; Donne's Correspondence of George III. with North, ii. 188; Walpole's Last Journals, ii. 338.

Eden's account of his negotiations with Fox for a compromise is printed in the Memoirs and Correspondence of Fox, i. 180.

Jonathan L. Austin was sent to London by Franklin to confer with the opposition. Boston Monthly Magazine, July, 1826.

Bancroft, x. ch. 5, gives a view of the state of feeling in England; and a reflex of tory opinions is found in Curwen's Journal.

For instances of the commercial distress which the ministry's action had brought upon England, see Stanhope, v. 133; Franklin's Correspondence; Adolphus's History, ii. 261; Burke's Works; Parliamentary History, xviii. 734, 951, 963, 964; xix. 259, 341, 710, 711, 1072; Walpole's Memoirs of George III. ii. 218.

Hozier's Invasions of England, ii., shows the concern prevailing after the alliance with France became known; and there is in Donne, ii. 176, an account of the blundering efforts of the English navy to intercept the French fleet, which left Toulon in April.

Toward the end of the year, two pamphlets, one by Sir Wm. Meredith, the other by David

Hartley, were printed in London, which had marked influence, as is described in Walpole's Last Journals, ii. 327.

Congress, 1778.

Bancroft, x. 349, says that though Congress sat with closed doors, the French envoys conveyed to their government the most complete reports of their discussions which are known. They are preserved in the French archives. See a representation of Congress at this time in the Life of John Adams, i. 282. Washington wrote to John Bannister, in April, his views of the political bearing of events. Sparks's Washington, v. 321. Cf. Christopher Marshall's Diary; Leake's Memoirs of General Lamb; Journals of Congress, and the lives of its members.

The Summer's Campaign, 1778.

Washington in April had submitted to his officers three plans of a campaign. Sparks's Washington, v. 320. A plan of his own is among the Sparks MSS. in Harvard College Library. Life of Muhlenberg, ch. 5.

The expected arrival of a French fleet, which might close the Delaware to succor, necessitated the British evacuation of Philadelphia, and Sir Henry Clinton began his march across the Jerseys towards New York, June 17th. For the march see Eelking's Hülfstruppen, ch. 10; Magazine of

American History, Jan. 1879, p. 58 ; a journal of Clinton's secretary in New Jersey Historical Society's Proceedings, vi. ; Diary of Jos. Clark in the same, vii. 93.

Monmouth, June 28, 1778.

The advance of Washington's army attacked the rear of the retreating British, who turned and forced back the Americans under Lee ; but the presence of Washington on the field, later, retrieved the day.

American Accounts. — Washington's letters are given in Sparks, v. 422 and App. No. 18, and in Dawson's Battles, ch. 37, and Kapp considers Dawson's account the clearest. Lives of Washington by Marshall, iii. ch. 8 ; and Irving, iii. ch. 34 and 35. Sparks's Correspondence of the American Revolution, ii. 150. Custis's Recollections of Washington, ch. 5.

Lee was brought to trial by court-martial, July 14th, for misbehavior and disrespect to Washington, under reproof. The evidence introduced is of importance. It was published separately, and is embodied in Dawson. Lee's defense is also given in Longworthy's Memoirs of Lee, p. 23. Cf. Sparks's Life of Lee ; Davis's Life of Burr, i. ; and Lee's letter in Reed's Joseph Reed, i. 369.

Other Accounts. — Heath's Memoirs, p. 186. Gen. Hull's Revolutionary Services, ch. 14. Drake's Life of Knox. Kapp's Life of Steuben,

p. 159. Quincy's Life of Shaw, ch. 4. Sargent's Life of André, p. 187. Hamilton's Life of Alexander Hamilton, i. 194. Hamilton's Republic of the United States, i. 471. Bancroft. x. ch. 4. Letters of Hamilton and Wm. Irvine in the Pennsylvania Magazine of History, ii. 139. Reed's Joseph Reed, ch. 17. Williams's Life of Olney, p. 243. Life of Anthony Wayne. The original orderly-book of Wayne is No. 2095 in the Menzies Catalogue. C. King's account in the New Jersey Historical Society's Proceedings, iv. Lossing's Field-Book, ii. 356, and his paper in Harper's Monthly, vii. 449; also see June, 1878. Barker and Howe's Historical Collections of New Jersey. J. W. De Peyster in the Magazine of American History, July, 1878, and March, 1879; also June, 1879, for letters. American Historical Record, June, 1874.

Carrington, in his Battles of the Revolution, gives one of the most intelligible accounts.

British Accounts. — Stedman, ii. ch. 22. Murray's Impartial History, ii. 448. Stanhope's England, vi. ch. 58. Clinton's dispatch is given in Dawson.

Maps. — Sparks's Washington, v. 430. Atlas of Guizot's Washington. Hilliard d'Auberteuil's Essais, ii. 271. Duer's Life of Stirling, ii. 196. Lossing's Field-Book, ii. 356. Carrington's Battles. Coffin's Boys of Seventy-Six.

The Sparks Collection in Harvard College

Library has some MS. maps copied from others belonging to Lafayette.

New York and Philadelphia, 1778.

The British retreated to Sandy Hook and crossed over to New York. Sargent's Life of André, ch. 11. Documents relating to the occupation of that city by the British will be found in the New York City Manual for 1863; and a plan from the London Magazine of 1778 is reproduced in the same manual for 1869.

For Arnold's career as commander in Philadelphia after the city was regained, see Sparks's Life of Arnold; his Washington, vi. 514; Irving's Washington, iv. ch. 2; Pennsylvania Archives, vi. and vii.; Reed's Life of Reed, ii. 48, 88, 93, 102.

The charges against Arnold and his answer are in Almon's Remembrancer, 1778–1779, p. 349.

Indian Depredations, 1778.

Wyoming, July 1st–4th. — The irruption into this valley by tories and Indians, with the fight and subsequent massacre, is described in Dawson's Battles, ch. 38, who gives the official documents. The panic-stricken refugees from the valley, flying eastward, crossed the Hudson at Poughkeepsie, where their exaggerated statements (Stone's Brant, i. 339) were first published, and formed the basis of the narratives in Thacher's Military

Journal, Gordon, Ramsay, Botta, etc., and they have been repeated in Drake's Book of the Indians. Marshall, in the later editions of his Life of Washington, modified his earlier statements. Contemporary accounts are given in Moore's Diary of the American Revolution, ii. More accurate views of the transactions were taken by Charles Miner in his original newspaper articles, and in his History of Wyoming, 1845 ; and Stone, in his Poetry and History of Wyoming, followed Miner. Stone, in his Life of Brant, and in his Border Wars, drawn chiefly from the Life of Brant, gives an account of the inroad, but contends that Brant was not present. Caleb Cushing reviewed the Life of Brant in the Democratic Review, claiming that Stone had not proved an *alibi* for Brant ; but Stone in his Wyoming (p. 192) reasserted his statement, and pointed out Campbell's confession of his error for making Brant present in the story as told in his " Gertrude of Wyoming," which poem is reprinted in Stone's Wyoming. See Brodhead's New York Documents. Peck, in his Wyoming, ch. 2, enforces Stone's argument, and gives various personal reminiscences.

Chapman's Wyoming has but a hurried account. Other narratives will be found in Irving's Washington, iii. ch. 37 ; Jenkins's Historical Address, July 3, 1878 ; Hollister's Connecticut, ii. ch. 15 ; Harper's Monthly, xvii. 306 ; Lossing's Field-Book, i. 352. Mrs. Ellet's Women of the American Revolution, ii., and her Domestic History of the Revolution; and the Appendix to Campbell's Tryon County.

Mohawk Valley. — The plans and actions of the enemy in the Mohawk Valley are described in Lossing's Field-Book, ch. 12; Stone's Brant, ch. 14; Campbell's Tryon County; History of Schoharie County, ch. 9; Dawson's Battles, ch. 36, etc.; Harper's Monthly, July, 1877.

Cherry Valley, Nov. 11th. — The slaughter at Cherry Valley is particularly detailed in contemporary letters in the Historical Magazine, June, 1866; Campbell's Tryon County, ch. 5; Dawson's Battles, ch. 45; Stone's Brant, i. ch. 17; Lossing's Field-Book, p. 268; Dunlap's New York, ii. 147, etc.

Brant. — Stone's Life of Brant. Drake's Book of the Indians, book v. ch. 5. New England Historical and Genealogical Register, Oct. 1848. Norton's Pioneer Missionaries, New York, 1859. W. C. Bryant in Beach's Indian Miscellany.

Border Warfare in General. — Beside Lossing, Schuyler, and Stone's Brant, see De Haas's Indian Wars of Western Virginia; J. H. Perkins in North American Review, Oct. 1839, an article also included in his Memoirs, ii. 281. A paper on the British and Indian coöperation is in the New York Historical Society's Proceedings, iii. There is much illustrative matter in the New York Documentary History, and in the Pennsylvania Archives.

Fiction. — Border and Indian traits and warfare during the Revolution are worked into the guise of fiction in Grace Greenwood's Forest Tragedy, and in C. F. Hoffman's Greyslaer.

The Rhode Island Campaign, August, 1778.

The French fleet under D'Estaing arrived at the Capes of Delaware in July, but the British fleet had escaped to New York, whither the French commander followed. He was unable to pass the bar of that harbor with his larger ships. Sparks's Correspondence of the Revolution, ii. 155.

Opening communication with Washington, a plan was formed for an attack on the British forces at Rhode Island. Irving's Washington, iii. 419.

A land attack was undertaken by Gen. Sullivan at the same time. Sullivan's letters are given in Sparks's Correspondence of the Revolution, ii. ; Rhode Island Historical Tracts, No. 6 ; Dawson's Battles ; Sparks's Washington, vi. Bancroft, x. ch. 5, questioned Sullivan's soldierly conduct, and T. C. Amory vindicated him in Massachusetts Historical Society's Proceedings, Dec. 1866, and in his Military Services of General Sullivan.

Shortly after D'Estaing and Sullivan had laid their plans by conference, Howe appeared off the harbor with the British fleet, reinforced. The French put to sea, but a general action was prevented by a storm, and D'Estaing returned to

Newport with a shattered fleet, and sailed for Boston to refit. Cf. A Candid and Impartial Narrative of the Transactions of the Fleet under Lord Howe, London, 1779. The British army on the island was now reinforced, and Sullivan retreated to the main-land. The abandonment of the attempt produced effects on the country that are set forth in Wells's Samuel Adams, iii. 38. The charges of Sullivan against the French came near disturbing friendly relations with the allies. D'Estaing's papers are in the Ministerie de la Marine et des Colonies at Paris. The French side of the controversy is presented in Chevalier's Histoire de la Marine française pendant la guerre de l'indépendance Américaine, ch. 3, and in an Extrait du Journal d'un Officier de la Marine, 1782, which gives a likeness of D'Estaing, and another will be found in Andrews's History of the War. The proclamation of D'Estaing to the former subjects of France in America, issued in October, is given in the Documents relative to the Colonial History of New York, x. 1165. See other authorities on the French auxiliaries under 1780.

Lafayette went to Boston to confer with D'Estaing. Heath's Memoirs. Lafayette's letters to Washington on the miscarriage of the expedition are in Sparks's Correspondence of the Revolution, ii. 181, 196. Lafayette's account of the campaign, told by himself fifty years later, when in this country, is in the Historical Magazine, Aug. 1861.

Accounts of this expedition, more or less full, are given in the following places: Bancroft, x. ch. 5. Hamilton's History of the Republic, i. ch. 17. Arnold's Rhode Island, p. 419. . Green's Rhode Island. Dunlap's New York, ii. Barry's Massachusetts, iii. 150. Rhode Island Historical Collections, vi. Moore's Diary of the American Revolution, ii. 85 ; also his Songs and Ballads of the Revolution, p. 231. Heath's Memoirs. Lives of Washington by Marshall, iv. ; by Irving, iii. ch. 36. Sparks's Washington, v. 29, 40, 45. Greene's Life of Greene, ii. 100, and Greene's letter in the Correspondence of the Revolution, ii. 188. Amory's Sullivan, p. 70. Memoirs of John Trumbull, p. 51. Stuart's Life of Jonathan Trumbull, ch. 32. Williams's Life of Gen. Barton, ch. 3. Glover's Orderly-Book in Essex Institute Collections, v. Major Gibbs's Diary, Aug. 5th–30th, in Pennsylvania Archives, vi. J. A. Stevens in Magazine of American History, July, 1879. Historical Magazine, iv. 145. Carrington's Battles. S. S. Rider's Rhode Island Historical Tracts, No. 6, gives the Centennial Address of S. G. Arnold, and reprints contemporary accounts, including the German narrative of Max von Eelking.

English Accounts. — The dispatches of Gen. Pigot, etc., in Gentleman's Magazine, Nov. 1778; in Dawson's Battles; in Rider's Rhode Island Historical Tracts, No. 6. Stedman's American

War, ii. ch. 23, 24. A Diary at Newport is in
the Historical Magazine, 1860. A loyalist view
in Jones's New York in the Revolutionary War,
ii. ch. 12.

Maps. — The Massachusetts Historical Society
preserves a plan of the campaign ; see its Proceedings, May, 1865. The Sparks Collection at Harvard College has copies of contemporary French
plans. There are contemporary British plans of
Newport and Narragansett Bay in the American
Atlas, Nos. 17 and 18. The Magazine of American History, July, 1879, gives fac-similes of Faden's Newport plan, 1777, made by Blaskowitz,
and also his Narragansett Bay, 1777. The Gentleman's Magazine, 1778, has a print of the battle
of Quaker Hill, Aug. 29th, which is fac-similed in
Lossing's Field-Book, ii. p. 83, where is also a
map of the campaign ; and others are in Rider's
Centennial volume ; in Marshall's Washington,
v. ; and in Carrington's Battles. There is a MS.
plan of attack in the Faden Collection in the
Library of Congress.

A subsequent British incursion at New Bedford
is noted in Ricketson's New Bedford, ch. 22, and
in the Appendix to Crapo's Centennial Address,
p. 58.

On Rhode Island's share in the war, at large,
see A. B. Gardner's Rhode Island Line in the
Continental Army ; B. Cowell's Spirit of Seventy-
Six in Rhode Island ; W. R. Staples's Rhode

Island in the Continental Congress, published by the State in 1870; G. W. Curtis's Newport, in Harper's Magazine, ix. 289.

Capture of Savannah, December 29, 1778.

A naval and military force from New York attacked the small American army defending Savannah and defeated it. Dawson's Battles, ch. 46. Simms's South Carolina. Stevens's Georgia, ii. 160. Marshall's Washington, iv. 97. Stedman's American War, ii. ch. 26.

The Vermont Troubles.

These were disputes between the governments of New Hampshire and New York as to jurisdiction over this territory, and the British government endeavored by emissaries to seduce the inhabitants of this region from their allegiance to the American cause. New York Documentary History, iv. 329, with map. Dunlap's New York, ii. 217. Belknap's New Hampshire, ii. ch. 26. Williams's History of Vermont. Madison Papers, i. Lossing's Schuyler, ii. 408. Wells's Samuel Adams, iii. 144.

Naval Actions, 1778.

For accounts of the blowing up of the Randolph, March 7th, see Dawson's Battles, Cooper's Naval History, Clark's·Sketches of Naval History.

Paul Jones's exploits in the Ranger, and his

capture of the Drake, are described in the several lives of Jones, and in Parton's Franklin, ii. ch. 8. Dr. Ezra Green's journal of the Ranger's cruise is given in the New England Historical and Genealogical Register, 1875. Cf. Annual Register, xxi. 176. Jones's instructions from the Commissioners in France are given in the Diplomatic Correspondence of the Revolution, i. 361, where are also various other letters.

Galloway's Letter to Lord Howe on his Naval Conduct, London, 1779, animadverts on his inaction in face of the inferior force of the colonists, and gives lists of their respective fleets.

James's Naval History and the Life of Admiral Keppel tell the story of the confronting of the English and French fleets in European waters.

A diary of the English fleet in the summer of 1778 is among the manuscripts of the Percy family, according to the 3d Report, 1872, of the English Historical MSS. Commission.

The Northwest, 1778–1779.

Bancroft, x. ch. 8, gives an account of the expedition, and of the bearings of this conquest of the northwestern territory, as influencing subsequent control by the United States. Accounts, more or less extended, are given as follows: —

Clark's own account, dated Nov. 19, 1779, has been edited by H. Pirtle, and published by Clarke of Cincinnati in 1869; and in the Appendix of this volume will be found Patrick Henry's private and public instructions to Clark, and Bowman's Journal of the Expedition, Jan. 27 to March 20, 1779. Stone's Life of Brant, i. ch. 16. Almon's Remembrancer, vi. 82. Dawson's Battles, ch. 40, for the attack on Fort Boone, Aug. 8th–20th. Jefferson's Writings, i. 221, and Randall's Jefferson, i. 248, 256, 273. Parton's Jefferson, p. 233. Girardin's History of Virginia. Pennsylvania Archives. Butler's Kentucky. Law's Colonial History of Vincennes. Imlay's Western Territory. T. M. Smith's Legends of the War of Independence, Louisville, 1855. G. W. Hill's Captivity of Christian Fast, an episode of the Indian invasion of the Northwest, in Beach's Indian Miscellany. Adventures of Daniel Boone. Doddridge's Notes on the Indian Wars. Heckerwelder's Moravian Missions. C. I. Walker's Address on the Northwest in the Revolution, before the Wisconsin Historical Society, 1871.

There is a sketch of Col. Clark in the Historical Magazine, June, 1857 ; another in Lewis Collins's Historical Sketches of Kentucky, which is copied in Pirtle's edition of Clark's letter to George Mason.

Prisoners of War.

For the early period of the war there is much illustrative matter in the several volumes of Force's American Archives. The memoirs of various suf-

ferers throw light upon prison experiences. Ethan
Allen's Narrative of his Captivity. Memoirs of
Andrew Sherburne. Adventures of Ebenezer
Fox.

Jersey Prison Ship. — Dring's Recollections of
the Jersey Prison Ship, ed. by Albert G. Greene,
1829, and again by H. B. Dawson, with an App.
1865. Thomas Andross's Old Jersey Captive.
Dunlap's New York, ii. ch. 10. Prisons and
Prison Ships in the Revolution, privately printed,
45 copies, New York, 1865. History of the Inter-
ments at Wallabout, 1808. Harper's Monthly,
xxxvii. 187.

Mrs. Ellet's Domestic History of the Revolution, ch. 10, 11. Onderdonk's Suffolk and Kings
Counties. George Taylor's Martyrs to the Revolution, 1855. Lossing's Field-Book, ii. 865.
New York Historical Society's Proceedings, Dec.
1861. Historical Magazine, 1866, supplement.
Pennsylvania Archives, *passim.* — Moore's Diary
of the American Revolution, ii. *index.*

An account of the " Fleet Prison " kept by the
Americans at Esopus, on the Hudson, is given in
Jones's New York in the Revolutionary War, i.
705.'

Much about the American prisoners detained
in England will be found in the Diplomatic Correspondence, the letters of Franklin, Lee, and John
Adams. Charles Herbert's Relics of the Revolution gives experiences in the English prisons.

Exchanges of Prisoners. — George Bancroft printed, New York, 1862, A Letter on the Exchange of Prisoners during the Revolution. More or less details will be found as follows : Washington's Writings, Sparks's edition, iv. 547, and generally throughout his correspondence ; v. 306; vi. 508, on the vacillating policy of Congress; and vii. 3, on the unwillingness of the British to treat on " national grounds." The Gentleman's Magazine, 1777, printed the correspondence of Howe and Washington. Irving's Washington, iii. ch. 2. Hamilton's History of the Republic. Graydon's Memoirs, ch. 8. A report of the Commissioners for settling a cartel detailing their unsuccessful negotiations, was printed in Philadelphia, 1779. Jones's New York in the Revolutionary War, i. 93, gives a loyalist view.

EVENTS OF 1779.

In General.

WASHINGTON was in camp at Middlebrook during the winter. Irving's Washington, iii. Greene's Greene, ii. 160. His views in January are given in a letter to Congress. Sparks, vi. 158. He resolved on a defensive campaign. Bancroft, x. ch. 9. Heath was in command east of the Hudson. Memoirs, p. 205.

Bancroft, x. ch. 10, summarizes the military movements in the north, and, ch. 13, in the south. Cf. Hildreth, iii. ch. 39.

The Journals and Secret Journals of Congress and the Diplomatic Correspondence hardly indicate the infelicitous bickerings of Congress. Greene's Historical View gives sections to Congress and to the relation of Congress to the States. Bancroft, x. 208. Washington to Mason in the Virginia Historical Register, vol. 96. Greene's Greene, ii. 170, 175. John Adams's Works, i. 292.

For the riots in Philadelphia, and the efforts to regulate prices, see Reed's Reed, ii. ch. 6.

For the British rule in New York, see the Memoirs of the Baroness Riedesel; New York City Manual, 1863; Letters of Major-General James

Pattison, a British officer in New York, Jan. 1779–Aug. 1780, in the New York Historical Society's Collections, 1875; Memoirs of Lieut. General Samuel Graham, Edinburgh, 1862, and abstracts in the Historical Magazine, Aug., Sept., Oct., and Nov. 1865.

Tryon in Connecticut, July, 1779.

Clinton dispatched a plundering expedition under Tryon, which invaded New Haven and destroyed Fairfield. Part of the plan was to draw Washington from the Highland fastnesses.

Hinman's Historical Collections of the part sustained by Connecticut in the Revolution. Stuart's Life of Jonathan Trumbull, ch. 37. Chauncey Goodrich on the invasion of New Haven in the New Haven Historical Society's Collections, ii. 27. Moore's Diary of the Revolution, ii. 180. Ithiel Town's Particular Services, a British account. For the destruction of Fairfield, Massachusetts Historical Society's Collections, iii. 103. Diplomatic Correspondence, ii. 253, for the Committee of Foreign Affairs to Lee, and, iii. 99, for Lovell to Franklin.

Wayne at Stony Point, July 16, 1779.

The defenses at this post and on the opposite side of the Hudson were the outworks of West Point, and protected King's Ferry, the crossing below the Highlands. Before the Americans had completed them, Clinton captured them in June. Sparks's Washington, vi. 292. Washington planned a surprise of the British garrison, and intrusted the execution to Wayne. Armstrong's Life of Wayne.

The contemporary accounts of his brilliant success will be found in Washington's letter to Congress, Sparks, vi. 298, and Wayne's account in the Appendix of the same volume. Moore's Diary, ii. 192. Pennsylvania Archives, vii.

Dawson has a special monograph on the assault, and gives a chapter to it in his Battles of the United States.

Marshall's Washington, iv. ch. 2. Irving's Washington, iii. 465. Lossing's Field-Book, ii. 175. Hull's Revolutionary Services, ch. 16. Reed's Joseph Reed, ii. 110. Harper's Monthly, July, 1879, by H. P. Johnston.

Steuben was interested as testing his bayonet instructions. Kapp's Steuben, ch. 11. Greene's review of Kapp in North American Review, vol. xcix. — an article reprinted in Greene's German Element in the War of Independence. Eberling's account of Steuben in the Amerikanisches Magazin, 1796. J. C. Hamilton's Republic of the United States, i. 443.

At the Centennial Celebration, July 16, 1879, Gen. Jos. Hawley delivered an historical address.

Maps. — Faden's English plan, showing also the works at Verplanck's Point, after surveys by

Simpson and Campbell, by John Hills, published
in London, March 1, 1784, is fac-similed in the
New York Calendar of Hist. MSS. p. 347. The
MS. plans used in the attack are in the Sparks
Collection in Harvard College Library. Other
plans are in the atlas of Guizot's Washington; in
Hull's Revolutionary Services, ch. 16; in Sparks's
Washington, vi. 304.

For an account of the medal given to Wayne
see Loubat's Medallic History of the United
States, where are also described the medals given
to Lieut. Col. De Fleury and Major Stewart for
good conduct in the assault.

Paulus Hook, August 19, 1779.

This was a brilliant advance, attack, and retreat
by Major Lee. This British post was where Jersey City now stands. See the general histories;
Marshall's Washington, iv. 87; Irving's Washington, iii. 475; Dawson's Battles; Quincy's Shaw,
p. 65; Reed's Joseph Reed, ii. 125; Duer's Stirling, p. 204; Moore's Diary, ii. 206; and S. A.
Green's paper in the Historical Magazine, Dec.
1868.

An account of the medal given to Major Lee
is in Loubat's Medallic History of the United
States.

The Neutral Ground.

This was the country in Westchester County
between the outposts of the British and American

lines.   See the general histories, Irving's Washington, histories of New York, and Bolton's Westchester.   For the interval of Burr's command see
Parton's Burr, ch. viii., and Davis's Burr.

Events that took place here are fashioned into
the substance of Cooper's novel, The Spy; and
II. L. Barnum's Spy Unmasked collates the nov-
elist's story with actual occurrences.   See other
imaginative renderings in Roe's Near to Nature's
Heart, Gleig's Day on the Neutral Ground in his
Chelsea Pensioners, etc.

Sullivan's Expedition against the Indians, July—September, 1779.

Stone's Life of Brant, i., gives a full account of
the Indian depredations in the spring and early
summer.   Washington had early given his attention to some plan of chastising the Indians, in
retaliation for their incursions into Wyoming and
Cherry Valley.   Sparks, vi. 183.   His instructions to Sullivan are in Sparks, vi. 264, and Historical Magazine, Sept. 1867.   Sullivan's comments in Sparks's Correspondence of the Revolution, ii. 264.

Gordon is unfriendly to Sullivan in his account.
Bancroft's strictures are noticed in T. C. Amory's
Military Services of Gen. John Sullivan, p. 97.

Accounts of greater or less fullness may be
found in O. W. B. Peabody's Life of Sullivan;
Stone's Life of Brant; Marshall's Washington,

iv. 105; and letters of Washington in Sparks's
edition, and in the Magazine of American History, Feb. 1879, p. 142; F. Moore's Correspondence of Henry Laurens, and his Diary of the
Revolution, ii. 216; Pennsylvania Archives, vii.;
Historical Magazine, Aug. and Sept. 1862, and
by N. Davis, April, 1868; Stuart's Jonathan
Trumbull; Lossing's Field-Book, i. 272; Hamilton's Republic, i. 543; McSherry's Maryland,
p. 14; Miner's Wyoming; Campbell's Annals of
Tryon County, ch. 6; Seaver's Life of Mary Jemi-
son, p. 278; and a little notice of the Campaign,
printed at Rochester, 1842.

There are several other contemporary records:
Bleeker's orderly-book of Gen. James Clinton's
brigade, printed 1865, edited by F. B. Hough.
Major Norris's journal in Jones's New York in the
Revolutionary War, ii. 613, notes. Barton and
Elmer's diary in New Jersey Historical Society's
Proceedings, ii. Jabez Campfield's diary, in the
same, 2d series, iii. 1873, covering May 23–Oct.
2, 1779. Gookin's, in the New England Histori-
cal and Genealogical Register, Jan. 1862. Hub-
ley's, in Miner's Wyoming, Appendix, p. 82. Rev.
Wm. Rogers's, with introduction and notes by
S. S. Rider, and map of the campaign.

Gen. Sullivan after this left the army and sat
in Congress for New Hampshire. His character
has been the subject of controversy between Bancroft and T. C. Amory, the former alleging that

Sullivan was a pensioner of Luzerne, the French minister. Amory's reply was entitled, General Sullivan not a Pensioner of Luzerne. Bancroft published in response the letter on which his charge was founded. Cf. Massachusetts Historical Society's Proceedings, Dec. 1866; Historical Magazine, Supplement vi. of 1866. An account of Sullivau and his genealogy is given in the New England Historical and Genealogical Register, Oct. 1865.

The Penobscot Expedition, August and September, 1779.

Massachusetts fitted out an armament, the land forces under General Lovell, and the fleet under Commodore Saltonstall, to dislodge the British from the Penobscot region. A British reinforcement sent from New York shut the Americans up within the bay, and their whole force was destroyed or scattered.

Accounts more or less full are found as follows : John Calef's Siege of Penobscot, with Journals, London, 1781; this and other documents are reprinted in Wheeler's Pentagoet (Castine), ch. 5 and 6. Williamson's Maine, ii. 471. Williamson's Belfast, ch. 12. Willis's Portland, ch. 19. Various other local histories detail the connection of separate sections with the expedition. Barry's Massachusetts, iii. ch. 14. Bradford's Massachusetts. Thomas Philbrook's Account in B. Cowell's Spirit of Seventy-Six in Rhode Island. Thacher's

Military Journal, p. 166. Heath's Memoirs, p. 235. Sparks's Correspondence of the Revolution, ii. 460. Ithiel Town's Particular Services. Boston Gazette, March 18, 25, April 1 and 8, 1782. Pemberton's Journal, in Massachusetts Historical Society's Collections, ii. 172. Journal of the Attack on his Majesty's Ships and Troops, July 24th, 1779, from the Nova Scotia Gazette, Sept. 14, 1779, reprinted in the Maine Historical Society's Collections, vii.

Maps. — In Calef's Siege of Penobscot, and in Wheeler's Pentagoet.

Briar Creek, March, 1779.

For movements in the spring in Georgia, see Stevens's Georgia, ii. 180; Moore's Diary, ii. 138; Lossing's Field-Book, ii.

Siege of Savannah, September 23—October 18, 1779.

Lincoln had been in command of the Southern department since Dec. 1778. Sparks's Correspondence of the Revolution, ii. 241. D'Estaing with a French fleet approached the town by water, and Lincoln marched from Charleston to invest it by land. An assault failed. The fleet went to the West Indies; the army returned to Charleston.

Contemporary Accounts. — Two Journals of officers of the fleet, edited by C. C. Jones, Jr., and published in folio. A Narrative of the combined attack, edited with notes, by F. B. Hough. Col.

14

Cruger's narrative in the Magazine of American History, Aug. 1878. Maj. Gen. Provost's Journal of the Siege in Gentleman's Magazine, 1779, p. 633. Original papers in the Historical Magazine, Jan. and Sept. 1864. A Journal in Frank Moore's Correspondence of Henry Laurens. Caroline Gilman's Letters of Eliza Wilkinson. Moore's Diary, ii. 221.

D'Estaing's orders are in the Magazine of American History, Sept. 1878.

Later Accounts. — Lee's Memoirs of the War, ch. 12. Moultrie's Memoirs of the American Revolution. Simms's South Carolina. Bowen's Life of General Lincoln. Lossing's Field-Book, ii. 736. Carrington's Battles, ch. 61. Stevens's Georgia, ii. 200. Flanders's Life of Rutledge.

British Accounts. — In Stedman's American War, ii. ch. 30, and in the English general histories.

Pulaski. — This general was mortally wounded in the assault. See Sparks's Life of Pulaski, and his North American Review articles, vol. xx. and xxiii. The account of Pulaski in Johnson's Greene, brought out a vindication of Pulaski by Col. Bentalou, 1824, which was noticed by Sparks in the North American Review, No. 47, which led to Remarks, etc., by Johnson, in rejoinder.

Maps. — In Stedman's American War; Jones's ed. of the contemporary Journals; Carrington's Battles; Lossing's Field-Book, ii. 736. Moore's

Diary of the Revolution, ii. 221. Two contemporary French MS. plans, one showing more of the country around than the other, are in the Boston Public Library, described in Dufossé's Americana, 1879. Dr. S. A. Green of Boston has another French MS. plan.

Paul Jones in British Waters, August and September, 1779.

Correspondence of Franklin and Jones will be found in Franklin's Works, viii. See letters in the Proceedings of the Massachusetts Historical Society, Oct. 1872. Cooper in his Naval History takes a favorable view of Jones's character. Dawson in his Battles, vol. i., gives a full collated narrative of the action between the Bon Homme Richard and the Serapis, Sept. 23d. Compare Peter Landais's account in his Memorial, printed in Boston in 1784, justifying his conduct, which gives a plan of the action. See also Parton's Franklin, ii. ch. 8; Preble's " Three Historic Flags " in the New England Historical and Genealogical Register, Jan. 1874; Headley's Miscellanies, ii.

A British view is taken in Allen's Battles of the British Navy, and in the English histories. For the effect in England of his exploits, see Albemarle's Rockingham and his Contemporaries, ii. 381.

Of the monographs on Jones, Sherburne, who had access to the archives of the United States government, and possessed some of Jones's private papers, particularly his correspondence with La Fayette and Jefferson, published the earliest authoritative life, in 1825. Five years later, a life was published in Edinburgh, based upon Jones's log-books and family papers, which was decidedly English in tone, and the papers used by its author, being shortly after brought to this country, Robert Sands had use of them and others, in preparing his memoir ; while in 1840, Mackenzie made the most readable narrative of all, by sifting the material of his predecessors. A more popular life is that by J. S. C. Abbott. S. P. Waldo printed a sketch of Jones in his American Naval Heroes, fifty years ago. See Lossing's illustrated paper in Harper's Monthly, xi. 145 ; and " Paul Jones and Denis Duval " in Hale's Ingham Papers, or the Atlantic Monthly, Oct. 1864 ; and in this last connection see Thackeray's Denis Duval with the notes appended. See a reactionary British view of Jones, in All the Year Round, 1870, or No. 1353 of Living Age, and a biographical account Fraser, April 1878.

Jones figures in Cooper's Pilot and in other tales by A. Cunningham and T. Mügge. Dumas's Le Capitaine Paul, is a sequel to Cooper's Pilot. See also Herman Melville's Israel Potter.

An account of the medal struck in Jones's honor, for his action with the Serapis, is given in Loubat's Medallic History of the United States.

Foreign Relations, 1779–1780.

The unhappy differences between Franklin and Lee and Izard still went on. Lives of Franklin by Sparks, i. ch. 11 and Works, viii. 444, and by Parton, ii. 379. John Adams's opinion of Franklin is given in Works, i. 319. Samuel Adams held a good opinion of Lee. Wells's Samuel Adams, iii. 120. Correspondence of Ralph Izard, edited by his daughter Mrs. Deas, one volume only published.

To put a stop to these disturbances, La Fayette, in Feb. 1779, carried over a commission to Franklin, as sole minister plenipotentiary, when Adams returned to America. Diplomatic Correspondence, iv. 307. Lee still filled his position as agent to Spain.

Congress was occupied with baffling the schemes of France which were aimed to secure a general peace, at the price of curtailing the limits of the United States westward, and giving up the navigation of the Mississippi to Spain. Bancroft, x. 349. Sectional differences resulted in a compromise, by which John Adams was appointed a commissioner to negotiate with Great Britain, and John Jay with Spain, thus terminating Lee's agency. The agitation which produced this result can be traced in the following : Life of John Adams, ch. 6, where the policy of France is represented as entirely selfish ; also his diary in Works,

iii. 186, 229, 259; his official correspondence, vii.
119, 120, 139, etc., which is full on the European
complications; his private letters, ix. 476. C.
F. Adams thinks the French translator of Botta
had access to Gerard's papers. Adams's commission and instructions are given in the Diplomatic Correspondence, iv. 339, and his letters are
continued in vol. v. and in his Correspondence
with Mercy Warren, Massachusetts Historical
Society's Collections, 5th series, iv. 378. Cf.
Parton's Franklin, ii. 394; Bancroft, x. 442.

For Jay's instructions and the question of the
free navigation of the Mississippi, see Rives's
Madison, i. ch. 6 and 8; Madison's Debates and
Correspondence, i. App.; Writings, iv. 441;
Jay's Life of Jay; Niles's Register, 1822; Bancroft, x. ch. 8 and 9; and for his letters to Congress, the Diplomatic Correspondence, vii. 171
and viii. (1781); Francis Dana's correspondence
from St. Petersburg, begins Aug. 1780, in Diplomatic Correspondence, viii. 239.

Lossing gives a summary of these diplomatic
manœuvres, in his Field-Book, ii. supplement.
Condorcet, Œuvres, viii., gives a view of the influence of the Revolution in Europe. Cf. Cape-
figue's Louis XVI. and contrast with Bancroft, x.
ch. 11 and 12.

For the combination of the northern powers in
an *Armed Neutrality*, 1778–1780, to protect them-
selves against British interruptions of their trade,

see Bancroft, x. ch. 12 and 20; Anderson's History of Commerce, ed. of 1790, vi. 362; note in Thornton's Pulpit of the Revolution, 457; Wells's Samuel Adams, iii. 109.

Bancroft, x. ch. 11, summarizes the abortive naval movements of France and Spain against England. Adams sent to Congress, 1780, a statement of Great Britain's naval losses since the beginning of the war. Diplomatic Correspondence, iv. 483; v. 234.

Adolphus, History of England, iii. ch. 40, points out the complications of England with the other powers. Cf. Stanhope, the Pictorial History and other general histories. The view of the expatriated loyalists are given in Curwen's Journal, and in Reminiscences of an American Loyalist, in Notes and Queries, 1876. The year was fertile in political tracts. A Short History of the Opposition was followed by Observations on the same, and again by a Defence.

The King and ministry made fresh efforts, 1780, to bring about a union with the opposition. Memoirs and Correspondence of Fox, i. 251. Walpole's Last Journals, ii. 422. Donne's Correspondence of George III. with Lord North, ii. 327. Stanhope's England, vii. 73.

Henry Laurens, late president of Congress, was sent to Europe, armed with credentials for concluding a treaty of alliance with the Netherlands. His instructions are given in the Diplomatic

Correspondence, ii. 453. The British captured him at sea, and securing his papers, discovered the complicity of the Netherlands, and declared war Dec. 20, 1780, against that country. Diplomatic Correspondence, ii. 461, v. 367. Donne's Correspondence of George III. with Lord North, ii. 350. Fitzmaurice's Shelburne, iii. ch. 3. Massey's England, ii. 382. Stanhope's England, vii. 81. Adolphus's England, iii. 221.

Laurens was confined in the Tower. South Carolina Historical Collections, i. Parton's Franklin, ii. 405.

John Adams's letters to the Dutch jurist, Calkoen, 1780, on the present state of affairs in America, were printed by Adams in London, 1786; reprinted, New York, 1789, and in the Correspondence of the late President Adams, Boston, 1809, and in Adams's Works, vii. 265.

Winter, 1779–1780.

This was an exceptionally severe winter. Jones's New York in the Revolution, i. 320; Greene's Greene, ii. 184; Leake's Lamb; Almon's Remembrancer, ix.

In December Clinton went south with a force for the capture of Charleston, leaving Knyphausen in command in New York. The river froze, but Washington was unable to take advantage of this natural bridge into the town, on account of the weakness and destitution of his troops, now hutted at Morristown. An Orderly-Book of Capt. Parker at Morristown, is in the New York Historical Society's Cabinet. See Irving's Washington, iv. ch. 1 and 4 ; J. F. Tuttle's Washington in Morris County, in Historical Magazine, June, 1871, p. 364 ; and Washington at Morristown, in Harper's Monthly, Feb. 1851, also Lossing's Field-Book, ii. Some account of the suffering of the troops will be found in Thacher's Military Journal.

Washington sent an unsuccessful expedition to Staten Island. Life of Pickering, i. ch. 17. Revolutionary Correspondence in Rhode Island Historical Society's Collections, p. 257. Historical Magazine, i. 104.

Bret Harte's Thankful Blossom is a tale of the Jerseys in 1779.

EVENTS OF 1780.

The Southern Campaigns in General.

UNABLE to make progress in the north, the British transferred the seat of war to the south, where the finally decisive conflicts of the war were fought, often hardly more than skirmishes as regards numbers, but exerting a determinate influence on the progress of political events.

/ Ramsay's American Revolution is the one, more particularly of the general histories, to serve the reader. Cf. Bancroft, x., and Hildreth, iii. ch. 40 and 41.

American Accounts. — Moultrie's Memoirs of the American War. Joseph Johnson's Traditions and Reminiscences of the American Revolution in the South, particularly concerns the upper country. Garden's Anecdotes of the Revolutionary War. Caruther's Revolutionary Incidents in the Old North State. Graham's Lecture, on the invasion of North Carolina in 1780–1781, is in W. D. Cooke's Revolutionary History of North Carolina. McRee's Life of Iredell, ch. 13. R. W. Gibbs's Documentary History of the American Revolution, 1776–1782, and another volume, 1781–1782, chiefly concerns events in South Carolina. W. G. Simms's South Carolina in the Revolutionary War. Johnson's Life of Greene.

G. W. Greene, in his Life of Nathanael Greene, iii. ch. 1, gives a description of the country and its inhabitants; and in ch. 2 he begins a review of events previous to the arrival of Gen. Greene.

Partisan Leaders. — The lives of Morgan, Sumter, Marion, and others, are sketched by Greene in the 7th ch. of his Life of Greene. Other accounts are in the Appendix of Lee's Memoirs of the War; and in C. B. Hartley's Heroes and Patriots of the South. There is a life of Morgan by Graham, and chapters on him in Custis's Recollections of Washington, and in Headley's Washington and his Generals. Sumter is depicted in Irving's Washington, iv. ch. 8. Lives of Marion have been written by Weems, Simms, and James; and Lossing has a paper on him in Harper's Monthly, xvii.

See a journal in the southern department given in the Historical Magazine, April, 1867 ; and in Parton's Life of Andrew Jackson, ch. 5 and 6, there is a picture of family vicissitudes in the Carolinas during this period.

British Accounts. — Col. Tarleton's Campaign of 1780–1781, London, 1787. Roderick Mackenzie published the same year in London, 1787, Strictures on Tarleton's Narrative, defending Cornwallis. Stedman's American War accuses Tarleton of misstatement and exaggeration. Stanhope and the other general histories. See also the Cornwallis Correspondence, i., for much in illustration.

Loyalists. — The narrative of Col. David Fanning, a tory in North Carolina, was privately printed at Richmond, in 1861. He practiced barbarities on the whigs. See the paper on a Carolina loyalist in Col. Chesney's Military and Biographical Essays.

Maps. — The American Atlas, by Mouzon and others. Political Magazine, London, Nov. 1780. Hilliard d'Auberteuil's Essais, ii. Marshall's Washington, atlas. Greene's Life of Greene, iii. Johnson's Life of Greene, ii. Carrington's Battles. Ridpath's United States, p. 342.

Tarleton gives a large map, showing the marches of his legion, and of the army of Cornwallis. Faden published in 1787 a map of Cornwallis's marches.

Collet, governor of Fort Johnson, made a map of North Carolina, which was published in London in 1770.

A large map of South Carolina and adjacent parts is given in Ramsay's Revolution in South Carolina. Cook's Province of South Carolina, engraved by Bowen, was published in 1773.

A large map of South Carolina and Georgia, made by Bull, Gascoigne, Bryan, and De Brahm, was published in 1777, both in London and in Paris; and, with additional surveys by Stuart, was reissued in London by Faden in 1780.

Archibald Campbell's Northern Frontiers of Georgia was published by Faden in 1780.

Siege of Charleston, March—May, 1780.

Arbuthnot with the English fleet, and Clinton with the army, advancing from Savannah, gradually inclosed Lincoln and the American army within the defenses of Charleston.

There is a monograph on the siege by F. B. Hough. See also Bancroft, x. ch. 13 and 14; Simms's South Carolina in the Revolution; Marshall's Washington, iv. 135; Irving's Washington, iv. ch. 3 and 5; Tarleton's History of the Campaigns of 1780–1781; Moore's Diary, ii. 269; A Journal of the Siege in the Proceedings of the New Jersey Historical Society, ii.; Carrington's Battles of the American Revolution, ch. 63; Massachusetts Historical Society's Collections, 2d series, iii., on Lincoln; Bowen's Life of Gen. Lincoln; and Lincoln's letters in Sparks's Correspondence of the Revolution, ii. 401, etc., as well as others from Woodford, Col. Laurens, etc.; Dawson's Battles; Sargent's André, p. 225; Moultrie's Memoirs of the American War, ii. 65; Ramsay's Revolution in South Carolina; Flanders's Life of Rutledge. The British gazetted account is in Gentleman's Magazine, June, 1780. For the political significance of this southern movement of the British, see Sparks's Washington, vii. 92.

Charleston in 1774 is described by an English traveler in the Historical Magazine, Nov. 1865, and Faden published views of Charleston in 1776, drawn by Lieut. Col. Thomas James.

The tory ascendency in South Carolina at this time is depicted in J. P. Kennedy's Horseshoe Robinson, a novel.

Maps. — An English MS. map of the siege is in the Faden Collection in the Library of Congress. Faden published a plan of the town and environs in 1780. A MS. plan of Charleston, by Cowley, 1781, is in Harvard College Library. See Ramsay's Revolution in South Carolina; Johnson's American Revolution in the South; Stedman's American War, ii. ch. 33, similar, but not the same with the one published London, March 1, 1787; Marshall's Washington, atlas; Lossing's Field-Book, ii. 765; Gordon's American Revolution, iii. and iv., for a map of the campaign; Moore's Diary of the American Revolution, ii. 258.

Waxhaws, May 29, 1780.

A defeat and massacre of Buford's regiment by the legion of Tarleton, who was sent out by Clinton after the capture of Charleston. See Dawson, Lossing, and, on the English side, Tarleton's Campaigns.

Ramsour Mills, June 20, 1780.

A deadly encounter in North Carolina between whigs and tories. See Historical Magazine, July,

1867, beside scanty accounts in some of the general histories, etc.

Springfield, New Jersey, June, 1780.

The British in New York, getting tidings of an insurrection in the American camp in the Jerseys, caused by want of pay, made an incursion into that State.   Histories of New Jersey.   Bancroft, x. ch. 18.   Marshall's Washington.   Gordon's American Revolution, iii. 368.   Historical Magazine, i. 104.   Irving's Washington, iv. 6.   Carrington's Battles, p. 502.   Sparks's Washington, vii. 75.   Lossing's Field-Book, i. 322.   Greene's Greene, ii., and Greene's letters in Sparks's Washington, vii. 506.

A tory view is given in Moore's Diary, ii. 285. A Journal of a British officer in New York, and in these excursions, Aug. 1779 to Nov. 1780, is in the Historical Magazine, i. 103.   Simcoe's Queen's Rangers.   The court-martial of Colonel Cosmo Gordon, a British officer, for neglect of duty in the action, was printed in London in 1783, and gives some details.

Maps. — Faden published, April 12, 1784, a plan by John Hills, showing the British forces at Elizabethtown Point, after their return from Connecticut Farms, June 8th, giving also the works erected to protect the army while passing to Staten Island, June 23, 1780.   Later maps are in Carrington and Lossing.

Bull's Ferry, July 21, 1780.

This was an effectual attempt by Gen. Wayne
to assault a blockhouse (near Fort Lee, on the
Hudson) garrisoned by refugees. Life of Wayne.
Sparks's Washington, vii. 116; Sparks's Correspondence of the Revolution, iii. 34, 37. Sargent's Life of André, who wrote in derision his
doggerel of " The Cow Chase," part of Wayne's
project being to gather cattle from the neighborhood. Lossing's Field-Book.

Summer, 1780.

During the inactivity of the northern army
Steuben exerted himself to reorganize the forces.
Kapp's Steuben, ch. 12–15. Chastellux gives an
account of camp life. Irving's Washington, iv.
ch. 13.

The British Government erected Maine into a
province called New Ireland, to serve as a foil to
the new Commonwealth of Massachusetts, now
reorganized under a new constitution. Bancroft,
x. 368. Barry's Massachusetts. Maine Historical Society's Collections, vii. The efforts which,
before this, had been made to protect the frontier
by the force under Col. John Allan are described
in F. Kidder's Military Operations in Eastern
Maine and Nova Scotia. Cf. Journal of the Ship
Hunter in Historical Magazine, viii. 51, and Ithiel
Town's Particular Services, etc.

In June martial law was declared in Pennsylvania to meet the emergencies of the time. Reed's Reed, ii. 208.

In July President Reed addressed Washington a long letter on the condition of affairs, which is in Sparks's Correspondence of the Revolution, iii. 15.

Washington's vigorous letter to Congress, in August, on the evils which, through the war, had arisen from short enlistments and the temporizing action of that body, and the want of uniform and concerted action by the States, indicates the wiser feelings of the patriots. Sparks's Washington, vii. 156.

A number of Washington's letters, 1780–1781, are printed in the Magazine of American History, Aug. 1879.

In August there was a convention of delegates from the several States to advise on a vigorous prosecution of the war, and to provide a generous reception for the French allies. The original MS. of their proceedings has been edited by F. B. Hough, Albany, 1867. ˙

The French Auxiliaries, 1780.

Lafayette gives Washington an account of his efforts to induce the French government to send troops and a fleet to America. Sparks's Washington, vii. 477. Lafayette's own arrival heralded their coming. Memoirs of Lafayette. J. C. Hamilton's Republic, ii. 15. The measures taken by Washington in anticipation of their arrival are detailed in Sparks, vii. Heath, July 12th, informs Washington of the fleet's arrival. Sparks's Correspondence of the Revolution, iii. 12. Heath's Memoirs, p. 243. Irving's Washington, iv. ch. 7. Washington's first letter to Rochambeau, July 16th, is in Sparks, vii. 110, and in App. No. 4 is Rochambeau's reply, where is also Lafayette's report of his interview with the French commander, held by Washington's direction.

The French took post in Newport harbor, where they were blockaded by the English fleet.

Contemporary Accounts. — Rochambeau's Mémoires, and his account in Walsh's American Register, ii. Letters of an aid of Rochambeau, written from Newport, Aug.–Dec. 1780, in the Magazine of American History, May 1879, etc. Letters in Rhode Island Colonial Records, ix. Luzerne's letter in Diplomatic Correspondence, x. Marquis de Chastellux's Voyage de Newport à Philadelphie, printed on board the French fleet in Newport harbor, and afterwards published in his Voyage dans l'Amérique Septentrionale. (Cf. Bibliographical Contributions of Harvard College Library, No. 6; the Sumner Collection, p. 8.) Count Ségur's Mémoires. Mémoires du Duc de Lauzun. The New Travels of the Abbé Robin, the Chaplain. The Journal of Deuxponts, 1780–1781, brought to light and edited by Dr. Samuel A. Green, in French and English. An English

version of the Journal of Claude Blanchard, a
commissary of the French army, which gives
daily experiences. (Cf. Revue militaire française,
new series, iii., and vol. ii., for 1870.) There
was printed at Amsterdam in 1783, another
French narrative, Journal d'un officier de l'armée
navale en Amérique, en 1781–1782. New England Historical and Genealogical Register, Oct.
1873, p. 409.

*General Accounts of the French Participation
in the War.* — Leboucher's Histoire de la guerre
de l'indépendance des États Unis. Thomas
Balch's Les Français en Amérique, 1872, covering
1777–1783. Cf. Tuckerman's America and her
Commentators, ch. 3.

Clinton's purpose to attack the French at Newport was thwarted partly by want of harmony
between him and the British admiral, and partly
by Washington's movements about New York.
Sparks's Washington, vii. 130, 137, and the general histories; Irving's Washington. Cf. Jones's
New York in the Revolutionary War, i. 358, etc.

For the subsequent plan of a concerted attack
on New York, see Sparks's Washington, vii. 171,
and App. No. 6; Mémoires de Rochambeau, and
the general works. The English blockaded the
second division of the French fleet at Brest, and
this caused, in August, the final abandonment of
the plan. The next month, September, Washington met Rochambeau at Hartford to devise further

methods of coöperation. Irving's Washington. J. C. Hamilton's Republic of the United States, ii. 49.

Maps. — The Political Magazine, London, 1780, has a map of Rhode Island and surrounding waters, showing the station of Admiral Arbuthnot in blockading Admiral Ternay.

Charles Blaskowitz's chart of Narragansett Bay and his plan of Newport were engraved by Faden in 1777 ; and Almon published the same year a map of Rhode Island, engraved by Lodge.

Gates in Command, June, 1780.

Gates was sent to take command of the southern army in June. Washington, in a letter to the President of Congress, traces the growth of Gates's sinister feelings towards him. Sparks, vi. 214. See the general histories, the lives of Gates, and G. W. Greene's summary in his Life of N. Greene, iii. 17. The chief original authority for Gates's campaign is the Narrative of Otho Williams, first published in Johnson's Life of Greene. It is valuable, though controversial in character. Lee's Memoirs of the War, ch. 18. The Letter on Gates's Campaign, published in 1822, by Gen. Thomas Pinckney, who was aid to Gates. Lives of Washington by Marshall, iv. 169, and by Irving, iv. ch. 8.

Camden, August 16, 1780.

Gates was confronted by Cornwallis at Camden, and the American army was routed.

American Accounts. — Gates's letter is in Sparks's Correspondence of the Revolution, iii. 66, 76. Greene's letter in Rhode Island Colonial Records, ix. 243. Bancroft, x. ch. 15. Hamilton's History of the Republic, ii. 120. Simms's South Carolina. Marshall's Washington, iv. 181. Irving's Washington, iv. ch. 8. Lives of Gates. Lossing's Field-Book. Dawson's Battles. Carrington's Battles, ch. 65. New England Historical and Genealogical Register, Oct. 1873.

De Kalb was mortally wounded. Kapp's Life of De Kalb. J. S. Smith on De Kalb in the Maryland Historical Society's Publications, 1858.

British Accounts. — Cornwallis's dispatches are in the Cornwallis Correspondence, i. 492, and in the Gentleman's Magazine, Oct. 1780. Rawdon's letters are preserved among the Percy papers, according to the third report, 1872, of the English Commission on historical manuscripts. Captured letters of Rawdon are in Sparks's Washington, vii. 554, and Almon's Remembrancer, xi. 156. Stedman's American War, ii. 210. Moore's Diary, ii. 310.

Maps. — A British plan is in the Faden Collection. Stedman, ii. ch. 34, the same published London, March 1, 1787. Johnson's Greene, ii. Carrington's Battles.

W. G. Simms's novel, The Partisan, covers the
events of this period, and for the events following
down to Greene's arrival, see his Mellichampe.

Arnold's Treason, September, 1780.

Arnold, who had, while in command in Philadelphia, circuitously opened correspondence with
Clinton, also approached Robinson to secure a
confederate. Sabine's American Loyalists. Sargent's André, Appendix. He then sought from
Washington and obtained the command at West
Point. Irving's Washington. Lossing's Schuyler, ii. 412. Hamilton's Republic, ii. 52.

While Washington was absent, holding a conference at Hartford with Rochambeau, Arnold
planned to betray the garrison at West Point.
For arranging details, Major André, adjutant-
general of the British army, was dispatched by
Clinton up the river, under a flag of truce, to an
interview with Arnold. This over, André, in
disguise, attempted to return to New York by
land. Near Tarrytown he was stopped by a party
of Americans; his papers found in his boots; and
word was incautiously sent to Arnold, who, finding the plan had miscarried, fled down the river
under a flag in a boat to a frigate of the enemy.

Contemporary Accounts. — The papers found
on André's person are in the State Library at
Albany, and they are printed in Boynton's West
Point, ch. 7, and elsewhere. Correspondence in

Sparks's Washington, vii. 520–544. The papers used by Sparks in writing his Life of Arnold are in Harvard College Library. Hamilton's letter to Laurens in Works, i. 172–182; also his letters to Sears and Miss Schuyler. Pennsylvania Packet quoted in Moore's Diary, ii. 333. Gen. Greene's letters in Rhode Island Colonial Records, ix. 246, and in the Revolutionary Correspondence in the Rhode Island Historical Collections, vi. Journal of General Matthews.

Clinton's official dispatches are preserved in the State Paper Office, and have been used by Sparks and others. His letters, Oct. 11th and 12th; his report to Lord Amherst, Oct. 16th; his secret letter, Oct. 30th. Extracts from his journal printed in Stanhope's England, vii. App. His statement, written at some length in his copy of Stedman (now in the Carter-Brown Library) is printed in Jones's New York in the Revolutionary War, i. 737; in Stanhope, vi. App.; in Sargent's André; and in the New York Tribune, May 24, 1875.

Joshua H. Smith was brought to trial for complicity in the plot. A report of his trial, edited by Dawson, was printed in New York, 1866. The Gentleman's Magazine, 1780, Supplement, p. 610, gave an account of the trial and printed the chief documents. Historical Magazine, 1866, Supplements 1 and 2. Smith's Narrative of the Causes which led to the death of Major André, London,

1808, was written for the English public, and must be cautiously used. It has been a disputed question if Mrs. Arnold was privy to the plot. Davis's Life of Burr, i. 219. Parton's Burr, p. 126. Stone's Life of Brant, ii. 101. Reed's Joseph Reed, ii. 373. Sargent's André, 220.

Washington gave in 1786 an account at a dinner-table of the treason of Arnold, which is reproduced in Richard Rush's Washington in Domestic Life, being letters addressed to his secretary, Lear, 1790–1797.

The Captors. — Williams and Van Wart's account of the capture is in the Historical Magazine, June, 1865. American Historical Record, Dec. 1873. Bolton's Westchester, i. Simms's Schoharie County, p. 646. Quincy's Journals of Samuel Shaw. Sargent's André, App.

Paulding in 1817 petitioned Congress for an increase of his pension, and Judge Egbert Benson vindicated the captors against aspersions of their character. Analectic Magazine, x. This Vindication was printed with documentary evidence, including proceedings of the Board that tried André, affidavits, etc. The Journals of the House, 1817, give Major Talmadge's recollections. Statements of one of André's guards, printed in the newspapers, 1817, are given in Jones's New York in the Revolutionary War, i. 734.

Loubat's Medallic History of the United States shows the medal given by Congress to the captors.

H. J. Raymond delivered in 1853 an address at Tarrytown in commemoration of the captors.

André. — Boynton's West Point reprints entire the proceedings of a board of general officers respecting Major John André, Sept. 29, 1780. The original MS. of these proceedings is in Washington; and Sargent (Life of André) collated the printed account with the original.

Accounts of André's connection with the plot will be found in P. W. Chandler's American Criminal Trials, ii. ; Earl Stanhope's Miscellanies, 2d series; Atlantic Monthly, Dec. 1860; Harper's Monthly, iii. and xxiii.; North American Review, by C. C. Smith, July, 1861; L. M. Sargent's Dealings with the Dead; Paulding's Paper in the Historical Magazine, Nov. 1857.

Dr. Thacher furnished some Observations on André's execution in the New England Magazine, May, 1834.

On the removal of André's remains to England, see United Service Journal, Nov. 1833; Sargent's André; Stanley's Westminster Abbey; Pennsylvania Historical Society's Memoirs, vi. 373; New York Evangelist, Jan. 30 and Feb. 27, 1879.

Memorials of André. — Sabin's American Bibliopolist, 1869–1870. Political Magazine, March, 1781. New Jersey Historical Society's Proceedings, 1876. Smith and Watson's American Historical and Literary Curiosities. Galaxy, Feb. 1876, on André and Miss Seward, and the latter's monody is given in J. H. Smith's Narrative, etc., and in other places.

Portraits of André. — In Smith; Political Magazine, March, 1781; Sargent's André; Moore's Diary, etc.

André's fate has given rise to dramas by Calvert, Lord, Dunlap, Haid, etc. For Arnold as the subject of fictitious stories, see W. G. Simms's Views and Reviews.

In General. — Bancroft, x. 395, follows only "contemporary documents, which are abundant and of the surest character, and which taken collectively solve every question." Hildreth, iii. ch. 41, gives an outline. Marbois, secretary to the French legation at the time, published Complot d'Arnold et Clinton, Paris, 1816, and G. W. Greene says it is "neither so accurate nor so complete as might have been expected." Cooper's Travelling Bachelor, says Sargent, gives "several particulars which possess value from those [Lafayette, etc.] that supplied them." Thacher's Military Journal and New England Magazine, vi. 363. Walsh's American Register, ii.

Lossing's Field-Book, ii. ch. 6, 7, and 8. Dunlap's New York, ii. ch. 13. Marshall's Washington, iv. 274. Irving's Washington, iv. ch. 9, 10, and 11. Sparks's Arnold. Sargent's André. Leake's Life of Lamb. Gen. Hull's Revolutionary Services, on André and Nathan Hale. Hamilton's Life of Alexander Hamilton, i. 262. Greene's

Life of Greene, ii. 227. Quincy's Life of Shaw,·
p. 77. E. G. Holland's Highland Treason, in his
Essays.

Boynton's West Point points out the military
importance of that post, and gives ch. 6, 7, and 8
to these transactions.

Lossing's Papers in Harper's Monthly, iii.,
xxiii., and again, May, 1876. Historical Magazine,
Aug. 1859; Aug. 1863; Supplement of 1866;
Dec. 1870. Niles's Register, xx. Southern Lit-
erary Messenger, xi. National Quarterly Review,
Dec. 1862. Cf. titles in the Menzies Catalogue.

Col. Trumbull gives an account in his Memoirs
(pp. 69, 317) of his arrest in London as a *pendant*
to André. Simcoe (Queen's Rangers, App.) offered to rescue André.

English Comment. — Sargent, ch. 22, gives the
characters of the members of the board that condemned André, to refute the claim, sometimes put
forward by English writers, of their unfitness to
act by virtue of their ignorance of law and prec-
edents; and also collates the different English
commentators on the justice of the execution.
Clinton's views are given in Sargent, p. 415.
Adolphus (History of England, iii. ch. 39) takes
an adverse view of the American grounds. Stanhope, in his History and in his Miscellanies, cen-
sures Washington and the court, and his position
is examined by C. J. Biddle in the Pensylvania
Historical Society's Memoirs, vi. (cf. Allibone, iii.

1204), and in the Historical Magazine, July, 1857.
Massey (History of England, iii. ch. 25) exoner-
ates Washington. A British estimate from the
Saturday Review, 1872, is given in Sabin's Amer-
ican Bibliopolist, Oct. 1872. Cf. contemporary
British view in Moore's Diary of the American
Revolution, ii. 393.

Jones, the loyalist, in his New York in the
Revolutionary War, i. ch. 18, judges Arnold to
have played "a noble and virtuous part."

Sargent thinks a vindication of Arnold (Remarks on the Travels of M. de Chastellux, London, 1787) was instigated by Arnold himself.

Maps. — Carrington's Battles, p. 512. Lossing's Field-Book, ii. 148. Guizot's Washington,
atlas. Sargent's André, p. 303. Marbois's Complot has a plan of West Point. Sparks's Washington, vii. 216, gives a map of the region. Maj.
Villefranche, a French engineer, made several
plans at this time, and they are given in fac-simile
in Boynton's History of West Point, viz.: map of
Fort Constitution, opposite West Point, p. 26;
map of the river and military positions, p. 45;
plan of the lower works at West Point, p. 79; of
all the works and river, p. 86. The same book
has a contemporary panoramic view of West
Point.

Note. — I have been favored by the Hon. Isaac N. Arnold of
Chicago with the proofs of the chapter on Arnold's treason,
which makes part of a Life of Arnold by that gentleman, now

in press. He has used the Arnold and Shippen papers, and sets distinctly forth the incentives to Arnold's plotting of treason. He does not think Mrs. Arnold guilty of any complicity ; and defends the action of the board that condemned André to death. Gen. King, the officer who had charge of André immediately after his capture, wrote, in 1817, a letter describing these events, which was first printed in the New Haven Palladium, 1879, and copied in the Boston Sunday Herald, Sept. 14, 1879. Cf. also Sargent's André.

The Northern Invasion, 1780.

The several attempts at invasion from Canada at this time are supposed, in F. B. Hough's Northern Invasion, published by the Bradford Club, New York, 1866, to have had connection with Arnold's plot, and they are outlined in Lossing's Schuyler, ii. 407.

Washington in Camp, October and November, 1780.

An account of Washington's camp at Totowa and Preakness in New Jersey, with a map and view of his headquarters, is given in the Magazine of American History, Aug. 1879.

King's Mountain, October 7, 1780.

Fergusson, one of Cornwallis's marauding officers, in endeavoring to rejoin that British general, was attacked by the mountain militia and defeated. This checked Cornwallis's advance. Marshall's Washington, i. 397. Irving's Washington, iv. ch. 14 ; Foote's Sketches of North Carolina ; Lee's Southern War ; Hamilton's Republic of the

United States, ii. 161; Bancroft, x. ch. 16; Lossing's Field-Book, ii. 629; Carrington's Battles; Dawson's Battles; Tarleton's Campaigns; Mackenzie's Strictures on Tarleton ; Moore's Diary, ii. 338; J. W. De Peyster in the Historical Magazine, March, 1869; Ramsay's South Carolina; Simms's South Carolina. J. S. Preston delivered a commemorative address in Oct. 1855, which was printed with a documentary appendix.

Leslie's Expedition into Virginia, October, 1780.

See the accounts in the general narratives. Leslie made his way to North Carolina to coöperate with Cornwallis. Parton's Jefferson, ch. 27. Sparks's Washington, vii. 269. Correspondence of the Revolution, iii. 141.

Map. — Political Magazine, Dec. 1780.

Greene in Command, October, 1780.

Late in the year Greene resigned as quartermaster-general of the army. Life of Pickering. J. C. Hamilton's Republic of the United States, ii. 41. Greene's Life of Greene, ch. 10. In October Greene was appointed to succeed Gates in command of the southern army. Washington's instructions to Greene are given in Sparks, vii. 271. Cf. Correspondence of the Revolution, iii. 116, 137; Greene's Greene, ch. 12; J. C. Hamilton's Republic, ii. 133, and his Alex. Hamilton, i. 308; and the latter's eulogy on Greene,

1789, in Works, ii. 481. Marshall's Washington, iv. 336. Irving's Washington, iv. ch. 15. Bancroft, x. ch. 22.

Steuben accompanied Greene as far as Virginia, where he was left in command, with orders to send forward reinforcements to Greene. See Kapp's Steuben, ch. 16 ; Greene's Greene, ii. ch. 3 and 5 ; and the Life of General Mühlenberg, who was under Steuben in Virginia. Randall's Jefferson, i. ch. 8.

Greene arrived on the field in December. Correspondence of the Revolution, iii. 165.

Mrs. Sedgwick's Walter Thornley gives the guise of fiction to events of this year.

EVENTS OF 1781.

Mutiny of the Pennsylvania Line, January, 1781.

· THESE troops, under Wayne, stationed at Morristown, without pay and supplies, revolted and marched toward Philadelphia to claim redress of Congress. Wayne visited their camp to expostulate. Clinton sent emissaries, whom they hung.

Wayne's letters to Washington in the Correspondence of the Revolution, iii. 192–199. Life of Anthony Wayne. Sparks's Washington, vii. 348, and the account in App. 10. Marshall's Washington, iv. 393. Irving's Washington, iv. 195. Hamilton's Life of Alexander Hamilton, i. 323, and Works, ii. 147. Amory's Sullivan, 181. Hildreth's United States, iii. ch. 42. Madison Papers, i. 77.

Pennsylvania Archives, viii. and ix. Hazard's Register of Pennsylvania, ii. 160. Bland Papers, ii. Reed's Life of Joseph Reed, ii. ch. 14.

Sir Henry Clinton's report is in Almon's Remembrancer, xi. 148. Jones's New York in the Revolutionary War, ii. 179.

Political Aspects, 1781.

On March 1st the final ratification of the articles of confederation was made. Journals of

Congress. Bancroft, x. ch. 19. G. W. Greene's
Historical View, p. 111. The executive business ⌣
was taken from committees and delegated to
heads of departments. Hamilton's Republic, ii.
ch. 28. R. R. Livingston became head of the
department for foreign affairs. Diplomatic Correspondence, xi. 201.

The want of power in Congress to compel the
States began to be seriously felt. Rives's Madison,
i. ch. 10. G. W. Greene's Historical View of the
American Revolution.

Bancroft, x. ch. 17, traces the beginnings of the
abolition of slavery ; and the origin of the appor-
tionment of five slaves as three persons is traced
in Rives's Madison, i. 424; Madison's Debates,
etc. i. 422; Journals of Congress, iv.

A new commission was formed to negotiate a
peace, and new instructions given. Life of John
Adams, i. 341; vii. 349. Rives's Madison, i. ch.
11. Madison Papers, i. Hamilton's Life of Alexander Hamilton. Flanders's Life of Rutledge,
p. 596. Franklin's Works, viii. 526; ix. Journals of Congress, vii. Diplomatic Correspondence,
vi. 3, for John Adams's letters. See under " Negotiations for Peace," 1782.

Lafayette's letters during his visit to Europe
are in the Diplomatic Correspondence, x.

Finances.

The question of the finances of the Revolution has had special treatment in Bancroft, x. ch. 7; Hildreth's United States, iii. ch. 40, 43; Greene's Historical View of the American Revolution, p. 137 (with tables of expenses, federal and state, with emission of Continental money in the Appendix), and his Life of Greene, ii.; Pitkins's United States, ii. ch. 16; Rives's Madison, i. 217, 229, and ch. 14; Madison's Debates and Correspondence, i. Sparks's Life of Gouverneur Morris, i. ch. 13 and 14; J. W. Schucker's Brief Account of the Finances of the Revolution, 1874.

Special or Local Aspects. — Felt's History of Massachusetts Currency; Amory's Sullivan, p. 187; Reed's Life of Joseph Reed, ii. 287; Mulford's New Jersey, p. 457, etc.

Continental Money. — Force's American Archives, 5th series, vol. ii. *index;* S. Breck's Historical Sketch of Continental Paper Money in the Transactions of the American Philosophical Society, 1843; Lossing's Field-Book, i. 317, and Harper's Monthly, xxvi.; National Quarterly Review, Dec. 1875.

Depreciation of the Paper Money. — Gouge's Short History of Paper Money; Greene's Greene, ii. 163, 243, 248; Moore's Diary, ii. 422; Rhode Island Colonial Records, ix. 282.

Loans in Europe. — Diplomatic Correspondence,

ix. 199; xi. 291; Franklin's lives and letters; Sparks's Washington, viii. 525. Col. John Laurens was sent in 1781 to negotiate a loan. His instructions are given in Diplomatic Correspondence, ix. 199, and for his efforts and success, ix. 195–249; Hamilton's Republic, ii. 150. John Adams secured a loan in Holland. Works, vii. 599.

John Adams's Relation to the Question. — Works, vii. 292, 355; viii. 193.

Hamilton's Views. — Writings, i. 116, 150, 223; his Life by J. C. Hamilton, i. 241, 352; ii. etc. J. C. Hamilton's Republic of the United States, i. 570; ii. 80, 100, 351, and ch. 35, etc. For the diverse views of Hamilton and Madison, see Rives's Madison, i. 433. A charge is made in the Republic of the United States, ii. 398, that Madison falsified the record of Hamilton's votes, which is answered in Rives, i. 437. Cf. Atlantic Monthly, Nov. 1865, p. 628.

Robert Morris was made Superintendent of Finance, Feb. 20, 1781, and entered upon his duties in May. Diplomatic Correspondence, xi. 347, 431. Pennsylvania Archives, ix. Sparks's Washington, viii. 136. Custis's Recollections of Washington. Bancroft's United States, x. 566. Franklin's Works, ix. 59, etc. Life of Morris in Hunt's American Merchants. Michael Nourse's account of Morris, 1781–1784, in Banker's Magazine, Feb. 1860. Albert S. Bolles in the Penn

Monthly, Oct. 1878, on the Financial Administration of Morris, also issued separately. Turner's Pioneer History of the Holland Purchase. Potter's American Monthly, Dec. 1775.

Greene's Campaigns in General, 1780–1782.

Greene, leaving Steuben in Virginia late in 1780, pushed on and took command of the southern army at Charlotte. His conduct of the campaign gave him a reputation second only to that of Washington; and though he never gained a decisive victory, his battles were always followed by the retreat of the enemy. The general works on the southern campaign have been referred to under 1780. The fullest record of Greene's own participation in it is in the elaborate life of him (1867–1871) by his grandson, George W. Greene. The same writer had already furnished a summarized narrative in the Life of Greene in Sparks's series of American Biography. Another Life of Greene, published in 1822, by Judge Johnson, who had possession of Greene's papers, had reflected on Gen. Lee, one of Greene's lieutenants, and this drew out a vindication of Lee from his son, Henry Lee, entitled The Campaign of 1781, which has an Appendix of original documents. G. W. Greene calls this book both " clever and lively, but too controversial to be perfectly trustworthy." Lee is the subject of a chapter in Custis's Recollections of Washington; and he wrote thirty years later, in 1809, his own recollections in his Memoirs of the War in the Southern Department.

Greene's own letters are given in Sparks's Correspondence of the Revolution, iii. 207, etc.; in Reed's Life of Joseph Reed, ii. 344, etc., and in the lives of him.

On the British side we have contemporary authorities in Clinton's Narrative of the Campaign of 1781 ; Cornwallis's Answer to Clinton, and another Reply to Clinton, likewise vindicating Cornwallis, all published in London, and reprinted in Philadelphia, 1865–1866.

Later summarized accounts will be found in Bancroft, x. ch. 22 ; Hildreth, iii. ch. 42 ; Irving's Washington, iv.; McRee's Iredell, ch. 14; Moultrie's Memoirs.

Contemporary likenesses of Greene and Cornwallis are in Andrews's History of the War and in Lee's Memoirs.

Maps. —Greene's Life of Greene.   Carrington's Battles, 540, 556.   Caruthers's Incidents in the Old North State in 1781, two series.   Balch's Les Français en Amérique.

The British in Virginia, January — May, 1781.

It was the British plan for Cornwallis to move north in the end and join the forces to be sent from New York to the James.   Clinton had already dispatched Leslie, who had reached Virginia, as already stated, Oct. 22, 1780. Arnold, the traitor, was now sent with a detachment, arriving Dec. 29th. Gen. Phillips arrived and superseded Arnold, March 26, 1781, and dying, May 13th, Arnold again took command, which he held till the 20th, when Cornwallis (arriving at Petersburg, as hereafter stated) ordered Arnold to New York and assumed command.

General accounts of transactions in Virginia during the summer, and of the inertness and unprepared condition of the Virginians, can be found in the histories of Virginia by Campbell, p. 168, and by Howison, ch. 4. Hamilton's Republic of the United States, ii. ch. 27, reflects on Jefferson, at the time governor, and lives of Jefferson by Tucker, i. ch. 6 ; by Randall, i. 295; by Parton, ch. 27, need to be compared. In Jefferson's Writings, ix. 212, 220, there are extracts from his diary, etc. Also Wirt's Patrick Henry ; Jefferson's Notes on Virginia ; Rives's Madison, i. 289; and Madison's Writings, i. 45.

Arnold's Military Movements. — Sparks's Life of Arnold. Marshall's Washington, iv. 387. Sparks's Washington, vii. 347. Correspondence of the Revolution, iii. 200. Irving's Washington, iv. ch. 14 and 17. Bancroft, x. ch. 25. Hamilton's Republic, ii. 170. Arnold's own report in Almon's Remembrancer, ii. 350. Kapp's Steuben, ch. 17–19, records that officer's watch upon Arnold's movements. Lossing's Field-Book, ii. 434,

546. Carrington's Battles. Life of Mühlenberg. Moore's Diary of the Revolution, ii. 384. The Life of Arnold, now in press, by Isaac N. Arnold.

British Accounts. — Simcoe's Military Journal of the Queen's Rangers, privately printed, 1787, and subsequently published in New York, 1843. Stedman's American War. Jones's New York in the Revolutionary War, ii. 177.

Washington was disappointed in not entrapping Arnold by aid of the French fleet. Sparks's Washington, vii. 410. This fleet encountered the British squadron, which succeeded in commanding the Chesapeake waters. Meanwhile, in April, Lafayette reached Virginia with a detachment of troops. For his movements, see Sparks's Washington, viii. 118, 509; Correspondence of the Revolution, iii. ; Marshall's Washington, iv. 418 ; Irving's Washington, iv. ch. 21 and 23. Lafayette's Memoirs and lives of him by Regnault, etc.; Bancroft, x. ch. 21; Dawson's Battles; Carrington's Battles, ch. 72 and 73 ; Kapp's Steuben, ch. 20, in which justice is hardly done to Lafayette ; J. A. Stevens's Expedition of Lafayette against Arnold, published by the Maryland Historical Society, 1878; Balch's Maryland Line, published by the Seventy-Six Society.

Simcoe, Stedman, and Moore's Diary.

Maps and Plans. — Carrington's Battles. Simcoe's Queen's Rangers.

Cowpens, January 17, 1781.

Cornwallis, advancing, sent Tarleton to rid his flank of Morgan, who encountered Tarleton at the Cowpens and defeated him. Graham's Life of Morgan, according to G. W. Greene, " a full and trustworthy narrative founded on authentic material." Morgan's papers were offered for sale in New Orleans, July, 1879.

Greene's Life of Greene, iii. 139. Marshall's Washington, iv. 342. Irving's Washington, iv. ch. 18. Correspondence of the Revolution, iii. 217. Bancroft, x. ch. 22. Dawson's Battles. Carrington's Battles, p. 546. Lossing's Field-Book, ii. 636. Simms's South Carolina. Moultrie's Memoirs, ii. Harper's Monthly, xxii. 163. Historical Magazine, Dec. 1867. Some details were picked up by Chastellux in his Travels, English translation, ii. 60. New York Historical Society's Collections for 1875, p. 476.

British Accounts. — Annual Register. Stedman's American War, ii. ch. 41. Tarleton's History of his Campaigns, with Mackenzie's Strictures on Tarleton.

Congress gave medals to Gen. Morgan, Lieut. Col. Washington, and Lieut. Col. Howard, which are described in Loubat's Medallic History of the United States.

Cornwallis and Greene.

In January Cornwallis detached a force to the region of Cape Fear River, and the Political Magazine, March, 1781, gave a map of the locality.

After Cowpens, Greene and Morgan united, and, Cornwallis pursuing, Greene conducted his famous retreat across the Dan River, when the British general in turn falling back, Greene recrossed the river in pursuit. Lives of Greene by Johnson and Greene, iii. Marshall's Washington. Correspondence of the Revolution, iii. 225, 233. Ramsay's Revolution. Lee's Memoirs. Histories of the United States by Bancroft, x. ch. 23, and others.

British Accounts. — Stedman, Tarleton, Lamb's Journal.

Guilford, March 15, 1781.

Greene offered battle to Cornwallis at Guilford Court House and was defeated. Lives of Greene by Johnson and Greene, iii. 176, and Moore's Diary of the Revolution, ii. 400. Sparks's Washington and Correspondence of the Revolution. Lives of Washington by Marshall, iv. 366, and by Irving, iv. ch. 19 and 20. Gordon's American Revolution. Bancroft, x. ch. 23. Lossing's Field-Book, ii. 594, 608. Dawson's Battles. Carrington's Battles, ch. 69.

Cornwallis's letters and dispatches are in Ross's Cornwallis Correspondence, i. 85, 506. Moore's

Diary, ii. 400. The discussion in Parliament upon the battle is noted in Macknight's Burke, ii. 437.

Maps. — MS. plans in the Faden Collection, Library of Congress. Tarleton's Campaigns. Stedman's American War, ii. ch. 41. Caruthers's Revolutionary Incidents, 2d series. Greene's Greene, iii. Carrington's Battles.

Greene's statement of the aspect of affairs subsequently, April 22, 1781, is given in the Rhode Island Colonial Records, ix. 380; Revolutionary Correspondence of the Rhode Island Historical Collections, vi. 284.

Hobkirk's Hill, April 25, 1781.

Cornwallis, unable to profit by his victory at Guilford, retreated to Wilmington, while Greene, pushing by Cornwallis's left flank, carried the war into South Carolina. Greene's Greene, iii. ch. 12. Lord Rawdon attacked Greene at Hobkirk's Hill, near Camden, defeating him.

Greene's Greene, iii. 241. Johnson's Greene, ii. 83. Gordon, iv. 81. Marshall's Washington, iv. 510, following Davie's MS. Lee's Campaign of 1781. Gibbes's Documentary History. Irving's Washington, iv. Lossing's Field-Book, ii. 676. Simms's South Carolina. Dawson's Battles. Carrington's Battles.

Stedman's American War, ii. ch. 42.

Maps. — Stedman, ii. 358, the same published,

with slight differences, by Faden, Aug. 1, 1783. Greene's Greene, iii. 241. Carrington's Battles, p. 576.

A series of minor reverses compelled Rawdon to fall back to Charleston. Greene's Greene. Bancroft, x. ch. 24.

Ninety-Six, May—June, 1781.

Greene laid siege to this post, and, on the approach of Rawdon with relief, assaulted it unsuccessfully and retired.

Greene's Greene, iii. 299. Johnson's Greene, ii., which apologizes for Sumter's harassing of Greene ; but see Greene's Greene, iii. 319. Marshall's Washington, iv. 524. Bancroft, x. ch. 24. Lossing's Field-Book, ii. 690. Dawson's Battles.

British Accounts. — Stedman, ii. ch. 43. Tarleton and Mackenzie. Jones's New York in the Revolutionary War, ii. 376.

Sparks's Correspondence of the Revolution, iii., gives various letters of Greene.

Maps. — Johnson's and Greene's Greene.

For Greene's camp life during the summer, see Greene's Greene, iii., and his letters to Washington in Sparks's Correspondence of the Revolution, iii.

W. G. Simms covers the events of the siege of Ninety-Six in his novel, The Scout, and the story is pursued in his other tales, — Katharine Walton, Woodcraft, Forayers, and Eutaw.

Eutaw, September 8, 1781.

Greene, advancing towards Charleston, was successful at first at Eutaw, but checked towards the close of the fight. Greene's Greene, iii. 384. Johnson's Greene. Marshall's Washington, iv. 542. Irving's Washington, iv. ch. 27. Bancroft, x. ch. 24. Lossing's Field-Book, ii. 698. Simms's South Carolina. Dawson's Battles. Carrington's Battles, ch. 71. Lee's Memoirs. Greene's Report to Congress. Stuart's Report to Cornwallis, — Moore's Diary, ii. 486. The medal given to Greene is described in Loubat's Medallic History of the United States.

Maps. — Johnson's and Greene's Greene. Carrington's Battles.

End of Southern Campaigns.

For final movements in South Carolina: Greene's Greene, iii.; Bancroft, x. ch. 28; Sparks's Correspondence of the Revolution ; and the histories of Ramsay and Moultrie. Some of Greene's letters are given in Reed's Reed, ii. 377, 468.

For the case of Isaac Hayne, who was hung by the enemy, see Greene's Greene, iii. 356; Ramsay's South Carolina, ii. 277 ; Moultrie's Revolution, etc.; Lee's Campaign of 1781.

For movements round Charleston in 1782, see Ellis's Count Rumford, p. 127.

Conquest of Georgia. — Armstrong's Life of

Wayne; Historical Magazine, May, 1860; Stevens's Georgia, ii. 240; Greene's Greene, iii. 435; Johnson's Greene; Lee's Memoirs; Marshall's Washington.

Siege of Pensacola.—Historical Magazine, iv. 166.

Cornwallis in Virginia, May, 1781.

Meanwhile Cornwallis, not regarding Greene's march to the south, moved north to Virginia, and reached Petersburg May 20th, superseding Arnold in command, as before noted.

Bancroft, x. ch. 23–25. Marshall's Washington, iv. 430. Irving's Washington, iv. ch. 20 and 21. Lossing's Field-Book.

Ross's Cornwallis Correspondence. Sparks's Correspondence of the Revolution, iii., gives Lafayette's letters, detailing his movements in the presence of the enemy.

In June, Tarleton raided to Charlottesville and Monticello. Tarleton's Campaigns. Life of Jefferson by Randall, i. 337, and by Parton, ch. 28. Harper's Monthly, vii. 145.

For movements about Williamsburg, see Denny's Journal in the Pennsylvania Historical Society's Memoirs, vii. 240.

The Allies in Virginia, 1781.

Washington had contemplated a combined attack by the Americans and French on New York, and, after the scheme was abandoned, he kept up the appearance of preparation to deceive the enemy. Sparks's Washington, viii. 54, 130, 517.

Stuart's Jonathan Trumbull describes the planning of the movement to Virginia. Washington, Aug. 2d, informs Robert Morris of his intentions. Diplomatic Correspondence, xi. 417. Heath (Memoirs, p. 298) was left in command on the Hudson, and Washington and Rochambeau moved south. Robin's Nouveau Voyage, translated as New Travels through America, Boston, 1784. There is a map of the march in Soulé's Histoire des Troubles de l'Amérique Anglaise. Lincoln had the immediate command on the march. Bowen's Life of Lincoln. Life of Timothy Pickering, i. 294. Journal of William Feltman. Diplomatic Correspondence, xi. 462, for Washington's passage through Philadelphia.

On Rochambeau and his participation, see Magazine of American History, July, 1879. The representatives of his family offered Rochambeau's papers to Congress in 1879.

Arnold in Connecticut, September, 1781.

Meanwhile, a marauding expedition from New York, under Arnold, was sent along the shore of Long Island Sound. The points of attack were New London, Fort Griswold, and Groton. See Hollister's, ii. ch. 17, and the other histories of Connecticut; Sparks's. Arnold ; Stuart's Life of Jonathan Trumbull, ch. 45; and Gov. Trumbull's

letter to Washington in Sparks's Correspondence
of the Revolution, iii. 403; Moore's Diary, ii.
479; Dawson's Battles; Carrington's Battles,
with plan, p. 630; Irving's Washington, iv. ch.
25; Caulkins's New London, ch. 32; Niles's
Principles of the Revolution; Hinman's Historical
Collections. Cf. Isaac N. Arnold's Life of Gen.
Arnold.

MS. plans of New London and Groton are in
the Faden Collection in the Library of Congress.

Cf. Tuttle's address at Fort Griswold, 1821;
C. Griswold's address in commemoration of Led-
yard in 1826; W. F. Brainerd's, 1825; and Rath-
burn's Narrative of capture of Groton fort, and
of the massacre.

Off the Capes of Chesapeake, September, 1781.

De Grasse, with a French fleet, had arrived
within the Capes to coöperate with the American
land forces, when Admiral Graves with a British
fleet appeared off the Capes. To engage him,
while De Barras, expected with a smaller French
fleet, made the bay, De Grasse stood to sea, and
the two fleets partially engaged, Sept. 5th, and
manœuvred for some days, till, his purpose accomplished, De Grasse drew off and returned to
Lynn Haven Bay, and the blockade of Cornwallis
was made complete. Stedman's American War,
ii. ch. 44, with a map. The Political Magazine,
1781 and 1784. John G. Shea edited in 1864 for

the Bradford Club two contemporaneous journals, showing the Operations of the French fleet, and gave a plan. Cf. also Chevalier's Histoire de la Marine française pendant la guerre de l'independance Américaine, Paris, 1877, ch. 7. Moore's Diary, ii. 476.

Siege of Yorktown, September—October, 1781.

The French secure within the Capes, Cornwallis, posted at Yorktown and Gloucester, was shut off from escape by water and from succor from Clinton, while Washington and Rochambeau opened their trenches on the land side.

Contemporary Records. — Washington's Writings, viii. ; Thacher's Military Journal; Colonel Tilghman's Diary, p. 103; Journal in Historical Magazine, March, 1864; Journal of William Feltman of the Pennsylvania line; Denny's Journal in Pennsylvania Historical Society's Memoirs, vii. ; papers in Almon's Remembrancer, xiii.

French Accounts. — Memoirs of Rochambeau, Ségur, and Dumas; De Fersen's Journal in the Magazine of American History, July, 1879; Chastellux's Travels. Robin's New Travels.

English Accounts. — Cornwallis's Correspondence. Cornwallis's letter to Clinton is in Robin's New Travels, App. Moore's Diary, ii. 512. A controversy between Cornwallis and Clinton gave rise to several pamphlets. Cf. Menzies's Catalogue, p. 79; and on this point see Ross's Cornwallis, i.

130; Jones's New York in the Revolutionary War, ii. 464, 466.

The return of Cornwallis to England gave occasion to Walpole to compare him as a general with the other British leaders.   Last Journals, ii. 499.

Stedman's American War.   Tarleton's Campaigns.   Simcoe's Queen's Rangers.   Robertson to Lord George Germain in Documents relative to the Colonial History of New York, viii. 814.

Correspondence and Articles of Capitulation.— Sparks's Washington, viii., App. No. 8.   Moore's Diary, ii. 508.   Ross's Cornwallis Correspondence, App.

Later Accounts. — Lee's Memoirs of the War, Force's edition.   Histories of the United States by Bancroft, x. ch. 35; Hamilton, ii. 263 ; Hildreth, iii. ch. 43 ; Ridpath, etc.   Lives of Washington by Marshall, iv. 472; Irving, iv. ch. 25, 26, and 28 ; and in the Recollections by Custis, ch. 6.   Lossing's Field-Book of the Revolution, ii. 508, and his Operations in Virginia Eighty Years Ago, in the Atlantic Monthly, June, 1862, also an article in Harper's Monthly, vii. 452.   Dawson's Battles of the United States.   Carrington's Battles of the Revolution, ch. 75.   Hollister's Connecticut, ii. ch. 18, etc.   J. E. Cooke's Virginia in the Revolution, in Harper's Monthly, June, 1876. Lives of Timothy Pickering, ch. 19 and 20 ; of Alexander Hamilton, by J. C. Hamilton, i. 384 ;

17

of Steuben, by Kapp, ch. 21; of Anthony Wayne; of Henry Knox, by Drake.

How the King received the news is told in Wraxall's Memoirs, 2d ed. ii. 108. Cf. Donne's Correspondence of George III. with Lord North, ii. 390. For the effect of the news in general: Walpole's Last Journals, ii. 474; Macknight's Burke, ii. 457; Annual Register, xxv.; Massey's England, i. 407; Parton's Franklin, ii. 448; Fitzmaurice's Life of Shelburne, iii. 123; Parliamentary History, xxii. 639, where the debate is given.

Maps. — The Political Magazine, Nov. 1781, has a contemporary map of the campaign, and a MS. one is in the Faden Collection. Hilliard d'Auberteuil's Essais, ii., gives a map of Virginia and Maryland; and a map by Fry and Jefferson, 1775, is No. 31 of the American Atlas. Sparks's Washington, viii. 158.

There was a French map of this part of Virginia published in Paris by Esnauts et Rapilly, and another of the Baie de Chesapeak, with a "plan de l'attaque." A German plan was made by Sotzman.

For the Siege. — Soulé's Histoire des Troubles de l'Amérique Anglaise, Paris, 1787. Gordon's History of the American War, iv. Ramsay's Revolution in South Carolina. Tarleton's Campaigns, ch. 7. Sparks's Washington, viii. 186. Atlases to Marshall's and Guizot's Washington.

Hamilton's Republic of the United States, ii. 263, following an English plan. Carrington's Battles, p. 646. Ridpath's United States. Faden issued in London, Oct. 7, 1785, a large plan of the siege, made by John Hills. That in Stedman's American War, ii. 412, is substantially the same with one published in London, March 1, 1787, but from a different plate.

Congress struck a medal in commemoration of the double surrenders of Yorktown and Saratoga, and it is described in Loubat's Medallic History of the United States. Cf. Sparks's Franklin, ix. 173.

For landmarks see Lossing's Field-Book, and Porte Crayon's Shrines of Old Virginia, in Lippincott's Magazine, April, 1879.

WINTER, 1781–1782.

The Situation.

THE French remained in Virginia. Parton's Jefferson, ch. 29. Washington went with the American troops to the Hudson. Sparks's Washington, viii., gives successive schemes of further concerted action with the French. Irving's Washington, iv. ch. 29 and 30. Kapp's Steuben, ch. 23. Lossing's Field-Book, ii. ch. 5. The question whether Washington was ever made a marshal of France has given rise to some dispute. See Historical Magazine, ii. 98 ; iii. etc. Potter's American Monthly, 1876, on Washington's order books. R. R. Livingston to the governors of the states on the next campaign in Diplomatic Correspondence, xi. 221. Reed's letter on the condition of affairs in Reed's Reed, ii. 371. Political movements, Rives's Madison, i. ch. 10.

EVENTS OF 1782–1783.

Various.

THOMAS PAINE was employed by Robert Morris, Feb. 1782, to sustain the action of Congress in the public prints. Diplomatic Correspondence, xii. 95. Sparks's Washington, viii. 345. Parton's Franklin, ii. 454. North American Review, No. 120, p. 40.

In general for the connection of Paine with the American Revolution, see lives of him by J. Cheetham, an English radical, and by G. Vale, somewhat sympathetic. In the Atlantic Monthly, for Nov., 1859, there is a paper on his first appearance in this country; for July, one on his second appearance, and in that for Dec., one on his career in England and France. M. A. Casey's Plea for a Patriot, in the Galaxy, xxi. Parton's Jefferson. Recollections of his residence in New York, in the New York City Manual, 1864. Potter's American Monthly, Feb. 1877. M. D. Conway in Fortnightly Review, March, 1879. Allibone, p. 1485, gives numerous minor references.

April, 1782. A plan to capture Prince William Henry, at this time in New York. Sparks's

Washington, viii. 262. Irving's Washington, iv. Historical Magazine, Feb. 1869, p. 130.

April, 1782. Loyalists hung in New Jersey a Capt. Huddy; and Capt. Asgill, a British officer and prisoner in the Americans' hands, was selected to suffer in retaliation. The case was one of perplexity to both Carleton and Washington. Diplomatic Correspondence, xi. 105, 128, 140. Sparks's Washington, i. 378; viii. 265, 301, 336, 361. Irving's Washington, iv. ch. 29. Correspondence of the Revolution, iii. Heath's Memoirs, p. 335. Franklin's Works, ix. 376. J. C. Hamilton's Republic, ii. 282. Political Magazine, iii. 472. Jones's New York in the Revolutionary War, ii. 232, 483.

May, 1782. Crawford's expedition against the Wyandottes on the Muskingum, near Sandusky, is the subject of a monograph by C. W. Butterfield, 1873.

The affairs of the loyalists on Long Island during 1782–1783. Ellis's Memoir of Count Rumford, 132, and Onderdonk's Queens, Suffolk, and Kings Counties.

June, 1783. The mutiny of troops in Pennsylvania and their insult to Congress. Rives's Madison, i. ch. 16; the histories of Pennsylvania; and W. P. Hazard's edition of Watson's Annals of Philadelphia and Pennsylvania, a book much improved over the original issue.

Fall of the North Ministry, March, 1782.

The tidings of Yorktown had reached London in November. Walpole's Last Journals, ii. The Life of Van Schaack, p. 267, gives the heads of debate in Parliament, Dec. 11, 1781. Cf. also Parliamentary History. On successive test questions the majority of the ministry gradually decreased. Parton (Franklin, ii. 452) describes the British intrigues in Jan. 1782, to alienate the allies.

Feb. 22, 1782. Gen. Conway's motion to put an end to the war was lost by one vote. Lyman's Diplomacy of the United States, i. 93. Walpole's Last Journals, ii. 505.

Feb. 28. Conway's renewed motion to put an end to the war prevailed, giving the first majority against the ministry. Debrett's Parliamentary Register, vi. 310–341. Walpole's Last Journals, ii. 509. Macknight's Burke, ii. 482.

March 28, 1782, Lord North resigned. Walpole's Last Journals, ii. 521. The condition of parties at this time is described in Bancroft, x. ch. 26. Cf. also for this period of the waning power of North, Donne's Correspondence of George III. with North, ii. 398, 429; Belsham's England, vii.; Stanhope's England, vii. 136 ; Massey's England, ii. 414 ; Adolphus's England; Pictorial History of England; Wraxall's Historical Memoirs, ii. 148; Cook's History of Party ; Russell's Memorials and Correspondence of Fox, i. 281; Russell's Life and Times of Fox, i. ch. 15; Fitzmaurice's Shelburne, iii. 129.

Negotiations for Peace, 1782.

Rockingham's demands of concessions by the King before he would consent to form a new cabinet, are given in Albemarle's Rockingham and his Contemporaries, ii. 452.

The party, late in opposition and now in power, was divided, Rockingham, the prime minister, being in favor of granting the United States their independence; but Shelburne, his colleague, represented the repugnance of Chatham to dismembering the monarchy. Albemarle's Rockingham, ii.; Fitzmaurice's Shelburne, iii. ch. 5, reviewed in Edinburgh Review, Jan. 1854, and in Quarterly Review, Jan. 1854. Sparks (Franklin, vii. 303) had copies of the Shelburne papers, then in Lord Lansdowne's hands, since used by Fitzmaurice. Russell's Memorials and Correspondence of Fox, i. 290, 294, and Life and Times of Fox, i. 281. Bancroft's United States, x. ch. 27 and 28.

July 1, 1782, Rockingham died. Walpole's Last Journals, ii. 544.

Meanwhile Sir Guy Carleton had arrived at New York to succeed Clinton, May, 1782, and had endeavored without success to open communication with Congress as commissioner of peace. Madison's Debates and Correspondence, i.; Rives's Madison, i. 331, 333.

On Rockingham's death Shelburne became prime minister, and Fox, representing the Rockingham party, divided the cabinet, and hoped to detach America from France, in treating through Grenville, his agent to Paris, while Shelburne sent Oswald in August on a similar mission, with the hope of inducing the acceptance of a plan for a separate parliament for America under the same king. Diplomatic Correspondence, iii. 373, 483; viii. 116; Sparks's Washington, viii. 328, 344; Rives's Madison, i. 336; Walpole's Last Journals, ii. 549, 583, and for Shelburne's character, unfavorably drawn, ii. 566, 623; Fitzmaurice's Shelburne, iii.; Stanhope's England, vii. ch. 66; Adolphus's England, iii. ch. 46–49; Belsham's England, vii. 325; Memoirs of the Court and Cabinet of George the Third; Russell's Memorials and Correspondence of Fox, i. 330, 343, 439, and Life and Times of Fox, i. 303; Life of John Adams, i. 362.

Congress had issued instructions to its Commissioners in Europe, June 15, 1781, Diplomatic Correspondence, x. 71; and again, Jan. 7, 1782, through Secretary Livingston, Diplomatic Correspondence, iii. 268, and Franklin's Works, ix. 128. See also, under 1781, " Political Aspects."

The proceedings of Congress, while the negotiations went on, are followed in their Journals; Madison's Writings, i. 61, 515; Rives's Madison, i. ch. 12; J. C. Hamilton's Republic, ii. ch. 31

and 34 ; Diplomatic Correspondence, *passim*. The Debates in Congress, Nov. 4, 1782, to June 21, 1783, are given in the Madison Papers, i. 187.

General summarized accounts of the negotiations are given in Bancroft's United States, x. ch. 26, 27, and 28 ; Sparks's Franklin, ch. 13 ; John Adams's Works, i. ch. 6 and 7 ; Pitkin's United States, ii. ch. 15 ; Marshall's Washington, iv. ch. 11 ; Knight's Popular History of England, vi. ch. 29 ; Hildreth's United States, iii. ch. 43 ; Greene's Historical View of the American Revolution. A tory view is taken in Jones's New York in the Revolutionary War, ii. 487, 491.

A correspondence had been opened between Franklin and Shelburne during the Rockingham administration. Bancroft, x. 535, and Lives of Franklin. Oswald had had an interview with Franklin April 16, 1782, and Franklin conducted the negotiations for some months alone. Franklin's Works, ix. 118 ; and for his journal of the negotiations, March 21 to July 1, 1782, Works, ix. 238–350. This journal is also in Bigelow's Franklin, iii. 66, and in the Diplomatic Correspondence, iii. 376, and many of Franklin's letters are in the same volume. Franklin's "Notes for Conversation " with Oswald are in Works, and in Parton's Life of Franklin, ii. 458. Franklin's unpopularity in England has sprung partly from what was felt to be his excessive care for the interests of America in his conduct of these negotiations. Cf.

Thomas Hughes in the Contemporary Review, 1879, or No. 1833, Living Age, p. 298. Jay came from Spain to Paris, June 23, 1782, and introduced his suspicions both of Great Britain's sincerity and France's purposes into the conduct of affairs. Diplomatic Correspondence, viii. 126, 128, 129, 163. Sparks's Franklin, i. 495; Parton's Franklin, ii. 476, 479. Madison's Debates and Correspondence, i. 518. Rives's Madison, i. 356, and App. D. Bancroft's United States, x. 559. J. C. Hamilton's Republic, ii. 476. Jay's Life of John Jay, i. ch. 6, assumes his suspicions to be well founded, and in Sparks's opinion needs to be read with caution. Sparks (Franklin, ix. 452) alleges the groundlessness of Jay's suspicions of the French ministry. Flanders's Life of Jay, ch. 12. Cf. C. F. Adams's Life of John Adams, i. 357, for a note on British secret agents near the American Commissioners. Arthur Lee at this time was holding opinions regarding the French alliance which excited suspicion. Rives's Madison, i. 340.

John Adams, meanwhile, though the head of the Commission, had been successfully achieving treaties with Holland, one acknowledging the Independence of America, April 19, 1782, and the other of commerce, etc., Oct. 8, 1782. Medals commemorating these are engraved in John Adams's Works, vii. and viii. For the progress and results, see John Adams's Works, i. 347, etc.;

iii. for Diary; vii. 501, for official correspondence; Bancroft, x. ch. 26; Lyman's Diplomacy
of the United States, i. ch. 3; Treaties and Conventions of the United States, 1871, p. 607.

The Holland mission accomplished, Adams,
Oct. 26th, joined Franklin and Jay in Paris, and
his letter to Livingston, Oct. 31, 1782, opens his
official correspondence. Works, vii. 652, continued in viii. Cf. his Life in vol. i. ch. 6 and 7;
his Diary, in iii. 300. Diplomatic Correspondence, vi. and vii., with extracts from his diary.
Parton's Franklin, ii. 486.

Laurens, released from the Tower (Madison's
Debates, etc., i. 175; Rives's Madison, 346; Parton's Franklin, ii. 404), joined the other Commissioners in Paris later. Diplomatic Correspondence, ii.

The negotiations were continued with the British agents, without the privity of Vergennes, and
directly in contravention of the instructions which
had been given by Congress. This was the result of the suspicions of Jay, now strengthened
by Adams's views, and helped by an intercepted
letter of Marbois, the French secretary of legation at Philadelphia, which the British agents
produced. The letter is given in Pitkin's United
States, ii. 528. Cf. John Adams's Works, i.,
App. D.; and i. 392, for Adams's views of the
policy of the French cabinet; and viii. p. 11,
for his views of his instructions. Flassan's Dip-

lomatie Française, vi. The whole course of the diplomatic relations with France is summarized in J. C. Hamilton's Republic, ii. ch. 32.

Conclusions were easily reached but upon three points : —

Boundaries. — The French proposal for dividing North America between the United States, Spain, and Great Britain is given in Fitzmaurice's Shelburne, iii. 170. A map showing the northern boundary as proposed by Oswald in Oct. and Nov. 1782, respectively, is given by Fitzmaurice, iii. 294, who says that the map with the line finally determined under the Ashburton treaty, 1842, is in the King's Collection in the British Museum. The original map is lost, and this loss led to the disputes, settled by that treaty. On p. 324 there is a copy of the official map, showing the rival claims for the boundary of Maine, with the line finally fixed in 1842, and a note on the two maps bearing upon the question. Cf. John Adams's Works, i. 377, and App. C. on the Maine boundary. A statement of the American view by Charles Sumner was circulated in England in 1839, and printed in the Boston Courier June 4, 1839. For a history of the dispute see Daniel Webster's Works, vol. i. p. cxxi; vol. v. 78; vi. 270; Gallatin's Memoir on the North Eastern Boundary, with map, New York, 1843, and the public documents of Great Britain and the United States.

The earliest map of the United States, as such,

with bounds defined according to the treaty of 1783, was published April 3, 1783, by John Wallis, London, and is fac-similed in Jones's New York in the Revolutionary War, ii. 313. Maps showing the bounds as fixed by the treaty were published at once in Philadelphia by Pursell, in Paris by Lattre, in Germany by Güssefeld, and in Amsterdam "d'apres Mr. Bonne." See also Political Magazine, Feb. 1783; Andrews's History of the War, etc. Gen. Chamberlain's Maine, Her Place in History, has a map showing the bounds of 1783 and the subsequent growth of the territorial limits.

The British had advanced claims as far west as the Penobscot and even the Kennebec, and to the territory south of the great lakes, under the terms of the Quebec Act, passed at the beginning of the troubles, but they were abandoned.

The whole question of the cession by Virginia of the northwest territory, and of the rival claims of other states and of land companies, as affecting the question of boundary, is gone over in Rives's Life of Madison, i. ch. 15. Cf. Journals of Congress; Madison's Debates and Correspondence, ii.; Thomas Paine's Public Good, an argument against the claims of Virginia; Histories of Virginia and of the northwestern states.

The question of the bounds and independence of Vermont has already been referred to under 1778. Congress was again engaged with the

subject during the period now under considera-
tion. Madison's Debates and Correspondence, i.
Rives's Madison, i. 465. Ira Allen's Political
History of Vermont. Stone's Life of Brant, ii.
199.

The Fisheries. — For the right to take fish
on the banks of Newfoundland, etc., see John
Adams's Works, i. 380 ; iii. 328 ; J. C. Hamilton's
Republic, ii. 482 ; Sabine's Report on American
Fisheries ; Wells's Samuel Adams, iii. 150.

The Loyalists. — The British agents endeavored
long to make the United States, rather than their
own government, indemnify the loyalists for
sacrifices ; but Franklin's intimation that an equi-
table equivalent would be the British indemnifi-
cation for ravages by their troops, stayed the claim.
Wilmot's Historical View of the Commission for
inquiry into the losses, services, and claims of the
American loyalists. Sabine's American Loyalists,
ch. 10 and 11. Jones's New York in the Revolutionary War, ii. 237, has a tory view, and in ii.
510, is given the New York act of forfeiture, in
1779. Franklin's Works, ix. 426. Wells's Samuel Adams, iii. 182.

The condition of the negotiations were somewhat affected by the political situation of Ireland.
Bancroft, x. John Adams's Works, i. 379. Memoirs of the Court and Cabinet of George the
Third, i. 66–136. Also by Rodney's defeat of De

Grasse and the French fleet in the West Indies.
Bancroft, x. ch. 27. James's and other histories
of the British navy. The Age of Pitt and Fox,
App., London, 1846.

Nov. 30, 1782, the provisional treaty was signed
at Paris. Lyman's Diplomacy of the United
States, i. ch. 4. Bancroft's United States, x. 59.
Hildreth, iii. ch. 45. Irving's Washington, iv. ch.
32. Treaties and Conventions of the United
States, 1871, p. 309. Stanhope's England, vi.
Diplomatic Correspondence, x. 109, 115. Austin's
Gerry, ch. 24. The Commissioners addressed Secretary Livingston concerning this preliminary
treaty. John Adams's Works, viii. 18. This
dispatch was laid before Congress March 12, 1783,
and for the views of Congress on the Commissioners' proceeding without the knowledge of the
French Court, see Rives's Madison, i. 352; J. C.
Hamilton's Republic, ii. 488; Journals of Congress.

Vergennes addressed Luzerne in Philadelphia
in deprecation of the want of confidence shown.
Sparks's Franklin, i. ch. 14; ix. 452. Livingston
sent a reproving letter to the Commissioners. Diplomatic Correspondence, x. 129; Rives's Madison, i. 372. Several drafts of a Reply are given
in John Adams's Works, i. App. F.; also see i. p.
375, and viii. 87, and Franklin's Works, ix. 532.

There is a correspondence of Jay and J. Q.
Adams on the treaty in the Magazine of American
History, Jan. 1879.

The story sometimes repeated, that Franklin at the signing wore the identical suit of Manchester velvet in which he was dressed when he was insulted at the Privy Council, is discredited. Sparks's Franklin, p. 488. Concerning the history of a portrait of Franklin, painted by Greuze, and given by Franklin to Oswald, and now in the Boston Public Library, see the Report of that library for 1872, App., with memorandum by Charles Sumner.

Jan. 20, 1783. The provisional treaty between Great Britain and France signed at Paris. Sparks's Washington, viii. 407, and the histories of England.

The provisional treaty of Nov. 30, 1782, was assailed in Parliament, and was one of the causes of the dissolution of the Shelburne ministry. Van Schaack's Life and Letters. David Hartley succeeded Oswald in the further negotiations for the definitive treaty. Rives's Madison, i. 497. John Adams's Works, viii. 78. Eight or nine months of fruitless diplomacy resulted in the terms of the provisional treaty being exactly agreed upon for the definitive treaty, signed Sept. 3, 1783. Congress ratified it Jan. 14, 1784; the King, April 9th; and Franklin notified Congress, May 13th. Works, x. 87, 95, 96. The treaty is given in Jones's New York in the Revolutionary War, ii. 664.

The Newburgh Addresses, March, 1783.

In Dec. 1782, the army had made representations to Congress, setting forth its sufferings from want of pay. Journals of Congress, iv. 206. Madison's Debates and Correspondence, i. 256. Rives's Life of Madison, i. 383.

Nothing satisfactory coming of this appeal, a movement of uncertain extent to demand of Congress a redress of grievances manifested itself in anonymous addresses to the army, calling for a meeting, and written, as afterwards acknowledged, by Maj. Armstrong, of Gates's staff. Hasty action was prevented by Washington's interposition. The original autograph of his address is in the cabinet of the Massachusetts Historical Society, and a fac-simile of it was issued by that society in 1876. The addresses, as written by Armstrong, are given in Sparks's Washington, viii. 551. More or less extended accounts of the proceedings incident to this attempt to coerce the civil by the military power will be found in Pickering's Life of Timothy Pickering, i. ch. 29, 30, and 31; Sparks's Washington, viii. 369, 393, 551; Marshall's Washington, iv. 587; Irving's Washington, iv. ch. 31; Rives's Madison, i. 392; Quincy's Life of Shaw, 101; J. C. Hamilton's Republic, ii. 365, 385, and his Life of Alexander Hamilton, ii. 68; Hildreth's United States, iii. ch. 45; Dunlap's New York, ii. 230; Journals of Congress, iv. 213.

Hostilities Cease, 1783.

Meanwhile, April 19, 1783, a publication of the cessation of hostilities was made in the camp at Newburgh. Sparks's Washington, viii. 425, and App. 13. Heath's Memoirs. Madison's Debates, etc., i. 437. Diplomatic Correspondence, ii. 319–329; x. 121; xi. 320.

On Washington's headquarters at Newburgh, see Lossing's Field-Book, and J. T. Headley in Galaxy, xxii.

May, 1783. The Society of the Cincinnati formed among the officers of the army. Kapp's Steuben, ch. 26. Heath's Memoirs, p. 381. Pennsylvania Historical Society's Memoirs, vi. Winthrop Sargent in the North American Review, Oct. 1853. Loring's Hundred Boston Orators, p. 184. The scheme was not approved by many. Wells's Samuel Adams, iii. 202. Austin's Gerry, ch. 25. Franklin's Works, x. 58. Chief among the tracts in opposition was Cassius's (Judge Burke of South Carolina) Considerations on the Society or Order of Cincinnati, 1783. The original Institution and Proceedings were printed at Boston, 1812. There have been various minor publications about the society, and there is an extensive History of the Massachusetts Society by F. S. Drake.

June 8, 1783. The circular letter of Washington to the governors of the states, taking leave of

them and expressing hopes for the future, is in
Sparks's Washington, viii. 439. Irving's Washington, iv. 394.

Oct. 18, 1783.   Proclamation disbanding the
army.

Nov. 2, 1783.   Washington's Farewell Address.
Sparks's Washington, viii. 491. Irving's Washington, iv. 402.

Nov. 25, 1783.   New York evacuated by the
British. Irving's Washington, iv. ch. 33. New.
York during the Revolution, New York, 1861.
Jones's New York in the Revolutionary War, ii.
504.   Histories of the City of New York.

Maps of the city at this time are in Moore's
Diary, ii. 498; Political Magazine, 1781; Dunlap's
New York, i.

Dec. 4, 1783.   Washington parts with his officers in New York.   Lives of Washington by
Marshall and Irving.

In Philadelphia, Washington deposited his accounts during the war, 1775–1783, in his own
hand,— a document now in the Treasury Department at Washington. A fac-simile of the MS
was published in 1837.

Dec. 23, 1783.   Washington resigned his commission to Congress at Annapolis. Sparks's Washington, viii. 504, and App. 14. Marshall's Washington, iv. 622.

An account of John Gray of Mount Vernon,
the last soldier of the Revolution, by J. M. Dal-
zell, was printed at Washington, 1868.

GENERAL RECORDS OF THE WAR.

Explanation.

IN the previous sections of this Handbook, special points of the conflict, arranged approximately in a chronological order, are illustrated by references to monographs, more or less confined in scope, and to parts of more general works. It seems convenient to add a survey of the principal works covering the whole period, and to indicate a few of the lesser ones, as typical; and also to mark some of the chief sources of contemporary information, comprehensive in their character.

American Contemporary Records.

The Journals of Congress begin Sept. 1774. Henry Armitt Brown delivered, in 1874, a centennial oration on the anniversary of the meeting of this Congress. The first volume of the Journals goes through 1775. After that there was a volume each year through the struggle. The volume for 1774–1775 was reprinted by Almon in London, 1775.

The Secret Journals of Congress begin 1775, when the Committee of Secret Correspondence began to communicate with agents in Europe, and the title of this committee was changed to the Committee of Foreign Affairs, April 17, 1777. These Secret Journals are concerned with their proceedings down to the close of the war. G. W. Greene says: " In using the Journals of Congress, I have constantly had occasion to regret the awkward separation of the Secret·Journals from the main collection, and the want of a new edition based upon an accurate collation of the original manuscript, and completed by the insertion of the fragments of debates and speeches scattered through the works of Adams, Jefferson, Gouverneur Morris, and other members of that body." These Journals — contemporaneous edition, 13 vols., and the reprint of 1823, 4 vols. — are but a selection from the originals preserved in the Department of State. There is a chapter on the Congress of the Revolution, and another on its relations to the states, in G. W. Greene's Historical View; and perhaps the best account of Congress from 1780 to the close of the war is found in Rives's Life of Madison, i.

The letters that passed between the officers or committees of Congress and its agents and ministers abroad are contained in the Diplomatic Correspondence of the American Revolution, 12 volumes, 1829–1830, edited by Sparks. After Aug. 10, 1781, the correspondence on the part of Congress was transferred to R. R. Livingston, the first Secretary of Foreign Affairs. Sparks used this publication of the government sometimes as a medium through his notes of his own arguments and inferences, for which he has been criticised.

Cf. North American Review, xxxii. on the Diplomatic Correspondence by Edward Everett; and xlvi. by George Bancroft, and xcii. by G. W. Greene, on the Documentary History; also the latter's Diplomacy of the Revolution in his Historical View, p. 173.

Washington's official letters had first been printed in Boston, New York, and London, 1795–1796, but Jared Sparks, in 1827, issued a pamphlet describing the papers of Washington (cf. Bancroft, ix. preface, p. 5.), and proposed a plan of publication of them; and between 1834 and 1837 he published the Life and Writings of Washington, 12 vols.,— an authority of the highest importance. Sparks's labors were great and extremely valuable, though his method of editing, in rectifying and dignifying language not originally intended for publication, has been censured by Lord Mahon (Earl Stanhope) and others, in 1851. In his own defense Sparks published pamphlets in 1852 and 1853. It was shown that much of the alleged tampering followed the language of Washington's letter books, which differed from the letters actually sent, and these last at the time were not accessible to Sparks, but the differences were made apparent on the publication of W. B. Reed's

Life of Joseph Reed, in 1847, where Washington's letters as sent were printed. In 1852 W. B. Reed reprinted the letters in dispute with marginal references, showing Sparks's omissions and changes and his own. Stanhope, after Sparks's explanation, gave his final views in the Appendix of History of England, vol. vi.

Cf. Allibone's Dictionary, iii. 1203 and 2596, for reference to spurious Letters of Gen. Washington to his Friends, 1776, published in London, and afterwards forming a part of Washington's Epistles, etc., New York, 1796.

In 1854 Sparks edited the Correspondence of the American Revolution, 4 vols., being chiefly letters addressed to Washington during the war, and a necessary complement to the letters of Washington. He says in the preface, in pursuance of his plan of editing, and after his controversy with Mahon: "Errors of grammar and obvious blunders, the result of hasty composition, have been corrected."

The measure of Sparks's labors for the history of the Revolution is taken in the Memoir of him, prepared by George E. Ellis, D. D., for the Proceedings of the Massachusetts Historical Society. Cf. also Historical Magazine, May, 1866, and the references in Allibone, iii. Col. Henry Whiting collected Washington's orders, 1778, 1780-1782, from the papers of his father, John Whiting, and published them, 1844. Inedited letters of Washington have been printed in various places, — Magazine of American History, Feb. 1879 ; Catholic World, Nov. 1867 (to Chastellux), etc.

In 1830 the late Col. Peter Force projected a documentary history of America from 1492 to 1789. In 1833 Congress ordered the publication of such portion of the American Archives as constituted series 4th and 5th of Col. Force's plan, covering 1774–1783. The 4th series as printed embraced the interval, March 7, 1774, to July 4, 1776, 6 vols. folio; and of the 5th series only 3 vols. ending with Dec. 1776, were printed, Congress ceasing to vote appropriations for it. The print showed a literal following of even obvious errors in the originals. In 1867 the library of books and manuscripts which Force had collected was purchased for the Library of Congress. A report of the Librarian of Congress (46th Congress, 1st session, Senate Misc. Doc. No. 34 — May 15, 1879) represents the manuscript material, 1776–1789 still unprinted as covering 230,000 foolscap pages, enough to make 30 volumes, matching those already printed. The librarian thinks it desirable to print it with " careful omissions and additions." The volumes as printed take a very wide scope in selection from contemporary printed records and manuscripts; but the indexes to each volume are very inadequate and inconsistent.

Niles's Principles and Acts of the Revolution

is a gathering of contemporary opinions and doings, without chronological arrangement, but with an index. It was reprinted in 1876.

Recitals of transactions and illustrations of views and manners will be found in the Diary of the American Revolution, a daily record, consisting of excerpts from the public prints and other original sources, compiled by Frank Moore, to which may be added the same compiler's Songs and Ballads of the American Revolution, and W. Sargent's Loyalist Poetry of the Revolution.

Thacher's Military Journal during the American Revolutionary War gives the experiences and observations of a surgeon.

The Familiar Letters of John Adams and his wife, Abigail Adams, with a memoir of Mrs. Adams, by Charles Francis Adams, give a picture of the feelings of the time, with glimpses of events, that is of extreme value. Other similar illustrations will be found in H. E. Scudder's Men and Manners in America One Hundred Years Ago. Cf. Mrs. Ellet's Domestic History of the American Revolution.

The newspapers of the day are of the first importance, and for the early stage of the conflict they are carefully used in Frothingham's Rise of the Republic, and Moore in his Diary of the American Revolution constantly gives extracts from them. The principal ones of New England are named on p. 7 of this Handbook, and others can be enumerated from the references of Frothingham and Moore. Rivington published in New York the principal paper in the British interest, known as The Gazetteer, 1773–1775, and as the Loyal and then Royal Gazette, after 1777. Hudson's Journalism in the United States. Buckingham's Specimens of Newspaper Literature. Sabine's American Loyalists, 2d ed. ch. 5 of introduction. Jones's New York in the Revolutionary War, i. 561.

The contemporary utterances of the pulpit are traced in Thornton's Pulpit of the Revolution, and in The Patriot Preachers of the Revolution. Cf. Sprague's Annals of the American Pulpit. J. T. Headley's Chaplains and Clergy of the Revolution.

A controversy was conducted in the Historical Magazine by H. B. Dawson and others, about the disloyalty of the Methodists during the war. Cf. the numbers for 1867, May, June, Sept. and Dec.

For the effect and traces of the eloquence of the time, see the lives of Patrick Henry and the other leaders; E. L. Magoon's Orators of the American Revolution; Frank Moore's American Eloquence; Rufus Choate's Address on the Eloquence of the Revolution. An account of the various conventions during the war is given in Jameson's Constitutional Convention.

Joseph M. Toner printed in 1876 the Medical Men of the Revolution, with a brief history of the medical department of the Continental army, containing the names of nearly 1,200 physicians.

Bancroft, in his prefaces, vols. vi., ix., and x., indicates the chief manuscript sources, public and private, in this country and in England and on the Continent, upon which he depends. He says of the military MSS. which he procured from Germany : " that they are, in the main, the most impartial of all which have been preserved." The Papers of Gov. Hutchinson of Massachusetts, Gov. Trumbull of Connecticut, of Gen. Heath, and of John Hancock, are in the Massachusetts Historical Society's Cabinet. The papers of Horatio Gates and Baron Steuben are in the New York Historical Society's Cabinet; those of Gen. Knox are in the library of the New England Historic Genealogical Society ; those of Hopkins and Foster in the Rhode Island Historical Society's library ; those of Arthur and Richard Henry Lee are divided between the libraries of Harvard College, American Philosophical Society in Philadelphia, and the University of Virginia ; those, both originals and copies, gathered by Sparks, are in Harvard College Library. The Journals of Gen. Henry Dearborn are in the Boston Public Library.

There is also a large mass of papers in the government archives, in those of the original states, and in the Force Collection in the Library of Congress.

The lives of John Adams, Samuel Adams, Thomas Jefferson, James Madison, Joseph Reed, Alexander Hamilton, Timothy Pickering, Generals Greene, Sullivan, Wayne, and other actors in the struggle, are based upon papers still preserved. The prefaces of such lives usually describe these collections. Other manuscripts have been mentioned in previous pages.

British Contemporary Records.

A Calendar of the Journals of the Lords was published in London in 1810; and general indexes of the Journals of the Lords, before 1779, and after 1780, were printed respectively in 1817 and 1832; and of the Journals of the Commons, covering 1714–1774, and 1774–1790, respectively in 1778 and 1796.

The Parliamentary Register, beginning 1774, was printed in London, 1775, and continued yearly till 1779.

Almon's Remembrancer was begun in London, June 15, 1775, but the second edition of the first volume of the Remembrancer has preliminary matter not contained in the earlier issue. Its purpose was to gather from English and American sources the fugitive and contemporary accounts of transactions, remembering chiefly, says Smyth, " such letters, speeches, and publications as serve to display the injustice of the design and the folly of the councils of Great Britain."

The Gentleman's Magazine, London Magazine, and other periodic publications of the day follow the current of events and variations of opinion, and the official reports of the officers in the field, when gazetted in London, were often reproduced in them. "Publications like these," says Prof. Smyth, lecture 26, "give the manners and opinions living as they rise, and seem to have been the precursors of the more ample and regular Annual Register."

Early American Histories.

There was printed in Boston, 1781–1785, An Impartial History of the War in America in three sections, which is in part a reprint of a work with a similar title, published in London in 1780, but with large alterations and additions to adapt it to the American public, and with a different appendix.

The Rev. Wm. Gordon, an Englishman, came to New England in 1770, and was settled at Roxbury, Mass., and beginning to collect material as early as 1777 (John Adams's Works, ix. 461), he returned to England after the peace, and published in London, in 1788, his History of the Rise, Progress, and Establishment of the Independence of the United States, 4 vols., a somewhat minute chronicle, and impartial in the distribution of praise and blame. He is thought not to have admitted some statements for fear of persecution in

England. Bancroft, ix. 123, says that, "notwithstanding its faults, it is invaluable, but is by no means free from tales that on examination are found untrustworthy." C. F. Adams says it has " a great deal of value with difficulty to be found in any other quarter." W. B. Reed, Life of Joseph Reed, i. 240, calls it " ponderous, curious, and ill-digested ; " and says the author had " access to much that was authentic, but made strange and often mischievous use of it," making his work " quite as much a British as an American version." Smyth praises him for his impartiality. See an account of Gordon and his history by J. S. Loring in the Historical Magazine, Feb. and March, 1862.

In 1790, Ramsay, a South Carolinian, published his History of the American Revolution, more concisely written than Gordon, and held to be superior to Gordon by Smyth.

A small History of the American Revolution, by John Lendrum, was printed in Boston, in 1795 ; and a History of the British Empire, 1765–1783, covering the war, was prepared by a "society of gentlemen," and printed in Philadelphia in 1798. A compiled Historical Journal of the · American War is given in the second volume of the Massachusetts Historical Society's Collections.

Mrs. Mercy Warren's History of the Revolutionary War, printed in 1805, is of interest as a reflex of intelligent comment by a contemporary, and intimate friend of leading patriots. She had differences with John Adams regarding the estimate to be put on some of them, and their correspondence on these points has been printed in the Collections of the Massachusetts Historical Society, 5th series, iv.

Early British Histories.

Erskine May says, "No part of English history has received more copious illustration than the revolt of the American colonies."

Capt. Hall's Civil War in America, 1780, never reached a second volume, and the first ends with 1777.

The continued narrative in successive volumes of the Annual Register, beginning with vol. xix., will show the course of British feeling, and these accounts are largely embodied in An Impartial History of the War in America, to 1779, published in London in 1780. The sections in the Annual Register are usually ascribed to Edmund Burke, and they were made into A Concise History of the Late War in America, published in the Columbian Magazine, in 1789, and separately in 1790. Cf. Wells's Samuel Adams, iii. 41.

Contemporary impressions, with the usual inaccuracies of hurriedly compiled histories, are found in Murray's War in America, 1778, and in Andrews's History of the Late War, 1785–1786.

Thomas Jones, a justice of the Supreme Court

of the Province of New York, and a loyalist, living on Long Island during part of the war within the British lines, and for another portion a prisoner in Connecticut, wrote in England, just after the close of the war, a History of New York in the Revolutionary War, which is largely, however, a history of the conflict generally. It remained in MS., and had never been used by any historical writer when it was first printed, in 1879, by the New York Historical Society, in two large octavos, edited with extensive notes by E. F. De Lancey. It is a valuable contribution to a history of the war from a side which has not yielded much of its kind, representing the common hearsay accounts at the time of many important transactions. The writer divides his condemnation in nearly equal proportions between the "rebels" and the ministry with their soldiers. The loyalists in his narrative are represented as abused by both. Simcoe's Journal of the Queen's Rangers was privately printed in 1787, and reprinted in New York in 1843. It begins after the battle of Brandywine in 1777.

The chief contemporary British authority is Stedman's History of the American War, 1794, a valuable record by an intelligent eye-witness, the author serving under General Howe, but having little faith in him as a general. Stedman is, however, of no authority in matters not military.

It has been asserted that his work was written by Dr. William Thomson.

Later American Histories.

Dr. Abiel Holmes's American Annals, 1492–1805, published 1805, and improved and continued to 1826 in 1829. It is a careful chronological arrangement of events, with references to authorities, and of importance in its day and still useful.

A History of the American Revolution of little value was published in Baltimore in 1822, purporting to be by Paul Allen, but said to be in great part by John Neal.

Timothy Pitkin of Connecticut published in 1828 a Political and Civil History of the United States, 1763–1797, two volumes, which Sparks calls a first attempt to disconnect political events from the military operations.

James Grahame's History of the United States comes down only to the Declaration of Independence. Originally published in 1836, it was re-issued in this country in 1845, under the supervision of Josiah Quincy, who was furnished with the MS. emendations left by the author. It is a well-sustained work by an ardent admirer of American principles.

As coming after much had been wrought by others, and as having had access to materials of the highest importance, particularly as regards the European relations of the contest, the volumes of Bancroft's History of the United States, covering the war, constitute the chief authoritative general narrative. Bancroft is controverted on points, but such have been mentioned in the progress of these notes. The original issue of this work, coming out between 1834 and 1875, makes ten volumes, of which vols. vii. to x. cover the Revolution. The plates of the several volumes have undergone correction and revision, and sets may not wholly correspond. In 1876 he reissued the whole in a revised centennial edition in six volumes, but this edition does not supersede the original work.

Lossing's Field-Book of the Revolution takes up the events, not in chronological sequence, but as they arose in his travels through the country in search of anecdotes and memorials of the contests, and he gives particular interest to the landscape and landmarks, in connection with their Revolutionary associations.

Col. Carrington's Battles of the American Revolution is a history applying the principles of military criticism ; and Dawson's Battles of the United States often gives the contemporary official accounts.

Mention can be made of only a few of the less distinctive or more condensed and popular general accounts. Hildreth's United States for the events of the war is too much summarized for any but those wishing a mere abstract of military events. Ridpath's United States is a convenient summary, with maps. The histories of the United States by J. H. Patton, Tucker, and J. A. Spencer; Mrs. A. S. Richardson's History of Our Country; C. E. Lester's Our First Hundred Years, — all are intended in one way or another to supply popular wants. C. C. Coffin's Boys of '76 offers the general reader a convenient gathering of plans of the various battles. Headley's Washington and his Generals was popular thirty years ago as a somewhat spirited portrayal of personal characteristics. Abbott's Paragraph History is an outline, something like an amplified contents-table of an éxtended history.

Later British Histories.

Belsham's Memoirs of the Reign of George the Third, 1760–1793, was published 1795–1801, and was afterwards embodied in his History of Great Britain, 1806. He espouses the side of the colonists, and Smyth considers him far more reasonable than Adolphus, whose History of England, 1760–1783, was published in 1802. Adolphus defends the king's ministers, and Smyth says that he very fairly puts the reader in possession of the opposing views of Chatham.

Beatson's Naval and Military Memoirs of Great Britain, 1804.

These early narratives, however, are largely followed by the later British historians. Earl Stanhope (Mahon), in his History of England, vol. vi., is not so favorable to the colonists as Massey, in his History, vol. ii. Cf. Reviews of Mahon in North American Review, July, 1852 (by J. G. Palfrey), and Jan. 1855. The account of the Reign of George III., in the Pictorial History of England, has a strong tory leaning. Knight's Popular History of England will show the average British views of recent days.

There are six lectures on the American war at the close of Smyth's Modern History, which express the better British feeling of sixty years ago, and they are accompanied by some advice on the best methods of studying the period. In treating of the preliminaries of the war he relies largely upon the debates in Parliament.

Sparks, in 1841, said of Smyth: "It would be difficult to find any treatise on the American Revolution confined within the compass of six lectures from which so much can be learned, or so accurate an estimate of the merits of both sides of the question can be formed."

There are very brief statements regarding the part borne by the various British regiments in the series of the Regimental Historical Records.

Of the less important British histories covering the war, mention may be made of Chalmers's Revolt of the American Colonies, for its legal bearing ; Bartlett's and Woodward's History of the United States, a pictorial record distinctively ; Mackay's United States ; the convenient and graphic summary, Ludlow's War of American Independence, in the Epochs of Modern History Series ; Tancock's England during the American and European Wars, 1765–1820, in the Epochs of English History series ; and popular histories by Cassell and others.

Green, in his Short History of the English People, says: " The two sides of the American quarrel have been told with the purpose of fairness and truthfulness, though with a very different bias, by Lord Stanhope and by Bancroft. The latter is by far the more detailed and picturesque ; the former, perhaps, the cooler and more impartial."

French and Italian Histories.

Various histories of the war were published in France, most of little value, except as reflecting incidentally the French sentiments, — such as Leboucher's Histoire de la Guerre de l'Indépendance des États Unis, which gives maps of the northern and southern colonies.

Sparks, however, Washington's Writings, viii. 135, says of Soulé's Histoire des Troubles de l'Amérique Anglaise, that it is " the best written and most authentic in the French language. The author had access to public documents, but all the particulars relating to the operations of Rochambeau's army are taken almost word for word from a narrative which had been drawn up by Rochambeau, and which was afterwards published as a part of his Mémoires. A large portion of Soulé's book was read in manuscript by Rochambeau and the Minister of War."

There is a paper on the French in the American Revolution in the Revue Militaire Française for 1870, ii. ; and various French narratives are mentioned in connection with the record of their participation in the war in previous pages. A list of French officers, appointed to the army by Congress, is given in Hilliard d'Auberteuil's Essais historiques, and is reprinted in the Magazine of American History, June, 1879.

An Italian, Botta, published in 1809 what was long accounted the best History of the American Revolution. Jefferson called it the best yet written in his day, but took exception to the speeches, which, after the manner of the ancients, are put into the actors' mouths. Bancroft styles it admirable. It was translated into English by G. W. Otis, of Boston, and is reviewed in the North American Review, xiii., by F. C. Gray.

A French translation of it appeared, with an introduction, in which the papers of Gerard, the French minister to Congress, had been used.

There was published in Genoa in 1879, under the editing of G. Colucci, the official correspondence of the Genoese ambassador in London during the American Revolution, — I Casi della Guerra per l'Indipendenza d'America, two volumes, — with an extended preface on the thirteen colonies. These dispatches, written by Francesco Ageno, begin in 1770 and end in Dec. 1780.

Biographies.

Most of the lives of the principal actors, covering but their personal experiences, can hardly be classed as general works, but from his position Washington has given his biographers grounds for making their works in large part extended narratives of the war.

In 1805 Marshall brought out his Life of Washington, and he had peculiar advantages in the use of Washington's papers, as well as from a personal knowledge of him, and by reason of his own participation in the conflict. He gave a sedate and trustworthy character to his work, which renders it still of prime interest, notwithstanding later developments, and notwithstanding a treatment of the subject that to some will appear dull. It was originally issued in five volumes, both quarto and octavo, and was reissued in 1832 in two volumes, without the introduction or colonial history.

Sparks's Life of Washington, making vol. 1 of Washington's Writings, and published also separately, is of excellent reputation for accuracy. Cf. Allibone's references to reviews of it in his Dictionary, iii. 2192. Guizot translated and condensed Sparks's twelve volumes into six, 1839–1840, and furnished a succinct and judicious introductory sketch, which preceded a life by De Witt, and which has also been printed separately as his Vie de Washington. C. W. Upham made up an Autobiography of Washington by detaching extracts from his writings, which has been successful in England, though the publication of it was stopped in this country, as infringing the copyright of Sparks. The most popular of the lives of Washington, however, is Irving's, which is gracefully written and shows respectable research.

Of the less important lives, reference may be made to those by Aaron Bancroft, Ramsay, Paulding, Mrs. Kirkland, Lossing, Headley, etc. The life by M. L. Weems was very popular at the beginning of this century, but it was worked up by a shrewd book-agent to insure a sensational popularity. Cf. Parton in the Magazine of American History, Aug. 1879, on the True and Traditional Washington. Of more condensed expression, see the addresses of Everett, Webster, Winthrop, etc., and the essays by Theodore Parker in his Historic Americans; by E. P. Whipple on Washington and the Principles of the Revolution, etc. Edward Everett wrote a condensed life for the Encyclopædia Britannica, which was published separately as a Life of Washington.

Cf. his Mount Vernon Papers, and the address which he delivered so widely in aid of the purchase of Mount Vernon. He tells the story of this address in the Massachusetts Historical Society's Proceedings, June, 1858. Lossing has a paper on Washington's Life-guard in the Historical Magazine, May, 1858.

Alexander Hamilton, as for a period one of Washington's military family, and as the exponent of marked views in administration and finance, is made the central figure of his son, J. C. Hamilton's History of the Republic of the United States, as traced in the Writings of Hamilton and his Contemporaries. This work has met hostile criticism from its attacks on the characters of the Adamses, Joseph Reed, Madison, etc., and from the obtrusiveness of the author's assumption that all papers, preserved in Hamilton's hand, but signed by Washington, were the work of the secretary. Cf. W. B. Reed's Life of Joseph Reed, i. 108; Sparks's introduction to Washington's Revolutionary Correspondence. G. W. Greene's Historical View, p. 385. J. C. Hamilton replied to his critics in the preface to his second volume. A more confined memoir of Hamilton's participation in the war is the same author's Life of Alexander Hamilton. J. T. Morse's Life of Hamilton, ch. 2, gives a summary of his Revolutionary career.

Joseph Reed, first Washington's secretary, then

adjutant-general, and later the President of Pennsylvania, was put in a central position, and the Life of him by W. B. Reed, 1847, is largely general. The character of Reed has given rise to controversy. In 1783 he published Remarks and an Address to the People of Pennsylvania, which brought out, in 1787, a Reply by Gen. John Cadwalader, which was reprinted in Philadelphia in 1848, and again in 1856, together with the " Valley Forge Letters," pronounced forgeries by W. B. Reed, under the title of Nuts for Historians to Crack; and both the Reed and Cadwalader pamphlets were printed in fac-simile at Albany, in 1863. There is also a pamphlet on this matter by John G. Johnson. Bancroft, in his volumes viii. and ix., took views that elicited a vindication of Joseph Reed from his grandson, W. B. Reed, entitled, President Reed of Pennsylvania, 1867, which is reviewed unfavorably to Bancroft in the Atlantic Monthly, June, 1867. Bancroft replied in Joseph Reed, an Historical Essay, 1867, which is rather favorably reviewed in Harper's Monthly, Feb. 1867. W. B. Reed issued a Rejoinder, 1867. Gen. Stryker, in his Reed Controversy, Trenton, 1876, showed that Bancroft had mistaken a Col. Charles Read for Joseph Reed, as being under British protection, and Bancroft corrects his centennial edition, accordingly, vol. v. Cf. Pennsylvania Magazine of American History, i. 114. A sharp controversy also arose between W. B. Reed and J. C. Hamilton, because of some statements in the latter's History of the Republic. Cf. Historical Magazine, Dec. 1867, supplement; also see 1866, supplement, p. 177; April, 1867, p. 249, and Jan. 1869, p. 45. See also President Reed, published at Morrisania, 1867.

For the political aspects of the war the lives of John Adams, Samuel Adams, Benjamin Franklin, James Madison, Gouverneur Morris, are of the chiefest importance. A less careless and clumsy manner had made the Lives of Richard Henry Lee and Arthur Lee, both by the younger R. H. Lee, of the first importance. The papers on which they are based are now part in the library of Harvard College, a calendar of which is now appearing in the bulletin of that library; part in the library of the American Philosophical Society in Philadelphia, bound in two volumes; and a third part in the library of the University of Virginia.

Naval Histories.

J. Fenimore Cooper's Naval History of the United States. Thomas Clark's Naval History of the United States, 1814. George F. Emmons's Navy of the United States, 1775–1853, a record of the vessels. Lossing's Field-Book of the American Revolution, i., Appendix. The lives of the several American commanders as named on previous pages. Cf. account of Com. Samuel Tucker in the New England Historical and Genealogical

Register, April, 1872. The records of the several states show much about their different participancy in this service. Cf., for example, the Pennsylvania Archives, first and second series.

C. D. Yonge's History of the British Navy, Allen's Battles of the British Navy, and other special monographs on the English side.

Portraits.

Various contemporary or nearly contemporary narratives have engraved likenesses of the principal public characters, some of which are mentioned in connection with their names as they occur in these notes. Such illustrated accounts are : James Murray's Impartial History of the American War, London, *no date*, giving Washington, Franklin, Hancock, Putnam, Lee, Arnold, Montgomery, George III., North, Germaine, Gen. Howe, Lord Howe, Earl Percy, Gen. Gage.

An Impartial History of the War in America, Boston, 1781–1785, giving Washington, Franklin, Lafayette, Greene, Samuel Adams, Montgomery, Knox, Lincoln, Warren, Hancock, Heath.

Impartial History of the War in America, London, 1780, giving Hancock, Samuel Adams, Washington, Putnam, Arnold, the Howes, etc., Boston Magazine, 1783–1786.

Geschichte der Kriege in und aus Europa, Nuremberg, 1776, giving Franklin, Com. Hopkins, Arnold, Putnam, Chas. Lee, Robert Rogers, Sullivan, D. Wooster.

Du Simitière's profile likenesses of thirteen of the patriots (including Arnold), engraved by Reading, were published in London in 1783.

Later portraits and mementoes are given in Smith and Watson's American Historical and Literary Curiosities.

It is not worth while to enumerate the appearance of such likenesses in all the later histories and biographies. The portraits of Washington and Franklin are very many in number, and have been the subject of special lists and examination.

Maps.

Contemporary. — A map of the colonies according to a survey of 1763 was made, and an engraved reduction of it appeared in London, 1766, in a collection of the Charters of the Provinces and the Proceedings in consequence of the Stamp Act. M. A. Rocques published at London, 1765, a set of plans of the country and of the forts in America, from actual surveys, which has a folding map of New York city.

Evans's map of the Middle Colonies, between Eastern Massachusetts, Ohio, and Virginia, published at Philadelphia, 1755, with an essay, was enlarged by T. Pownall, late governor of Massachusetts Bay, to include New England and part of Canada, and published in London by Almon in 1776, and was subsequently reissued, revised by Major Holland.

Peter Bell's map, according to the treaty of 1763, appeared in a History of the British Dominion in North America, 1773. The same year there was a map issued at Paris, by Bonne, which was reproduced at Leipsic in the Geographische Belustigungen, 1776; and again in 1776, at Nuremberg, there appeared another map of the colonies in the Geschichte der Kriege in und aus Europa. In 1779 a map was given in the History of the War in America, published at Dublin; and a large one the next year, 1780, came out in the Impartial History of the War in America, published at Dublin. Other maps appeared in the Political Magazine, April 17, 1780; in Soulé's Histoire des Troubles de l'Amérique Anglaise, Paris, 1787, and in the German version of it; in Hilliard d'Auberteuil's Histoire de l'Administration de Lord North et de la Guerre; in Boucher's Histoire de la Derniere Guerre, Paris, 1787; and in Gordon's American War.

Miscellaneous.

Ben: Perley Poore's Political Register gives the federal officials from 1776. A collection of rosters and personal items will be found in Saffell's Records of the Revolutionary War, New York, 1858. A convenient list of the general officers at the beginning and close of the war is given in G. W. Greene's Historical View, p. 452; and the same work has a section on the foreign element in the war.   The Last Men of the Revolution, by E. B. Hillard, 1864, is an account of the seven Revolutionary pensioners then surviving.

Sparks's Washington, v. 542, gives a statement of the effective force of the British army in America, at intervals, from 1777 to 1782, as derived from the State Paper Office.

A table showing the number of troops furnished by the several states is printed in Niles's Register, July 31, 1830 ; in G. W. Greene's Historical View, pp. 454, 455 ; in Hildreth's United States, iii. 441, and elsewhere.   Cf. W. Sargent on the Army of the Revolution, in North American Review, lxxvii. ; a chapter in G. W. Greene's Historical View of the American Revolution ; and Von Bulow's criticism of the military conduct of the war, in the Historical Magazine, 1865.

There are treatises on the employment of negroes as soldiers by George H. Moore and George Livermore.

Judge Charles H. Warren's paper on the buff and blue uniform of the Continentals is in the Massachusetts Historical Society's Proceedings, Jan. 1859.

There is a paper on martial law during the Revolution by A. B. Gardner in the Magazine of American History, i.

For the caricatures of the period, see Parton's article in Harper's Magazine, July, 1875, afterwards included in his History of Caricature.

The spirit of the Revolution is depicted in such novels as Cooper's Chainbearer, J. L. Motley's Morton's Hope, L. M. Child's Rebels, J. K. Paulding's Old Continental, John Neal's Seventy-Six, S. J. Hale's Grosvenor, Miss Sedgwick's Linwoods, etc. Other novels have been referred to in connection with the particular events which they illustrate.

The War of the Revolution is part of the series of visions that make up Joel Barlow's Columbiad, 1808.

The literature of the Revolution is illustrated in two chapters of G. W. Greene's Historical View of the American Revolution, in sections of Duyckinck's American Literature, and in Griswold's Prose Writers and Poets of America. Allibone's Dictionary, under the names of writers, will furnish data and references. The Songs and Ballads have been collected by Frank Moore, and the Loyalist Poetry by Winthrop Sargent.

The intellectual and material condition of the Revolutionary period is considered as the starting-point of the subsequent development of the country, in the conglomerate volume, by various writers, The First Century of the Republic; a Review of American Progress, New York, 1876; a series of papers, the most of which originally appeared in Harper's Magazine.

20

INDEX.

⁎ *Reference is commonly made but once to a book if repeatedly mentioned in the text, but other references are made when additional information about the book is conveyed.*

www.ingramcontent.com/pod-product-compliance
Lightning Source LLC
Chambersburg PA
CBHW020939030726
47496CB00005B/1261